0427787S

61

2 3 AUG 2023

WITHE...
EAST SUSSEX CCC

KT-428-253

£2.00   9/23

0027

MARINER'S ARK

Peter Tonkin

This first world edition published 2015
in Great Britain and the USA by
SEVERN HOUSE PUBLISHERS LTD of
19 Cedar Road, Sutton, Surrey, England, SM2 5DA.
Trade paperback edition first published 2015 in Great
Britain and the USA by SEVERN HOUSE PUBLISHERS LTD.

Copyright © 2015 by Peter Tonkin.

All rights reserved.
The moral right of the author has been asserted.

British Library Cataloguing in Publication Data

Tonkin, Peter author.
  Mariner's ark. – (A Richard Mariner adventure)
  1. Mariner, Richard (Fictitious character)–Fiction.
  2. Severe storms–Pacific Ocean–Fiction. 3. Yacht
  racing–Fiction. 4. Sea stories.
  I. Title II. Series
  823.9'2-dc23

ISBN-13: 978-0-7278-8448-0 (cased)
ISBN-13: 978-1-84751-584-1 (trade paper)
ISBN-13: 978-1-78010-632-8 (e-book)

Except where actual historical events and characters are being
described for the storyline of this novel, all situations in this
publication are fictitious and any resemblance to living persons
is purely coincidental.

All Severn House titles are printed on acid-free paper.

Severn House Publishers support the Forest Stewardship Council™ [FSC™],
the leading international forest certification organisation. All our titles that
are printed on FSC certified paper carry the FSC logo.

Typeset by Palimpsest Book Production Ltd.,
Falkirk, Stirlingshire, Scotland.
Printed and bound in Great Britain by
TJ International, Padstow, Cornwall.

For Cham, Guy and Mark, as always.

And with thanks to John Kiehle of Aeroscraft and Captain Andy Dogherty for their help and advice.

ONE

Robin Mariner woke into the last good day at an unusually early hour for her. She did so not because she knew things would grow worse and worse after today until her own life and those of many she cared for would be at risk – or even suspected that this could ever happen or happen so soon. Not because of the morning noises from the adjoining suites, the stirring of stewards busily delivering room service along the endless corridors outside, or because of the intensifying beams of sunshine bursting into her accommodation. Not even because it was coming up to teatime in her jet-lagged head.

She woke simply because her back was cold enough to make her shiver, and that was enough. Or nearly so.

It took Robin a moment to realize that the chill along her spine running from her shoulders to buttocks was what had disturbed her, and an instant more to work out what was causing it. She had a hazy memory of falling asleep in a tangle of bedclothes stark naked, with her equally bare-skinned husband Richard curled against her, their bodies fitting together like a pair of spoons. She was still nude now and the bedding remained in a mess, but Richard was missing – and his absence caused chilly tremors powerful enough to wake her.

She blinked, opening her grey eyes wide, though it cost her some effort to do so. She untangled her right arm from the bedclothes and felt behind her, discovering more icy vacancy. 'Oh, you *bloody* man,' she grumbled. 'Where in heaven's name have you gone to now?' But even in her half-awake bleariness, she knew the answer to that one: the only thing capable of dragging her loving husband away from a bed she occupied in her current state was a different sort of female altogether.

And this one's name was *Mary*.

After a moment's sleepy indecision, she rolled on to her back and sat up, pulling the bedclothes into some sort of order, wriggling her hips and digging her heels into the mattress until her derrière slid up the bottom sheet and the pillows gathered into a backrest behind her shoulders. At least the friction warmed things up a little, she thought. Enough to stop her shivering, at any rate, and smooth the goosebumps that had risen along her arms and legs. A moment's further reflection established that her sleepy head was clear – nothing lingering from the jetlag or the wine she'd consumed rather too freely last night. She sighed with relief. Then she looked around blearily.

And caught her breath.

For Robin found herself sitting in a sizeable if tumbled double divan at the heart of the Art Deco perfection of a long-vanished age, in the midst of a suite of rooms that might have graced the old Savoy or Strand Palace hotels in London during the years between the two world wars. It was as though she was Mrs Simpson, recently returned with her freshly abdicated Edward, still impressed by how that nice Herr Hitler was organizing things in Germany. Or, given where she was, like Daisy Buchanan coming to after an illicit night of passion with the mysterious Jay Gatsby.

Immediately opposite her, well clear of the foot of the bed, was a built-in unit of honey-coloured wood with drawers, closets and a make-up table, behind which stood a mirror, its crystal surface filled with the reflection of the almost identical fittings that surrounded the head of her bed. In the centre of the bed sat her own temptingly tousled reflection, like one of Russell Flint's nudes painted as president of the Watercolour Society after 1936. Bang on time with the decor, in fact, she reckoned. Without further thought she pulled the Egyptian cotton sheet up over the all-too-perky coral tips of her breasts, which had not smoothed down with the goosebumps, ran a hand through the jumble of her golden curls and looked away with a sigh that tacitly admitted that the mother of two university-age children – twins, no less – would be unlikely to catch the eye of Sir William Russell Flint. Sir Peter Paul Rubens was looking more and more likely, she thought darkly. He of the adjective *Rubenesque*, meaning 'plump, voluptuous . . .'

To her left, the king deluxe suite stretched inward above a modest prairie of blue, fan-patterned carpet, past more honey-coloured wardrobes towards the main door leading out into an apparently endless corridor beyond the bathroom, from which issued the unmistakable aroma of her errant husband's Roger and Gallet aftershave. To her right, across Richard's deserted half of the bed, the suite stretched through a doorway panelled in pale golden wood into a reception room with a table and chairs beneath a pair of portholes whose curtains stood wide, through which the sun was pouring in as it rose distantly above Bixby Park, Grissom Island and the outwash of the Los Angeles River as it ran into Queensway Bay.

Robin blinked again as her memory slipped more clearly into place. She was in an exclusive superior suite aboard the legendary North Atlantic cruise liner *Queen Mary* in her anchorage at Long Beach, California. Built in the John Brown shipyards on the River Clyde and commissioned by the Cunard line in 1936, it was famously the first of their queens whose name did not end in '*ia*'. Holder of the Blue Riband for the fastest crossing between Europe and America from the late thirties to the early fifties and now, the better part of eighty years after her maiden voyage, it was one of the top hotels in Los Angeles and Long Beach. Her interior spaces represented the acme of late thirties Art Deco after the fashion of Messieurs Bouwens and Expert in the *Normandie*, presenting the pinnacles of work by artists and designers such as Gilbert Bayes, Alfred Oakley and Agnes Pinder Davis, whose legendary but long-vanished carpeting had once graced these very decks. Not that Robin wouldn't have been just as happy wallowing in the steely stark twenty-first century ambience of the Hyatt or the Westin up in LA. Or even the Renaissance out at LAX.

But to be fair, Robin decided at last, she was quite satisfied. Satisfied in more ways than one, in fact. She glanced down the length of the gently curvaceous body outlined by the tangled sheet like an Egyptian mummy in its wrappings, and gave a sensuous little wriggle of her hips which were anything but mummified. In spite of the temptations of twenty-first-century luxury, her relentlessly romantic husband Richard had found the promise of the bygone elegance *Queen Mary* offered irresistible. So here they were.

Or, at least, here *she* was – but where the hell was *he*?

Richard and Robin had arrived on BA flight 283 at LAX yesterday, touching down at 16.30 local time and piling into a limousine just before 18.00; one a.m. in London and in their heads. The limousine, a Lincoln Town Car, had been booked by Richard in spite of the fact that their business partner and friend, Nic Greenbaum, had offered his company chopper. Instead, the American limousine had whisked them down highways 405 and 710 in sufficient comfort for Robin to power nap. And, as she was eight hours behind London time, that had been the least she required, for she had already been up and about for nearly twenty hours.

They'd arrived at the *Queen Mary* at 19.30 and gone straight to their suite to unpack. They'd showered one at a time in the dual purpose bath and shower – Richard finding the shower head a little low for his six-foot-four-inch frame, though it suited Robin's more svelte five foot eight inches fine. Then they had changed into the closest thing they had packed to eveningwear. They'd been booked into the Sir Winston restaurant at 21.00, an hour before last orders, their table beside the windows with breathtaking views across Long Beach; just a couple of decks, in fact, above the portholes in their suite.

Robin was not certain she approved of the restaurant's overly familiar name – her mother's father had been an occasional visitor at Chartwell after the Churchills had retired there; like Sir Winston and Sir William Russell Flint, he'd been a noted watercolourist. But she'd certainly approved of the decor, the table, the view and the food. And the fact that, chopper or not, Nic Greenbaum and his daughter Liberty had been seated at the table waiting for them when they arrived. They'd proposed that the Mariners should join Nic on a cruise down to his new property in the Mexican resort of Puerto Banderas. They'd been dressed to the nines, in acquiescence to the five-star restaurant's exacting dress code. And with a bottle of the most divine domestic Chablis chilled to perfection, all ready and waiting.

Robin rolled out of bed on that thought and paused, looking at herself in the mirror, her right hand automatically patting the pale, not quite Rubenesque curve of her tummy as she wondered how much she regretted the cordon-bleu but calorie-laden oysters Rockefeller and beef Wellington with asparagus and truffle mash she had consumed, along with rather too much of the Chablis.

Richard had also tucked into the oysters – though he had chosen to share a chateaubriand steak with Nic, while Liberty had settled for the Ahi tuna and green salad. The girls chatted about sailing, for which they both had a passionate expertise and on more than one occasion had been fierce rivals, while the boys discussed the business that had called the Mariners to cross the pond – and the North American continent behind it.

As ever, thought Robin, there were several situations that overlapped, all of which could, with luck, be dealt with in the next few days before the Mariners snatched a bit of R&R time in Mexico. Richard's huge container vessel *Sulu Queen*, inbound from Hong Kong, was due to dock in the port of Los Angeles multiuse terminal soon after midnight. If all went to plan, she would be emptied of her cargo of Chinese iron within the day. Iron produced in Guangzhou then shipped down the Pearl River to the huge Kwai Tsing container terminals and on to the Heritage Mariner vessel, destined to support the renaissance of the US's West Coast shipbuilding industry now that the voracious appetite of China's domestic house boom had slowed so suddenly. The plan was to turn the huge vessel round within the day, Robin knew. A day during which Richard was due to go aboard her and discuss matters with her captain, Captain Sin Heng Son, while the hull was reloaded with containers full of machine parts, top-end domestic appliances, disassembled motorcars from the General Motors Advance Automotive Division in North Hollywood, several thousand gallons of California wine in bottles of various shapes and sizes, and several farms-worth of biologic-ally engineered corn, soy, alfalfa and beets. All due to be loaded within forty-eight hours so *Sulu Queen* could turn round and sail again, and all destined for various parts of China's society, economy and agronomy; a virtuous circle of trade negotiated by Heritage Mariner's office in Jardine House, No. 1, Connaught Place, Hong Kong Central. Richard had been holed up there for most of the last few months while Robin had taken care of the day-to-day business back in London.

That day – *today* – was also one in which Nic wanted to show his old friends round his latest toy, a multi-billion dollar gin palace yacht called *Maxima*, built for him by Edminston at the Dunya shipyards in Turkey, which had just been delivered dull-grey emergency control beside them. Above the huge helms, brass trumpets gaped like the bells of French horns, communicating with the identical system of controls down in the engine room and – when necessary – with the emergency control room far below. And the engine room telegraphs stood beside them, marked with every command from full ahead to full astern, stand by, stop and finished with engines.

That last command brought a wry smile to Richard's lips, for he entertained a more recent memory – of the liquefied natural gas transporter *Sayonara* that was controlled by computers and had been taken over by pirates who had reprogrammed her command systems so that finished with engines had in fact started her final, near-fatal run to a terrifyingly deadly impact with a floating nuclear power station off the coast of Japan.

Without thinking, he pocketed his cell phone with its automatic text alerting him to the safe berthing of *Sulu Queen*, which had arrived unnoticed during the shenanigans at midnight last night. He'd only noticed the text when he'd called Robin. He strode forward towards the twin helms until he was brought up short by the equally effulgent brass rail designed to keep casual visitors away from the priceless equipment. He hesitated, overcome by a sudden boyish desire to climb over the barrier and explore the forbidden area further. After a moment, good sense prevailed and he stepped back, contenting himself with walking to the starboard extremity of the bridge, where he could look out over Queensway Bay past Grissom Island and over Long Beach into the dawn. But then something deep below his consciousness led him back across to the port side. And that was where Robin found him when she arrived at last, gazing narrow-eyed away westward, as though he could see over the grey bulks of Terminal Island, past *Sulu Queen* in her berth and distant San Pedro to the depths beyond the San Pedro submarine escarpment and away across the Pacific.

'Wow!' said Robin as she arrived. 'No wonder you wanted to show me this! I've never seen anything so beautiful. Shall we climb over the barrier and play with it a bit? Bags I try one of those wonderful wheels.'

Then Robin stopped speaking for an instant. And not because she had noticed Richard's preoccupied westward stare. Instead, she crossed to the opposite extremity of the bridge to the one he was occupying and looked eastward while he looked west. 'Hey,' she said a moment later. 'What do you make of that?'

Richard tore his frowning gaze away from the dark sky over the far Pacific and turned. 'What?'

Robin just gestured eastwards. And there, apparently static, a wall of fog stood where it had suddenly appeared, reaching right across Queensway Bay and Long Beach harbour as far as Seal Beach and Marina Vista Park less than five miles distant, a towering white cliff, sitting, waiting, like a rattlesnake about to strike.

'That's pretty impressive,' she said. 'Strange, too.'

'And then some,' he agreed, glancing over his shoulder at the distant, western sky. 'There's something up with the weather . . .' Then he shook his head as though clearing it of its forebodings. 'Let's go down to breakfast,' he suggested. 'Nic's chopper's due to pick us up at ten.'

THREE

In fact, Nic's chopper touched down at 10.15 a.m. It landed at the Island Express helipad, 1175 Queen's Highway, just behind the huge white dome of the Carnival Cruise Lines building, above which the three black-topped red funnels atop *Queen Mary* stood tall. Nic was aboard himself, but Liberty was not. The six-seater passenger cabin of the little Bell executive 429 was empty apart from the man himself. 'Look,' he said as Richard and Robin climbed aboard, strapped in and put on the headphones that allowed them to communicate. 'I'm sorry to be late but I've been forced to change plans with no notice. I've dropped Liberty down at *Maxima* where she's getting ready to go aboard *Katapult8*, and I'll take you to her as well if you insist, but I'm on my way to a meeting of the Chamber of Commerce and I'm only just going to make it in time as it is. Something's come up . . .'

'Something bad,' hazarded Robin, who had never seen her

friend looking so concerned. She had to raise her voice over the gathering roar as the Pratt and Whitney motors throttled up and the helicopter swooped upwards.

'Could be,' he said. 'That's why they've called a meeting of the local great and good. And one or two hangers-on, like me.' He gave a self-deprecating grin that banished the worry from his lean, boyish face. But not, Robin noticed, from his eyes. 'You heard of something called an ARkStorm?'

'Not since that Russell Crowe movie *Noah* came out,' said Richard lightly. 'And there were one or two people in England back at the beginning of 2014 who were thinking of arks as well. Especially on the Somerset Levels and down along the Thames towards Windsor . . .'

'Yeah. The floods. I remember.' Nic nodded. 'Well, as ever, anything you Limeys can do us Yanks can do bigger and better. Come along to the meeting and listen to this guy. He's from the USGS.'

'The United States Geological Survey?' said Richard, more seriously. 'Are they expecting an earthquake? Then yes, we'd better get going. The Chamber of Commerce, right?'

'The Los Angeles Area Chamber of Commerce.'

The main briefing room at the LA Chamber of Commerce building, 350, Bixel Street, was packed. Nic was right, thought Richard. They had made it just in time, and it looked like there was standing room only. Robin took what appeared to be the last seat on the end of the back row. Richard and Nic, both tall men, were happy to stand behind her, leaning against the rear wall, looking over the top of the assembled audience. The young USGS representative looked chipper and confident. But in spite of what Nic has said, the scientist was not a man. The ID tag on her lapel said Dr Dan Jones, though, which explained Nic's confusion.

Summoning PowerPoint frames up from her laptop on to the overhead system, and speaking into a Bluetooth ear and throat piece that linked remotely to the PA system, the scientist began her briefing at once. 'I'll start now, ladies and gentlemen,' she said as Robin sat down, her quiet tones booming around the room, amplified by the speakers. The audience of local businessmen and women settled to a tense hush.

The USGS logo flashed on to the screen. It was replaced almost immediately by another, more sinister emblem. Within a grey circle sat the stylized outline of an ark with a jagged bolt of black lightning splitting it down the middle. Beneath the circle were the words ARkStorm. 'My name is Danielle Jones,' began the scientist. 'I won't bore you with my qualifications. You can check me out online if you feel the urge. I work for the USGS National Oceanic and Atmospheric Administration division – NOAA for short. I am also consultant to the Federal Emergency Management Agency and the California Emergency Management Agency. My specialism is in floods: their prediction and their management. During the last five years and more my team, my associates and I have been planning for, preparing to face, and watching out for early warning signs of what has become known as an ARkStorm. I can see one or two smirks – NOAA has an ARk, of course – but in fact this is no laughing matter.

'Put at its most simple, an ARkStorm is one continuous wet weather event that is likely to last, non-stop, for in excess of forty days and nights. Just like Noah's flood in the Bible, in fact. And it could, really and truly, bring our world close to the edge of total destruction. Our particular piece of it here in California. An ARkStorm is not a series of individual severe weather events like the Pineapple Express storms that can come at us in California up from Hawaii, as they did in LA in 2012 and in San Francisco in 2014, or like the series of six consecutive depressions that hit the west and south of Great Britain between December 2013 and February 2014. No. I'm talking about something more akin to the monsoon that hits various areas of the Indian subcontinent. But something much more powerful and sustained than the average monsoon. Uninterrupted rainfall on a state-wide basis in which more than three metres – ten feet – of precipitation will fall everywhere from the coast to the Sierra Nevada during six weeks of unremitting torrential downpour. Imagine the San Joaquin Valley becoming an inland lake; everywhere from Chico to Caleinte under several feet – maybe metres – of water. Sacramento, Stockton, Fresno, Bakersfield . . . And that's just part of it. You guys at the coast will suddenly find not only storm surges and spring tides rolling upslope, swamping the docks and coastal city blocks, but there'll also be a couple of million tons of water upstate and inland with nowhere to go but downslope and over the top of you as it all washes back out to sea.'

Dr Jones reached for a glass of water beside her laptop and took a long, thoughtful sip as she watched her words begin to sink in and the amusement die out of the faces in front of her. Nic put his hand up as though he were back at a lecture hall in Harvard. 'This has happened, right? You're not just theorizing, Dr Jones. This has happened before. Here.'

Dr Jones nodded. 'One hundred and fifty-some years ago. December of 1861 to January 1862,' she confirmed. Suddenly the ARkStorm logo was replaced by the first in a series of old sepia-coloured photographs. 'This is Sacramento at that time,' she said. 'What it looked like by the end of January 1862.' The buildings astride the main street of Sacramento stood tall. But between them, instead of a road there was a deep lake and men in boats were rowing across it. Suddenly everyone in the room was paying very close attention to Dr Jones indeed.

She looked around, seeming to meet every pair of eyes there. 'Beginning in early December 1861 and continuing forty-five days into January 1862, an extreme storm struck California. Between ten and twelve feet of water fell. That's three to four metres; twice the depth of the deep end of your swimming pools. And on every square metre of land. This caused severe flooding, turning the Sacramento Valley into an inland sea, requiring Leland Stanford to take a rowboat to his inauguration as Governor of California, and ultimately causing the state capitol to be moved out of Sacramento altogether because it was totally underwater, as these contemporary photographs show.'

More old photographs appeared. It was just possible to make out a sign saying 'Coffee Warehouse' above the water in one of them. Dr Jones continued gently, 'So was San Francisco, which suffered an enormous amount more damage than it was to do forty-four years later in the famous earthquake of 1906 and the fire that succeeded it. In which, I might add, all the photographic records of the catastrophic San Francisco floods were burned. So what we have is mostly from Sacramento newspapers and state archives.'

Pictures followed at an increasing rate – photographs and daguerreotypes from the newspapers of the time, local and national. 'Inundation of the State Capital: K Street from the Levee'; 'The City Of Sacramento From the Pavillion' . . . In each picture, city blocks stood like fleets of ships becalmed above an inland sea large enough to be generating waves. In the distance, churches stood on tiny islands that had once been hillocks. Rowboats bobbed like cockleshells. Desperate men looked out across the devastation as though contemplating the end of the world.

Dr Jones cleared her throat. 'Lakes formed in the Los Angeles Basin, Orange County and the Mojave Desert. Something if, if it happened now, would surely peeve the guys at the solar electric generating system they brought online in 2013 covering three and a half thousand acres out there. It's not fitted for hydro-electric back-up! That alone would mean two and a half billion dollars down the Suwannee and nearly twenty per cent of the state's electricity with it. Well, back in 1862, that's what happened: the Mojave Desert became a lake more than ten feet deep. The mouth of the Santa Ana River moved six miles and the largest community between Los Angeles and New Mexico, Agua Mansa – which means smooth water, ironically enough – was completely wiped off the map. Forever. Nobody knows how many people died.

'The storm destroyed one-third of the taxable land of California and bankrupted the state. And this, remember, was at a time when there were 379,994 residents, according to the Census of 1860. Now there are more like forty million. In Sacramento there were 13,785 citizens in 1860. Now there are three quarters of a million. You see where I'm heading with this? According to our latest calculations, independently of business premises, state and federal institutions, warehouses, schools, hospitals and so forth that would be inundated, we're talking nine million flooded homes. Nine *million* . . .'

'OK,' came a voice from the front. 'So that's the worst-case scenario. But just what is an ARkStorm and why are we talking about it instead of keeping the businesses you mentioned afloat? That's *afloat* in the other sense of the word.'

'I guess if you think back to your fourth-grade geography or science lessons, you'll all remember learning about the water cycle,' answered Dr Jones. 'I'll have to rely on your memories. I didn't bring any PowerPoints with me—'

'Check online,' suggested Robin loudly.

'Sure,' acquiesced Dr Jones good-naturedly, and in less than a minute a big diagram from the USGS was up on the overhead, reminding the audience of what they may or may not have learned at school.

'We can skip all the detail about volcanic steam, sublimation, desublimation and fog drip,' Dr Jones informed them bracingly. 'But it's clear to see that what we have here is an ever-renewing system. Rain falls. It ends up in rivers and lakes, groundwater run-off and all the rest until eventually it reaches the oceans from where it evaporates, filling the air with water vapour. The water vapour becomes rainfall which goes into rivers, lakes and what have you, and the cycle starts all over.

'But I guess when you guys were fourth-graders, your teachers probably told you that the water vapour was spread pretty evenly through the atmosphere. Well, nowadays we know it's more complicated than that. The air up above our heads is actually full of streams. We can be absolutely certain of this now we have information from the Global Precipitation Measurement, or GPM, core observatory satellite that was launched back in 2014. The GPM mission was designed to build on the Tropical Rainfall Measuring Mission. That's TRIMM to anyone into acronyms. TRIMM is also a joint mission between NASA and the Japan Aerospace Exploration Agency. It was launched in 1997 but only measures precipitation in the tropics. The GPM core observatory satellite has extended coverage from the Arctic Circle to the Antarctic Circle. And what both satellite systems are showing us at the moment is a stream – what we call an atmospheric river – of humid air forming over the Pacific Ocean with the potential to come right for us. You've all heard of the jet stream, I'm sure. There's one up above us at the moment, about ten miles above us, in fact, right at the top of the troposphere. It's three miles in diameter, give or take, and three thousand or so miles long. It's a river of air that flows round and round the globe. It moves like a bat out of hell and anyone thinking of flying to Europe will probably get to ride along with it.

'That's just one stream, though it's the best known. But there are others, much lower in the atmosphere. And they are effectively rivers of air that is so humid it is just on the point of precipitating. Unlike the jet stream, these atmospheric rivers can be hundreds of miles wide, but just like the jet stream they can be thousands of miles long. And also like the jet stream, they tend to move from west to east because of the way the Earth turns on its axis. And under certain circumstances they can blow in off the Pacific right over the West Coast here. Once every couple of centuries, in fact, on average.

'Then all it takes is the elevation of something like the Sierra Nevada to push this incredibly humid air upwards and make the rain start pouring down along a storm front that can be as wide as the entire Californian coast. And it won't stop coming down until the whole of that atmospheric river has gone over the top of us and dumped every last drop of moisture it contains on to our businesses, homes, families and loved ones.

'Like I said, the stats show that we can expect one every couple of centuries. And it's well past one hundred and fifty years since the last one, which means, by definition, that the odds are narrowing. And also because, like I said, our weather sats, TRIMM and GPM, are beginning to pick up what looks like an atmospheric river coming our way. Because we at the USGS and NOAA think there may be an ARkStorm due to hit us within the next seventy-two hours and stay right above us, raining fit to burst, for forty days after that,' said Dr Jones. 'Just like in the Bible. And that movie with Russell Crowe.'

FOUR

'Is that what you were looking at, Richard?' demanded Robin, shouting over the roaring of the Bell's rotors, too impatient to wait for everyone to fit their headsets on. 'When you were looking away to the west? An ARkStorm on the way in?'

'I don't know,' answered Richard more quietly, his headset in place. 'There was just something . . . But Doctor Jones said it was seventy-two hours out . . . Nic, can you ask your pilot to take us up as high as possible? We're heading south-west back to the Long Beach docks anyway, and the higher we go the further I'll be able to see out over the Pacific.'

'Like you're going to see more than one of the USGS satellites,' said Nic, unsure whether to be incredulous or impressed. 'That's not forecasting, that's witchcraft.' But he shrugged and went forward to talk to the pilot. At once the chopper began to gain altitude and, as it did so, the vista all around it widened. Richard pressed the slightly broken aquiline jut of his nose against the starboard window, straining to see above the haze that cloaked the grey city blocks away out past the cost and over the sullen grey-green of the ocean. His mind began to fill with the rest of what Dr Jones had told the Chamber of Commerce. The governor, slipping into the decisive mode of a couple of his more dramatic predecessors, Regan and Schwarzenegger, had already called in the National Guard. And the USGS had backed him forcefully enough to alarm the president and the power brokers up on Capitol Hill. Containers full of medical supplies, emergency rations, heating and clothing were on the way, apparently. Everything from chemical toilets to mobile hospitals, all packed in containers and loaded into – or on to – every form of transport available. Preparing for the worst without panicking the populace.

There was an evacuation plan that would slip into place when the rain began to fall – but not until then. This wasn't going to be like an earthquake – total destruction in a couple of minutes, then aftershocks, fires and so forth. A city and its infrastructure wasn't going to be reduced to rubble in little more than a heart-beat. It wasn't going to be Mount St Helen's – or Pompeii and Herculaneum. Folks would get wet as they moved. Soaked and shaken – especially if the storm fronts were powerful. He remembered how it had been in the south of England in February 2014 with hurricane-force winds in the Western Approaches, along the south coast and up through St George's Channel and over the Isle of Anglesey. But if push came to shove the vast majority of Californians would have days, possibly weeks before things became impossible.

The only exceptions would be the unfortunate people living along the western, coast-facing slopes of the Sierra Nevada, for those steep surfaces would begin to wash away in the first few hours, taking everything and everyone with them. He closed his eyes for a moment, summoning up a sketchy map from the depths of his

near-photographic memory. There would be more towns than
Wishon inundated by Bass Lake and the offspring it would all too
swiftly spawn. North Fork would be among the first, he supposed,
washed down towards Yosemite, lock, stock and barrel . . .

But at this point in his darkening thoughts, Richard's concentration was disturbed. 'Oh my God,' Robin said to Nic. 'What
in heaven's name is that? It looks like something out of *Mars
Attacks!*'

'The Graf Zeppelin meets the Starship *Enterprise*, perhaps,'
Nic allowed.

The mention of the *Enterprise* was too much for Richard, a
card-carrying Trekkie. 'What is it?' he asked, blinking his eyes
wide and looking away from the darkening distance westwards.
Robin and Nic were on the inland side of the chopper, looking
south-eastwards towards Anaheim – another of the west-slope
areas that might find itself in the first firing line, he thought as
he crossed to crouch beside them. And there, above the grey haze
of morning, framed against the distant sage of the Santa Ana
Mountains, was an airship. Looking like the Goodyear blimp
crossed with something out of the *Terminator* movies, it gleamed
silver in the clearer inland air, aptly enough seeming to be sailing
just above the historic settlement of Silverado itself. Its frame
was too flat for a cigar shape, and as it moved through the air
with slow majesty its silhouette seemed to flatten further still,
almost like a flying saucer. Richard could see what Robin meant
about *Mars Attacks!*, not to mention *The War of the Worlds* and
The Day The Earth Stood Still. Then it lengthened again and tall
tail fins became apparent. Suddenly it looked more like a submarine. One of the sleek new *Virginia*-class boats – given a slightly
flattened hull. 'What sort of size is it?' whispered Richard, awed.

'Difficult to be sure,' said Nic. 'I'll see if the pilot can tell us
how far away it is, then we can guesstimate, at least.' He
unstrapped yet again and vanished into the cockpit once more.

'What does she look like?' asked Robin. 'I mean, she reminds
me of something so much . . . I just can't put my finger on it . . .'

'Thunderbird Two!' said Richard. 'She looks like Thunderbird
Two!'

Nic returned after a few minutes, his head packed with information imparted by an enthusiastic, well-informed pilot. 'The

pilot gave me the whole skinny,' he announced. 'Apparently the thing's got quite a rep among the local flyboys. Her name's Dragon Dream. She's two hundred and fifty feet long and a hundred feet wide, and she can lift the better part of thirty tons. She's the half-scale prototype. There are plans afoot to build one twice as big, but this one is awesome enough to be going on with. Technically pretty advanced by all accounts. Works using helium rather than hydrogen like the old airships did, and controls lift by compressing and decompressing the gas rather than picking up and releasing ballast. The main propulsion units can generate vertical lift as well as horizontal thrust into the bargain. She moves at about a hundred and fifty knots in still air. They plan to use her for general transport, of course, but there's apparently quite a sales pitch about her being perfect for disaster-relief work. Got the army sniffing around. And some of the NGOs. She can pick up and put down anything up to the size and weight of a fully-packed standard container. That's a full-sized TEU – twenty-foot equivalent unit, I guess. No need for any on-ground infrastructure – landing strips and so forth. She can just hover at any given height and lower or pick up anything beneath her. Flame-proof aluminium skin. And helium doesn't burn, of course. So she's even fireproof – within certain limits. Broiling the pilots, melting the controls and so forth just doesn't happen. And as long as she can sit still; as long as she doesn't get blown all over the place like a kid's balloon. Apparently she's on the last of a series of test flights over LA. In a day or so she's off down to Mexico City. The guys who built her, Aeroscraft, have headquarters here in Tustin and offices down there too. Tustin to Mexico City will be her first big test run.'

FIVE

Long Island Docks were a mess. There was no other way to describe them. From Nic's helicopter the sight was one of confusion, overcrowding and confrontation. The normally well-ordered expanse of waterfront was packed with conflicting armies of men, materiel and transport. From the air it was obvious the whole place was heading for gridlock pretty quickly, and by the time the Bell actually reached *Sulu Queen*'s berth the whole place was at a standstill.

It seemed clear to Richard that the governor's call had resulted in not only truckloads of National Guard and ancillary vehicles choking the roadways and backing up along Interstates 710, 405 and 110, but trainloads of freight cars which were all running into the rail yards like cholesterol into the veins of a heart-attack patient. Shiploads of aid were doing the same to the berthing facilities which had looked from the air like an overcrowded marina, but with massive freighters and tankers instead of bustling little pleasure boats.

And it appeared that the stevedores and longshoremen – whose huge machines for lifting and laying the twenty-foot equivalent units of the containers had been utterly overwhelmed – were on the point of walking out into the bargain. Certainly, there was no evidence at all of the usual well-ordered bustle that told of them being efficiently on-task. There was no movement at all, in fact. The whole place was frozen. Petrified.

And being on ground level, or deck level several metres higher, simply made the situation clearer, thought Richard half an hour later, looking down on the half-laden length of *Sulu Queen* and at the jetties beside her packed with stalled trucks and piled containers, with groups of angry and frustrated men dwarfed by massive immobile cranes and gantries.

Nic's helicopter had just managed to find space and permission to touch down on the dockside. It dropped Richard as close to *Sulu Queen*'s gangway as possible then powered up to lift off as he leaped out and ran, doubled over beneath the rotors, towards his mighty vessel. After half-a-dozen steps, Richard was tempted to run back through the mayhem and jump aboard before the chopper could swoop up and away towards the distant golf ball of *Maxima*'s radar equipment, with the upended black composite jumbo-jet wing of *Katapult8*'s mainsail immediately behind it, her next destination the relative quiet of *Maxima*'s helipad. But duty called. And he had promised to be on *Sulu Queen* by the time the afternoon watch was called. A glance at his Rolex warned him he had better hurry up or he would be late going aboard.

lengths or one standard forty foot – stood a cell guide with a
lashing bridge reaching up above it. The cell guides were effectively metre-wide walls reaching right across the ship, from the
level of a notional main deck down to the bottom of the in-hull
storage areas. These were designed to hold the containers securely
in place while the ship was laden and safely at sea. There were
walkways running along them from port to starboard at what
would have been deck level – metre-wide passages running from
side to side along the tops of the interior cell guides. Walkways
deserted now, for there was nothing to be done until the docks
started working properly again. Walkways which, when the ship
was more fully laden, would anchor the metal lashing rods
designed to reach across the ends of the container towers as they
rose above deck level and hold them secure up to the top of their
safe lading instructions, which was, of course, just below the
square top of the vessel's own container-handling gantry. But at
the moment there was nothing piled there at all.

'Then, if there's nothing to be done, perhaps we should grab
a bite to eat as well, Captain,' he suggested mildly, suddenly
aware that breakfast had not featured largely in this morning's
activities, and last night's chateaubriand suddenly seemed an
unsettlingly distant memory. Captain Sin was gave a deep sigh
of ill-contained fury and led the way below.

Like her cargo, *Sulu Queen*'s cook was from Guangzhou. His
speciality, therefore, was Cantonese cuisine. As Richard and the
fuming Captain Sin settled into their chairs, they were confronted
with a range of steamed and lightly stir-fried delicacies. Richard
chose steamed dim sum dumplings, sweet-and-sour pork and
steamed spare ribs with pickled plum and soy bean paste, stir-
fried rice, Chinese broccoli and Brussels sprouts. It was a cuisine
familiar to him from his recent trips to Hong Kong. Subtle, sweet
and substantial – very different from the spicy Szechuan food
he had enjoyed up in Shanghai. But he noticed that his pork, like
Captain Sin's beef, had been stir-fried rather than deep-fried; the
coating of the pork nuggets was soggy rather than crispy, though
tasty nonetheless.

'I banned all deep-frying in the galley,' explained Sin curtly
when Richard commented. Talking about something other than
the overwhelmed port officials – together with the calming effect

of lunch – allowed Sin's accent to return to the urbane American-
tinted English he usually spoke. He leaned towards Richard
earnestly. As he did so, the sun, just beginning to wester in the
early afternoon, struck through a port hole powerfully enough
to frame his round shoulders and basket-ball head. It shone
through his protuberant ears, making them glow like pink stained
glass. The effect was droll but a little disturbing, almost as
though his rage was sending steam out of them – the comic-book
cliché apparently coming to life. His words, however, were not
funny at all. 'The weather was too unsettled. Indeed, it is only
now that we are in port that I allow stir-fries. When we were at
sea we only ate boiled or steamed food.' He unbent slightly, his
round face losing a little of its hectic flush. 'I have eaten sufficient steamed chicken to last several lifetimes. But I thought we
were likely to face quite enough challenges without having the
galley awash with boiling oil – or, more likely, bursting into
flames. I like my spare ribs broiled, not my chefs. I had promised
the cook and the crew that I would reinstall the deep-fat fryer
and perhaps even allow deep-fat frying in the big wok if all
went well here.' His face clouded into a frown once more. 'That
simply adds to the frustration we all feel that things are not, in
fact, going well. I believe some of my officers and crew would
trade almost anything for a dish of salt-and-pepper shrimp or
twice-fried crispy sweet-and-sour pork like their mothers used
to make.' He leaned back out of the light and his ears stopped
glowing. But, like the top sections of his plump cheeks, they
remained a hectic red.

Richard forced speculation about Sin's face to the back of his
mind, and thoughts about the food aboard his ship as well. For
Sin's words struck a chord. 'So the passage over was rough?'
he asked with a frown. He knew better than most what it must
have cost to confiscate a Cantonese chef's deep-fat fryer. And
forbidding him to fry in his wok was almost unheard of.

Captain Sin shook his head in a curt negative. 'It was not as
I expected – feared, rather. Or as the weather predictors threatened. It was . . .' He leaned closer. 'Like the Legend of Dschou
Tschu, where the young man Dschou Tschu goes into the forest
and the great grey ghost tiger stalks him. The tiger who is so
powerful that his roaring becomes a terrible storm. A *tai fun*. It

was as though we were little Dschou Tschu and the storm tiger was stalking us all the way over from the Fragrant Harbour . . .'

Richard's lips twitched towards a smile of familiarity at the old Chinese name for Hong Kong, but then his lean face folded into a frown. Captain Sin was not a man given to sudden flights of fancy or extravagantly imaginative ideas. That, indeed, was part of his strength as a good, solid, utterly reliable commander. But the image of a storm tiger stalking *Sulu Queen* as she came east across the Pacific chimed all too vividly with what Dr Jones of NOAA had said about the impending ARkStorm, and with his own unsettled feelings every time he looked away westwards across the Pacific. He had a sudden, disorientatingly vivid mental image of Sin's mythic beast, a monster, miles high, made of granite-coloured cloud banded with anthracite-black stripes, its rain-grey foreclaws brushing the ocean's restless surface, its jaws a thousand miles wide and its eyes the yellow of lightning bolts, prowling out of the western Pacific and eastwards towards California, dragging a tail of destruction behind it that was longer than the jet stream. A sense of renewed urgency stabbed through him. Something deeper even than the wish of a businessman with possibly millions of dollars riding on getting *Sulu Queen* back on schedule. Suddenly he wanted his ship, his wife, his friends and himself well away from California – and as soon as humanly possible.

SIX

'**M**y *God*,' breathed Robin. 'She's just so *beautiful*!' And, right at the back of her mind, was a wicked little thought that, compared to her current quarters aboard *Queen Mary*, this was very much more like the steely, stark twenty-first-century ambience of the Hyatt or the Westin up in LA that she hankered after in spite of Richard and his boyish enthusiasm for the bygone age that *Queen Mary* represented.

The neat little Bell settled on *Maxima*'s helipad like a dragon-fly, its tail pointing out over the edge of the third upper deck, snub-nose pointing at the smoked glass doors into the rear bridge deck and the ladder up on to the flying bridge that bisected them. Everything aboard seemed to be white paint and blond wood, from the golf balls of the navigation equipment she wore like a crown at her highest point to the sections that folded out and down to water level. Robin loosened her safety belt and slid the door open, pulling off her headset as she did so. The noise of the motors died, leaving only the slowing thrum of the idling rotors. A breeze brought to her nostrils not the smell of avgas or dock water she had expected, but something like the aroma of a Rolls Royce car salesroom. She climbed out, stooping automatically and running a thoughtless hand through her hair as the downdraught undid what little coiffeur she had bothered with after her shower this morning. Equally automatically, she crossed to the rear of this deck to pause beneath the Bell's tail rotor and look down.

Immediately below her the second deck stepped out towards the stern, the pale wood of its flooring lost under a confusion of deck chairs and tables. Then the main deck stepped out and back sternwards again, at its centre a swimming pool whose forward edge was lost underneath the overhang of the gallery above it. And, beyond that, the whole of the yacht's aft section had been folded out, providing a platform a foot or so above sea level from which swimmers could enter the ocean or sailors could climb aboard the motor boats and jet skis clustered there. Though there were, in fact, no bathers. And the men beside the boats and skis seemed to be crewmembers running checks and maintenance. Even from the outside, the extravagance was astonishing. In any other context it would have been offensive to see this much money squandered on a rich man's toy.

But Nic was old money, thought Robin with unusual indulgence. His forbears had rubbed shoulders with the Astors, the Livingstons, the Roosevelts, the Dudleys and the Winthrops: Uncle Tom Getty and all. His father's summer home was in Hyannis Port, next along from the Kennedy compound. It was in the waters of Nantucket Sound that the old man had taught his granddaughter Liberty to sail, a skill which she in turn had taken to Olympic standard. Now she and her all-female crew were getting ready to give *Katapult8* a really tough shakedown run south towards Mexico tomorrow. With *Maxima* in close pursuit, if she could keep up.

Nic had used the fortunes of Greenbaum International to enormously good effect. It was he who funded initiatives like Self-help International, giving men and women in an astonishing range of countries the chance, the skills and the tools to work their way out of poverty. He was behind the MicroBank projects that loaned tens and hundreds of dollars at no interest to women all over the world who were fighting to start their own micro-businesses and earn enough to raise and educate their families. Not just money either – schooling where it was needed, too, not to mention peer-to-peer tutoring and business advice. Everywhere from Mauritania and Manila to the Maldives and Mexico, women who had lost their husbands to war, drugs, AIDs, the lure of big cities, restless feet or roving eyes were supported in their attempts to work and trade themselves out of poverty, and to teach their own sons and daughters through their experience and their example to follow in their footsteps.

But on the other hand, it was also Greenbaum International that gave tens of thousands and hundreds of thousands annually to projects designed to combat a range of diseases, including AIDs, tuberculosis and the creeping danger of malaria as global warming spread the climate that deadly Anopheles mosquitoes could live in wider and wider, higher and higher. Year after year, Greenbaum International won the International Ethical Industry Award – the Nobel Prize for businesses.

It had been Nic – and Richard – who had funded the project where Liberty and Robin exercised their love of sailing as they raced in opposite directions across the Pacific, in specially designed yachts, to bring the world's attention to the dangers of the rotting rubbish floating in the Sargasso Sea at the heart of the Northern Ocean. A dead sea of rubbish and plastic the size of Texas and growing. There was hardly a cause or an initiative designed to protect nature and support those fighting to live well within it anywhere in the world that was not getting support, guidance or expertise from Greenbaum International.

So if Nic wanted a new toy, he was welcome to it in Robin's book. Even a toy that must have cost a good deal more than *Sulu Queen* herself. There had been something like this at the last

International Boat Show Robin had visited, priced at a cool fifty million pounds. 'A little extravagant, eh?' asked Nic quietly, appearing like a genie at her shoulder. 'What do you Brits say? Over the top? Is that what you're thinking?'

'Something like that,' she allowed grudgingly.

'It kept half of the shipwrights in Istanbul employed for the better part of a year,' he exaggerated cheerfully. 'Not to mention designers and interior decorators from all over the world.'

'Money well spent, then.' She shrugged.

'Money well *invested . . .*' he teased. 'A bit like the old Cunard Line keeping John Brown shipyards on the Clyde busy during the great depression of the nineteen thirties with your current accommodation.'

'Your magnanimity knows no bounds,' she riposted – and then felt that she had gone too far, for the phrase came out more tartly than she had meant.

But he didn't seem to notice. 'You don't know the half of it,' he continued. 'When we go below I'll show you my pictures of Dahlia Blanca. Get you ready for the other part of this little jaunt.'

'Dahlia Blanca?'

'Named for the national flower of Mexico. Kept half of the builders in Jalisco busy for the better part of a year. Architects from Guadalajara to Mexico City, interior designers, painters, carpenters, tilers, rug-weavers, antique dealers, artists, landscape gardeners, plumbers, electricians, pool installers, cooks, house staff, grounds staff, security staff . . . Not to mention the guys who've built the marina and secure accommodation waiting for this little lady down there. And, of course, land agents, estate agents, local government agents, central government agents and lawyers from Chihuahua to Cancun. Heaven alone knows how many Mexican families will make it through to the next *Dia de Muertos* because of Dahlia Blanca and *Maxima*.'

'Dahlia Blanca is your little pied-à-terre in Puerto Banderas and where we'll be staying, I take it?'

'Some pied,' he answered, leading her forward once more through the smoked-glass doors and past the reflection of the Bell's little snub nose. 'Some terre. Wait till you see it.'

But Robin found herself too distracted to answer. And in truth, her breath had been taken away. For as he finished speaking she found herself standing beside a column of pure, clear crystal perhaps two metres in diameter. It reached from above her head down through the deck at her feet into a seemingly bottomless well, the shaft of which was banded with darkness and varicoloured light. Its glassy facade was wrapped in fans of silver which seemed to cling in dazzling cobwebs to its exterior, catching the light and shimmering like the surface of the sea. It was only when she saw something moving upwards out of the banded depths in the middle of it that she realized it was hollow. And that it was the lift to the lower decks.

SEVEN

The Port Authority Building at 301 East Ocean Boulevard was almost as choked as the docks. Which was hardly a surprise, thought Richard, but at least a visit there would let him know how soon the docks would be clear so *Sulu Queen* could unload, reload and return to her tight schedule. There were a lot of people impatient to ship stuff in and out through the gridlock at the dockside, and the men and women who worked in this building were the first port of call for those who wished matters to be expedited pretty bloody quickly. Not least among these was Heritage Mariner, given Richard's gathering worry that an ARkStorm might be approaching like a monstrous, mythical tiger prowling along the wake of the *Sulu Queen*.

Richard and Captain Sin came to a standstill at the back of a crowd that seemed to be intent on invading Suite 1400. The squat Sin could see nothing except for the backs of the crowd in front, and was too full of his own importance to rise on to his tiptoes like a child. So he just stood and fumed with yet more frustration. Richard, well aware of the Oriental concept of *face,* was careful not to remark on this. He was easily able to look over the tops of the heads packed along the hall between himself and the suite's closed door. And he was not alone in being able to do so. On the way over here in a miraculously mobile taxi, they had not only avoided the worst of the traffic jams but had also come past West Broadway, one block up, and picked up Antoine Prudhomme from Southey-Bell, a legal-trained executive from the local shipping agents Heritage Mariner shared with Greenbaum International, who was there to explain – and apply as necessary – any legal implications concerning the hold-up, particularly in regard of a lawsuit against the port authority if Richard wished to proceed in that direction.

Antoine was Richard's equal in height but he lacked the Englishman's deep-chested solidity. Somewhere in his maternal great-grandmother's French Creole genes lay a far more willowy figure, passed on to him several generations down the line. Every time Richard met Antoine he was put in mind of the paintings of Modigliani and El Greco with their brightly coloured but strangely elongated figures. But the effect was at least partly illusory – Antoine had played basketball at college, city and state level. Only a catastrophically broken ankle had stopped him turning professional – and left him with a slight but permanent limp. So he settled on a good degree from Loyola Law, LA, and a career with Southey-Bell instead.

Now the two tall men stood shoulder to shoulder in a kind of *entente cordiale*, looking over the crowd. 'I don't know what I can do,' Antoine was declaring. 'Get on to our paralegals and sue the port authority, I guess.' He pulled a hand back over his fashionably short, prematurely grey, tightly curled hair. He gave a peculiarly Gallic shrug.

'Let's not get carried away,' said Richard, unapologetically English in his hesitation to get combative attorneys involved at the drop of a hat. 'You're enough of a litigator to be going on with, Antoine. Why don't we see if there's anything we can do to help before we reach for more law.'

The big double doors into the suite opened as he spoke and a harassed-looking man called, 'Come on in, folks. Come in and sit down. There should be room. We'll deal with each and all of you just as quickly as we can, though I can't promise we'll get anything moving in the immediate time frame.' He waved them all in, his arms stick-like as they protruded from the short sleeves of his immaculately laundered white shirt. His tie was also short and failed to reach his belt buckle, despite being loosened so he could unbutton his collar.

The crowd surged forward again as the official stood back. Richard, Antoine and Sin went with them. Richard forgot all about calling Robin as he tried to work out which group they should join – if there was anyone else here on a mission similar to theirs. Sin was the only man in a naval outfit, so it was no use looking for other officers or shiphandlers judging by their uniforms. Most of the rest of the vociferous crowd were in jeans and T-shirts or lightweight business suits. Men off the vessels, and their owners' corporate lawyers, Richard calculated. Sailors and sharks. But there were several other heavy-set men in Day-Glo protective clothing whose faces were little short of murderous – longshoremen, Richard guessed. And, finally, several more purposeful-looking men and women who filled their army-issue camouflage-patterned outfits to bursting.

Richard assumed the squad in new-issue alternate ACUs were National Guard or regular army advisors sent to help them. Help was what he needed but also what he had to offer, so the men in camos seemed the best place to begin. Especially as, unlike the longshoremen, they looked calm and controlled. He started searching for someone wearing officer pips. His eye soon fell on a compact, decisive, dark-skinned individual whose ID flash showed his name to be Guerrero and whose gold, leaf-shaped badges revealed he was a major. It only took a moment for Richard to shoulder his way through the crowd with Antoine and Sin close behind, so that when the muscular guardsmen sat down, the three Heritage Mariner men were sitting right beside them.

'Good afternoon, Major Guerrero,' said Richard easily, leaning forward and sideways as they settled into their chairs. 'I'm Richard Mariner of Heritage Mariner Shipping.' He reached across in the introduction and shook hands with the major, whose youthful, dark chocolate eyes regarded him calculatingly from behind black lashes that would have flattered a model in a make-up advert, and from beneath raised eyebrows. 'These are my colleagues, Captain Sin and Antoine Prudhomme.'

'Jose Guerrero. Major, California National Guard, Sacramento Division.' The handshake was firm and dry. The nod to the other two curt but courteous.

'Good to meet you, Major. My ship *Sulu Queen* is half laden and stuck in her berth, unable to discharge or load up – not that we have any idea where her next cargo actually is at the moment.' Richard continued companionably, 'What's *your* problem?'

'Comparable to yours, sir,' answered the major easily, with only a trace of a Mexican accent. His voice was almost as deep as Richard's, its tone calm and thoughtful. 'I have a consignment of containers on the dockside. Emergency supplies, everything from field hospitals to chemical latrines – freighted down from Mather, Sacramento on the orders of the governor himself, with me and my people riding shotgun. They've been taken off the freight cars and just dumped on the dockside while I try and work out where they'll be most useful if the people at NOAA are correct with their weather predictions.'

'Back in Sacramento, from the sound of things,' said Richard.

'That's as may be, sir. But my orders are to make them available to the authorities here in LA, and at the moment I can't even move them west out to Fort MacArthur or east back inland to the National Guard HQ at Los Alamitos. They're stuck on the docks now. Holding everything else up, as far as I can ascertain.'

'Then you need to get them moved, Major!' intruded Captain Sin abruptly.

'Or you and the governor will be looking at a series of crippling lawsuits,' added Antoine. 'Not just from Heritage Mariner but from half the people here, as far as I can reckon.' This turned one or two heads nearby, Richard noted. Lawyers hearing the word *lawsuit* almost subliminally, like Great Whites scenting blood.

'OK, Antoine,' said Richard. 'Let's not rush to judgement here.'

Major Guerrero was opening his mouth to add his two cents' worth. But whatever he was about to add was cut off by the harassed-looking official who had invited them all in here. He was standing in front of a huge schematic of the Long Beach docks overlain with pictures of the chaos Richard had observed from Nic Greenbaum's helicopter. 'Good afternoon, ladies and gentlemen,' he began, pulling off his glasses and beginning to polish them with the tip of his tie. 'My name is Kurt Carpenter, terminal manager for the section your freight is snarled up in. I'm aware of the problems you are all facing,' he gestured widely to the big picture on the screen behind him, 'but in order to get them sorted out most quickly and efficiently, we'd be best to start with individual cases . . .'

One of the solid-looking men in Day-Glo yellow stood up. 'Problem's simple, Mac,' he said. 'We got more TEU boxes on the dockside than we can move. Twenty- and forty-foot equivalents both, as a matter of fact. We got nowhere to put them. No one's willing to freight them out from under our feet – not on trucks or railcars or ships. Everyone's wanting to bring shedloads more stuff in – no one wants to take anything out. Until the dockside is cleared of some of this stuff, it's total gridlock. There's nothing we can do.'

'I know the governor's ordered emergency supplies,' Carpenter answered. 'But I don't know where he wants it put. Or who he wants to move it.' The room was silent for a moment, with everyone looking at everyone else. Richard was looking at Major Jose Guerrero, his expression thoughtful.

'Is there anyone here who knows what the governor has actually shipped in?' asked Carpenter. 'All I know is it's in nearly one-hundred-and-twenty-foot TEUs.' He waved a flimsy piece of paper, clearly some sort of manifest.

The major stood up. 'Major Jose Guerrero, Sacramento Division, California National Guard,' he said calmly. 'I reckon a lot of the stuff you're worried about is to do with me and my guys. I can give you a detailed inventory for each container and all, but I guess we really don't have the time. Overall, it's just emergency equipment. Hospital supplies, emergency rations, bedding, chemical latrines, generators, the gas to keep them working and so forth. The sort of stuff we need in place if the health and welfare infrastructure of the city starts collapsing. My orders were to get it to a National Guard base for unpacking and distribution, but somehow it's ended up on the dockside here. I suppose someone must have thought this was the nearest freight yard. Maybe it is, I don't know; I wasn't briefed on that aspect. But the fact is I want to shift it all out to Fort MacArthur or inland to Los Alamitos as soon as I can. They've both been briefed to take some of it. But Los Alamitos would be the best

bet for me if we can get it all up on to I710, which is supposed
to be a five-minute drive away from the dock. Then across town.
Only, as far as I can tell, my consignment is stuck on the
waterfront. And it's at least part of what's holding things up, like
a cork in a bottle. I've called for trucks and trailers to come down
but apparently the guard's got nothing that'll handle twenty-foot
containers. The army's got all sorts of stuff, from tank transporters
to trailers, but nothing they can spare immediately. Certainly
nothing that's actually designed for containers – or to be able to
shift a hundred of them.'

'Couldn't get trucks into them even if they did have,' said the
man in the Day-Glo vest. 'And sure as shit not tank transporters!
Not through the gridlock we have here.' He gave a bark of dry,
humourless laughter. 'Roads are blocked. Quayside's clogged.
We even have trouble moving our cranes up and down on the
dock. That's why we stopped unloading everything.'

'So I can't move my stuff?' demanded the major, frowning.

'Nope. And if it don't get moved, then it looks like nothing
gets moved,' shrugged the man in the Day-Glo vest. 'But there's
no way you're going to freight it out of there, even if you had
the trucks. Not with everything from the Pacific to the Interstate
snarled up. Like I say . . .' He gave a brief, unexpected grin.
'. . . What you might call a *Mexican standoff* . . .'

'Put it on a ship,' said Richard mildly. His voice was not loud
but it carried across the silence that followed the longshoreman's
less-than-tasteful joke.

'What?' asked the longshoreman, swinging round to face the
new idea and the man who had proposed it.

'Put it on a ship out of the way,' Richard persisted. 'Clear the
blockage, free up the harbour and the Interstates, then take it off
again and freight it out when everything else is clear. MacArthur,
Los Alamitos, wherever.'

'What ship?' demanded Kurt Carpenter, his voice wavering
between hope and doubt. 'We'd need permissions from here to
Thanksgiving. We'd need clearance from the relevant captains
. . . Agents . . . Owners . . . *Christ* . . .'

'I can't speak for the Almighty or his Son,' said Richard, rising
to tower beside Major Guerrero as every eye on the room became
fixed on him. 'But I've got all the rest covered. My name is

Richard Mariner. I'm the CEO of Heritage Mariner and owner of *Sulu Queen*, the container ship docked in the middle of this mess and half laden. I have my captain and my agent's lawyer here.' He paused, aware that he was stretching a point about the lawyer. But Antoine wisely stayed silent. 'And I'm telling you,' he continued smoothly, 'if you can get Major Guerrero's containers to *Sulu Queen*'s berth you can load them aboard her with my blessing and leave them there until the docks are clear – she can accommodate more than four thousand TEUs and she has plenty of room to spare. Then you can take them off again when everything's running smoothly on the docks and freight them out. No problem. That way we'll maybe get the rest of *Sulu Queen*'s old cargo off and her new cargo on, and perhaps even get her back out to sea before the bad weather hits too hard.'

'Sounds like a plan,' said Carpenter. 'Is this something you can do, Mr Molloy?'

'I guess,' answered the man in the Day-Glo vest. Then he seemed to make up his mind. 'Sure. I know *Sulu Queen*. My team's been unloading her since the port officials gave us the all clear this morning. We can get some of the TEUs aboard her and see how things go from there. Good plan, Mr Mariner. Thanks.'

'OK,' said Richard, his bland gaze skating over Antoine's uncertain expression and Captain Sin's outraged one. 'Let's get to it.'

EIGHT

Robin went from 'stunned' to 'overwhelmed' as Nic showed her round his new toy. With her experienced eye taking in every detail as though *Maxima* were a boat she was just about to command, she walked at his side from the engine room with its showroom-new Caterpillar twin diesel motors capable of cruising at twenty knots, where she'd met the engineer and his little team. They walked through the galley where the chef was putting the finishing touches to the light luncheon he was just about to serve, through the eight palatial state rooms and the cavernous internal common areas where various crew members were tidying up and making beds after the crew of *Katapult8* had departed for the morning shakedown aboard their own vessel. They stopped at the command bridge where she met Captain Toro, his first officer and the navigating officer – and finally the flying bridge where she met the communications officer and the electrical officer who were running checks on the navigation and communication equipment up above their heads – and where it was possible to watch Liberty and the crew of *Katapult8* as they left off their preparations to take their multihull out tomorrow and came back aboard *Maxima* to wash-up and eat.

Robin, Nic, Liberty and *Katapult8*'s all-woman crew lunched at a table on the middle outer deck, with the tail of the Bell above them and the swimming pool below. Robin knew all of them well – she had raced with and against them in the past. If anyone could shake *Katapult8* down and really get the best out of her revolutionary 'flying hook' design, it would be these women. Though, even having seen the massive Caterpillar 3,516–6,200-horsepower diesels in the engine room below and discussed their massive potential with the men who maintained them, she doubted that *Maxima* could keep up if *Katapult8* got the wind in that huge jet-wing sail of hers. The gin palace might be capable of twenty-five knots at a push. *Katapult8* was capable of forty-five, especially when the long, sleek hulls lifted right out of the water and she sat just on the hook-shaped hydrofoils that generated hardly any drag to slow her as she flew.

As they tucked in to the lunch, *Katapult8's* crew debated whether they should rush back aboard as soon as they were finished or whether there might be time to take advantage of the warm afternoon for a quick dip in the swimming pool, which filled much of the aft section of the deck they were looking down on. After all, the plan was to run *Katapult8* south as fast as she would go and shake her down for the next Olympics, while *Maxima* shadowed her, then they would all meet up in Puerto Banderas and enjoy some R&R in Nic's newly built estate down there. However, Liberty didn't take much persuading to let her crew indulge themselves. The next couple of days threatened to be hard going, even if the weather predictions were overcautious. Earlier incarnations of *Katapult* had boasted comfortable accommodation for four. But this was the equivalent of a formula-one racer, not a family camper. There were berths but they were little more than strengthened hammocks. And there were supplies – though nothing tasty and nothing hot. Nor, indeed, facilities to heat anything up, in any case. It was a thousand miles down to Puerto Banderas and Liberty was reckoning on at least fifty hours' tough sailing – sheer, solid grind. If the wind really got up they would find themselves working very hard indeed. Or swimming in far more dangerous waters.

So the crewmen finishing the maintenance on the jet skis and inflatables around the folded-down stern section were soon treated to the distractingly attractive sight of four lithe bikini-clad bodies swimming like mermaids in an aquarium, for the act of folding down the stern revealed that the aft wall of the pool itself was made of toughened glass. And that was the reason they gave, much later, to explain why they failed to check the final item on their maintenance itinerary: the Spurs line-and-net-cutting system.

While Liberty and her crew relaxed, Nic took Robin round the rest of the boat's interior then, finally, after another hour or so, down to see his 'pictures' of Dahlia Blanca as Liberty and her crew went back to *Katapult8*. The minute Robin realized what he had in mind, she thought, you've got to be kidding me! But she said nothing, all too well aware that Nic was cheerfully winding her up. He settled her solicitously in the front row of the on-board cinema and popped a SIM card into the slot beneath the seventy-five-inch flat-screen TV that took up half the wall. Nic's 'pictures' sprang to life.

A swooping camera – clearly a helicopter-shot – sailed low across a wide blue sea towards a wall of jungle. In full, in-your-face, 3D, the blue-backed in-running waves whipped downwards out of shot at the bottom of the wide screen, replaced for an instant by a foam-edged white sand beach, but the precipitous, jungle-clad slopes washed threateningly towards the camera like a solid green tsunami. Between the leaves, trunks and creepers of the canopy, bare earth and sheer rock walls gleamed, running with steams and waterfalls. It was hard to get a sense of scale, but the angle of the shot made it all seem huge, precipitous and terribly threatening. Robin found herself leaning back in her seat as though the jungle were bursting out of the screen like an avalanche to crush her. But at the last moment the camera angle changed giddily and instead of rushing further up the precipice it turned to follow the crest of the ridge itself. Now the tops of the huge trees whipped under the shot like the waves at the start, reminding Robin of the rainforests of Africa; of the Virunga National Park clinging to the slopes of volcanoes on the Congo–Rwanda border. Equally untouched. Equally dangerous.

On the left-hand side of the wide screen, another ridge rose higher and, distantly, another rose higher still, reducing the sky to a shred of blue as thin as the strip of white that had been the beach. It was like an enormous staircase, Robin realized. An unimaginable wall of mountainside, stepping down and down beneath the jungle canopy to that tiny ribbon of beach and then the huge Pacific.

'This is like Keats's Peak in Darien,' said Nic cheerfully, 'where the poet imagines the Spanish explorer and conquistador Cortez looking at the Pacific for the first time – in the poem about Chapman's Homer. "*Or like stout Cortez when with eagle eyes he star'd at the Pacific – and all his men looked at each other with a wild surmise – silent, upon a peak in Darien*",' he quoted sonorously. Then he spoilt the effect by adding, 'Shit, it probably *is* that *peak in Darien*! On a less highbrow note, though, it's also where ex-Governor Schwarzenegger came to film the *Predator* movie. The jungle's that thick, wild and remote . . .'

But no sooner had Nic made the point than the trees stopped. The camera was suddenly swooping low over the outskirts of civilization. A sizeable town clung to the lower steps of the mountainside, overlooking the rolling Pacific. Tall trees were replaced in the blink of an eye by taller hotels. The mountain slope on the left of the screen fell back into a wide, dry river valley, on whose flat floor stood an airport. On the right, the inclines were suddenly divided into city blocks, and a kaleido-scope of red-tiled roofs, flat roof gardens, hotel tops with satellite dishes and lift housings came and went. And among them, all along the straight-ruled streets below and the upper ones winding like serpents into the wild greenery above, were blue pools, gleaming the iridescent scales on a butterfly's wing. Made brighter, Robin suddenly realized, contrasted against the early evening gloom gathering outside *Maxima* herself.

A larger river swept out of the distant jungle on the left and rolled down, step by step, fall by fall and pool by pool on to a broad, winding, island-filled stream that opened into the inrushing ocean. Robin had an instantaneous glimpse of ne· ˙ marinas coupled with ancient commercial dock facilities. A tall, gracefully arched bridge. A massive breakwater lined on one side with warehouses and on the other with tall hotels. Then the camera whirled away, dipped and started to rise again. And there, reaching out of the precipitous heart of a jungle-clad cliff, on the edge of a placid lake at the foot of a tall waterfall, there was a vision of pure white. As though a Carrara marble outcrop had been transported here from Italy's Amalfi coast and then carved into the shape of a fantasy by Frank Lloyd Wright, the building half clung, half floated above the vertiginous cliff slope that tumbled down to the northern outskirts of the town as they cut into the vegetation on the lower slopes and stood low above the long white beach leading back down to the old commercial dock and the broad mouth of the river.

The camera wheeled once more with stomach-churning abruptness and soared onwards towards the beautiful white house. Again, the size of the picture was difficult for Robin to judge. What she at first assumed was an outreaching balcony, edged with a low white wall, was suddenly revealed to be a huge garden with shady palms, elegant topiary and manicured lawns fit for a golf course, at the rear of which lay a half-covered swimming pool that must have been near Olympic size. The camera swooped over this, under the awning which extended from an upper veranda and in through cavernous doors made of smoked-plate glass in a zoom that would have flattered Alfred Hitchcock or Orson Welles into a massive, Mexican-styled open-plan area, all decorative tile and white adobe.

Robin was just beginning to come to terms with the abrupt transition when her phone went off. She pulled it out automatically. Richard's face filled the screen. 'It's Richard,' she told Nic. 'I'd better take this.'

'OK,' said Nic amenably. He reached forward to freeze the screen. 'We'll look around the inside when you're finished. But remind him we're meeting up for dinner tonight. The Sky Room, Breakers Hotel, Ocean Boulevard. Be there at eight; we're all booked in. My treat this time.'

'God,' said Robin. 'Look at the time. I'd better get back and change pretty damn quickly . . .'

NINE

Both of his companions were silent – though it seemed to Richard to be a *speaking* silence, as Jane Austen might have put it – down to the taxi rank outside the port authority building. Neither could or would put into words what they were thinking, but Richard reckoned that Antoine had some pretty serious worries about the legal implications, which might be well above his pay grade. Sin was simply smouldering at the thought of taking containers that did not contain his cargo aboard before he could begin to unload the containers that did contain his cargo – and get on with the job he was being paid to do. But before Richard had even snagged a cab or either one of them had begun to unburden their soul, Jose Guerrero joined them. 'Nice move, Mr Mariner,' said the major affably. 'But I'm not sure you've thought it all through.'

That makes three of you, thought Richard. 'How's that, Major?' he enquired affably.

'If you're taking my containers on board your ship, then I guess you're taking me. And my command.'

'That's fine by me,' answered Richard. 'Captain Sin?'

'We have little room for supernumeraries,' observed the captain rudely. 'But if you insist, Captain Mariner, we would try and find suitable accommodation. How many men are there in your command, Major?'

'Half a dozen. Four men, two women. Logistics. Medics.'

'That will be no trouble. We can supply food and rest areas. If you eat Chinese rather than Mexican, that is, and if you have nothing beyond basic requirements. I assume we will not be providing overnight facilities.'

'That depends on how fast the docks are cleared,' said Richard, cutting into the increasingly acid exchanges. 'But if push comes to shove, I expect you can manage something, Captain Sin.'

'If push,' snapped Sin, 'comes to shove.' He spat the final word as though 'shove' was one of his obscure Chinese insults, like *sons of rabbits*.

As he thought this, Richard opened the rear door of the cab that had pulled up in obedience to his signal. 'Are you riding down to the docks with us, Major? Or waiting for your own people?' he enquired, calmly and courteously.

'I'll wait,' answered the major shortly, reacting to Sin's tone rather than Richard's emollience. 'And I trust you – and we – will be able to get through the traffic jams down to the dockside.'

As it happened, the cab was able to avoid the worst of the jams by scooting down West Ocean Boulevard and Pico Avenue – more or less the reverse of the route that had brought them safely up here earlier – so that Richard, Antoine and Sin were dropped within walking distance of *Sulu Queen*'s gangplank little more than a quarter of an hour later. Even so, a long, grey evening was beginning to draw in. As he walked through the unnatural quiet of the dockside, Richard suddenly realized he still hadn't called Robin. He dialled her mobile and her face filled the screen almost at once.

'God,' she said as contact was made. 'Look at the time. I'd better get back and change.'

'Change?' asked Richard. 'What for?'

'Dinner, you dope. Nic's taking us to the Sky Room at the Breakers Hotel. We're due at eight. It's a "good luck" meal for the girls on *Katapult8* and a "thank you" to us for last night. We'll have missed the sunset by more than an hour but the view should still be spectacular.'

'*So's the food!*' called Nic, from seemingly far away.

'Eight o'clock,' said Richard. The clock in the top of the screen told him it was well after five now. He looked up at the thickening overcast. 'Wouldn't have been much of a sunset tonight in any case,' he said. 'You hitching a ride on the Bell?'

'*Yes, she is!*' called Nic as Robin hesitated for a moment.

'Ask Nic if he can he pick me up where you dropped me at lunchtime.'

'Sure, Richard,' called Nic. 'Be there at six!' And Richard began to wonder whether Robin had her cell on speakerphone.

'You get that?' asked Robin.

'I'll be there if I can get *Sulu Queen* sorted out.'

'We'll be there if Nic can get the girls back off *Katapult8* in time. He's gone off to call then in now.'

'Gotcha. Come in, *Katapult8*, your time is up! Something like that?'

'Something like that, lover,' she answered.

By the time Richard was standing at the spot Nic's Bell had dropped him off more than six hours earlier, the docks were beginning to come to life again. The security lights were on and an urgent bustle was building beneath their yellow brightness. The crane beside *Sulu Queen* was lifting the first few TEUs and loading them aboard his vessel with pinpoint accuracy and practised forethought – heaviest at the bottom of the columns, lightest at the top. Stevedores and crewmen were securing the lateral lashings in place, tightening turnbuckles and twistlocks as though *Sulu Queen* might set to sea with the one-hundred-and-twenty-foot TEUs of the National Guard's equipment stowed aboard.

Which was why, during much of the intervening time, Major Guerrero had been standing stolidly on the far side of Captain Sin to Richard, while Antoine had been monopolizing the ship to shore, talking things through with the senior legal officers at Southey-Bell, calling Richard through as and when he needed the owner's weight to back up what they were doing – and proposing to do.

But, at last, Richard had felt confident enough to leave them to get on with it. Hard hat and security vest in place once more, he followed one of the few officers not involved with loading the ship back down the walkway towards the gangplank. Now, on his right, instead of that vacancy with its Rubik's cube floor there was a wall of red, lead containers, ridged for strength, battered but still strong, stinking of oil, metal and rust. And this time, the vacancy was on his left hand, for the dockside was slowly being cleared of the first of the containers that had been choking it.

Normally it would have taken little more than a minute to lift a container from the dockside and position it aboard, but the process was slowed by several factors. The major's containers were not well placed and had to be moved from the side of the rail tracks before the cranes could lift them. They had also been offloaded from the trains that brought them down here without regard to contents or, crucially, weight. Furthermore, because they were going on to a vessel that was fundamentally unprepared to receive them, there was often an unusually lengthy discussion between the longshoreman and the lading officer as to precisely where each container should be deposited. A one hundred minute task, therefore, was threatening to stretch out to five hours and more. It was out of the question that Richard should have to wait until the better part of midnight to see everything completed here. Especially as Captain Sin and his crew were perfectly capable, if less than happy. Major Guerrero was able to take any decisions regarding National Guard matters and Antoine – a bachelor gay in the old-fashioned use of the term – had no calls on his time and was content to stay aboard and oversee any unexpected legal snags.

When Richard clambered aboard the Bell it became immediately clear that Nic had been more than generous in offering him a lift. The six seats in the passenger compartment were filled. Nic himself, Robin, Liberty and the crew of *Katapult8* were packed in tight. Richard hesitated, feeling a little like a mackerel invading a sardine tin. But Nic waved him forward with a grin. 'You're riding shotgun,' he shouted over the roar of the Pratt and Whitney motors. 'The co-pilot's seat's still empty.'

Richard folded himself as tightly as he could and oozed into the cockpit like toothpaste sinking back into the tube. Even so, the wiry pilot had to squeeze hard against the side window to let him through. Richard gingerly unfolded himself into the co-pilot's seat and buckled his seat belt tightly. The Bell jumped into the air. Richard had seen enough of the docks for one day, so he looked across at the man in control.

And blinked.

The pilot's skin was darker than Antoine's Creole colouring, but not quite dark enough to be African-American or West Indian. Her hair was curled thickly enough to camouflage the headpiece of her earphones. The stem of the built-in microphone almost touched the fullness of her chiselled lips. She shot him a glance from eyes that were unsettlingly like Major Guerrero's – long lashes framing milky whites and black-coffee pupils almost as dark as the irises at their centres. Her nose and cheekbones were sharp, as was the intelligence behind those arresting eyes. 'All secure, Cap'n?' she growled.

'Yup,' was all he could say.

And the Bell went up like a rocket lifting off.

TEN

The cab dropped Richard and Robin outside the Sky Room on South Locust Avenue at seven fifty-five p.m. and they hurried through the increasingly humid atmosphere under the bright thrust of the awning and into the restaurant section of the Spanish baroque fantasy of the Breakers Hotel. They crossed the lobby and entered the lift, which obligingly whisked them upwards almost as fast as Biddy McKinney, Nic's chopper pilot, had done.

Richard had watched, fascinated, as the pilot sent the Bell soaring across the docks and down into the Island Express helipad. Robin held a pilot's license and was a gifted helicopter pilot. He was well used to watching her taking control of a range of helicopters, but Biddy seemed to him to have something extra. A special gift – almost an ability to become one with her machine. It was at once fascinating and faintly disturbing. Like something out of the long discontinued *X-Files*.

'What's the matter, Cap'n?' she'd growled after a moment or two under his piercing stare. 'Ain't you never seen a woman of colour fly?'

His answer had begun a brief but intense conversation, during which he'd discovered her name and a great deal more about her. Not least that she was born and raised in Enterprise, Alabama, educated at the Enterprise Ozark Community College before joining the army and eventually transferring to the First Aviation Brigade at nearby Fort Rucker – *Mother Rucker* to those who knew and loved it. Among her other duties there, she'd worked her way up to warrant officer and served with the Aviation Technical Test Centre as a test pilot for choppers, so there were hardly any she didn't know her way around. She loved army life, flying and working under the command of Major General Magnum but, when her last tour of duty had come to an end, she'd discovered with some surprise that her reputation had spread beyond the realms of the aviation brigades, the state of Alabama and the United States Army Air Service – so much so that there were men willing to make her offers that were hard to refuse.

Mr Greenbaum had made the best of them, so here Biddy was. And, she had to admit, spending much of her time in corporate luxury in her quarters aboard *Maxima* – which were hardly less lavish than the guest suites – and pottering around in a pretty little new-generation Bell 429 was more like a long vacation on full pay as far as she was concerned. Moreover, she was off to Mexico tomorrow for a three-day cruise followed by a week or so in the most well-appointed building she had ever come across. As she had flown the chopper from which they had shot much of Mr Greenbaum's Dahlia Blanca video, she'd known exactly what she was talking about. The weather up here in California might be darkening down, but the future looked bright to ex-Warrant Officer Biddy McKinney.

The elevator doors opened several seconds and eighteen floors later. Richard and Robin stepped shoulder to shoulder into the Sky Room and Biddy vanished from Richard's mind, overwhelmed as he was by his immediate surroundings. The maître d', who introduced himself as Mario, greeted them and, at the mention of Nic's name, led them to a table in the corner. As they followed him, Robin looked around, caught between amusement and surprise. The whole place was like *Queen Mary*'s younger sibling. The ship's 1930s Art Deco fittings were echoed here in the stylish restaurant by furnishings every bit as palatial, but from the 1940s. And Mario's quiet speech of introduction and orientation mentioned the later cohort of Hollywood stars. In place of Greta Garbo, the Astaires and their generation, famous in the pre-war years, he talked of post-war regulars like Clark Gable, Errol Flynn and Cary Grant, who had famously come here to sip their cocktails and look down over Long Beach in the company of Elizabeth Taylor, Rita Hayworth and Ava Gardner. Robin

glanced across at Richard and shook her head. His grin was just
as wide as it had been aboard the *Queen Mary* last night. Any
wider, she thought, and the top of his head would fall off.

'This is Mr Greenbaum's table,' announced Mario as he pulled
out a chair for Robin. 'Here in his favourite corner.'

But this corner was no hideaway, no secluded spot, Robin
thought. Two long picture windows met to form it, offering a
breathtaking view across lower Long Beach towards the ocean,
from the cranes standing tall under the security lighting above
Sulu Queen right the way round past *Queen Mary* to Grissom
Island and White Island in the outwash of the Los Angeles River,
to distant Seal Beach beyond. Under a low grey sky that looked
like the roof of a squat mineshaft, the city spread out like the
strike of a lifetime in a diamond mine. Like the sales tray in
Tiffany's – points of jewel brightness beneath a coal-black cover
of velvety darkness.

Robin and Richard were still discussing the impressive but
slightly unsettling view when Nic, Liberty and her crewmates
arrived. No sooner had they settled in their chairs than the
menus and wine lists were presented. Robin was charier tonight
and settled for an alcohol-free evening like her teetotal husband.
The sailors were also careful – the last thing in the world they
needed when they got underway in the morning was a hangover.
Nic cheerfully fell in with the general abstemiousness and the
sparkling water flowed.

As it was with the wine list, everyone was careful with the
menu, thinking less about having a great gastronomic adventure
tonight than about whether they might regret it tomorrow. They
all settled for asparagus soup and Caesar salad. A certain amount
of oysters Rockefeller and seared Ahi had been consumed last
night, so the table settled for blue lump crab cakes, jumbo shrimp
and, on Liberty's recommendation, truffle *pommes frites*. Then
they got to work on the main courses.

For Richard this meant Colorado rack of lamb, heirloom
carrots, Brussels sprouts, spiced croquette potatoes and mushrooms. Robin went for the veal chop with mushrooms, carrots
and asparagus, while big meat-eater Nic chose rib-eye with
more asparagus and yet more truffle *pomme frites*, with no
thought at all for the health of his cardiovascular system, thought

Robin. A decision he would have had a hard time making were he not a widower bereft of a solicitous life partner's good sense. The crew of *Katapult8* variously went for pasta, salmon and black cod. From the dessert menu, those thinking of their waistlines choose the chef's trio of sorbets, while the rest went for the 'chocolate therapy'.

The conversation was about the view and the ambience to begin with, then about the menu and the food. But Liberty soon started needling her father about tomorrow. 'That fat gin palace of yours won't stand a chance,' she announced. 'It could have twice as many Caterpillar diesels and pull horses by the thousand but it won't even *see Katapult8* after an hour or so, except on radar maybe, let alone keep up with her.'

The gauntlet she threw down so calculatedly included Richard and Robin, who were also due to be aboard *Maxima* for the run down to Puerto Banderas. Nic smiled indulgently and remained silent, but Richard rose to the bait. 'OK,' he said. 'It's *put your money where your mouth is* time. What do you bet?'

Liberty's eyes went wide, then narrow. 'What do you know?' she demanded.

'Nothing you don't know.'

'It's the weather, isn't it? It's this ARkStorm – if it ever arrives!'

'If it arrives,' interrupted her father forcefully, 'then we'll all be running south of it as fast as it's possible to sail or motor.'

'That is part of the point,' added Robin. 'Your father wants you, *Katapult8*, *Maxima* and all of us well out of the way before the heavens open.'

'But I can't see how a storm, even a once-in-two-centuries event, is going to make us go slower and you go faster,' persisted Liberty, paying no attention to Nic or Robin, focused entirely on Richard and his challenge.

'That's for me to know and you to guess,' he answered blandly.

'There'd be winds along a storm front,' persisted Liberty, glancing at crewmates, Florence Weary and Emma Toda. 'It's the *calms* we need to worry about.'

'Maybe that's it,' said Flo thoughtfully. 'Maybe he's reckoning that if the ARkStorm streams in here there'll be light winds or dead calms to the south of it. What d'you think?'

All four yachtswomen looked at Richard. He raised his

eyebrows and presented his blandest face. After a moment he took a mouthful of lamb and began to chew slowly and silently. As he did so, suddenly but spectacularly in the background, the Tino Productions orchestra went into their opening number. Aptly enough, it was Billie Holliday's 'Stormy Blues'.

The table rather split into two camps after that. Liberty's crew went into a huddle, whispering among each other, and even started to make obscure notes on a folded napkin, letting the astonishingly good food go cold while they tried to second guess what Richard was up to – and to come up with something that they could put up against him in the wager.

Robin tried to brighten things up between Richard and Nic by describing in exhaustive detail everything she had seen aboard *Maxima*, including a long and detailed description of the 'pictures' of Dahlia Blanca. But when it became clear that neither man was paying attention, she turned her own attention to her recently arrived chocolate therapy dessert and let them all get on with it. The orchestra moved on to Buddy Holly's 'Raining in My Heart'.

Halfway through dessert, Liberty looked up. 'You're on,' she said. 'What's the wager, Richard?'

'Winner's choice,' he answered easily. 'I trust you, and you know you can trust me. Whatever the winner demands of the loser.'

The band moved on to Wynonie Harris' 'Stormy Night Blues'. 'Within reason,' said Flo and Emma together.

'Oh ye of little faith,' laughed Richard. 'Reason is my middle name.'

'Right!' decided Liberty with a captain's authority. 'Winner's choice.'

'Given,' added Robin severely, 'that the last thing Richard and Nic had us all race against each other for turned out to be worth several million dollars.'

'That's another story altogether,' said Nic. 'Though I still get letters of thanks from all the charities it went to – and the Tokyo University's Earth Sciences and Climate Change department.'

'Me too,' added Richard. 'And from the British Antarctic Survey.'

'Right,' said Liberty, taking control once again, noting that the dessert plates were empty and the hour was getting late. 'That's all for now. Bedtime, ladies. We're up early tomorrow.'

'Up *and out* early,' added Flo with a meaningful glance at Richard.

'That's what I'd recommend,' he advised easily. 'But the tide will be against you until ten, so I'd spend the early hours getting ready for a Le Mans racing start then or thereabouts.'

The orchestra segued into Arlen and Koehler's 'Stormy Weather'.

'What in heaven's name was that all about?' demanded Robin as she, Richard and Nic rode down in the Sky Room's lift a quarter of an hour later with T-Bone Walker's 'Call it Stormy Monday' echoing out of the restaurant behind them.

'Making assurance double sure,' he answered.

'He's lit a fire under the girls' tails,' said Nic. The lift stopped, the doors opened and they began to cross the lobby.

'That's *not* a mental image I want to hold on to,' said Robin as they approached the door out on to South Locust. 'But . . .'

'They'll be off as fast as humanly possible tomorrow. The second the tide stops running against them, as near as I can judge,' Nic said.

'That's the plan. I thought you wanted them out from under this as early and as fast as possible,' said Richard as they stepped out on to the pavement and a cab pulled up in front of them.

'Especially as Florence and Emma seem to think you'll demand a range of inappropriate forfeits if they lose,' observed Robin tartly.

'Fear not, my love – you know you're all the woman I can handle,' said Richard piously.

'Well, let's just hope you're man enough for me.' As she spoke, something fell from the lowering sky and shattered on the side-walk at their feet. It took them a moment to realize that it was a single raindrop. But it hit the dusty ground hard enough to make a sound as threatening as a silenced gunshot. And it left a mark on the dry pavement big enough to suggest that it must have been about the size of a baseball.

Richard looked down at the little puddle that had formed instant-aneously at their feet, then up at the low, leaden, under-lit cloud cover. 'And it's maybe just as well,' he added, his tone suddenly sober and serious, 'that we're currently staying in the only hotel in Long Beach that's actually designed to float . . .'

ELEVEN

One hour later and a thousand miles further south, Carlos Santiago was wearily bringing his fishing boat, *Pilar*, into harbour. Carlos and *Pilar* were equally tired, battered and superannuated. It was coming up to fifty years since *Pilar* slipped into the water off Encinitas, California. She had been called *Miss Ellie* to begin with, and had set out on a hopeful career under the firm hand of James Hardy, the man who had commissioned her. Carlos had been celebrating his fifteenth birthday round about then, learning the art of fishing from his father. How the boat he named *Pilar* after his wife came to him he had no clear idea, for he could not read the American records that told her story and was happy to accept the assurance of the man who sold her that she was a strong and reliable lady. And so she had proved to be – even though the woman for whom she was named died in childbirth, forcing him to raise their beautiful daughter alone.

Now he and *Pilar* were old and the town in which he had grown up, buried his wife and raised his daughter and seen *her* married was strange to him nowadays; full of strange buildings, strange people, strange accents and languages, strange sights and smells. A new breakwater big enough to have hotels stood on the seaward side of it. A new six-lane highway reached over the juncture of the inner marina and the outer docks. It was a haven for tourists and pleasure boats. Billionaires and drug dealers. Less and less room for honest working fishermen like himself.

As Carlos Santiago helmed the worn-out old trawler towards this strange new land, feeling the Pacific rollers begin to gather under her keel as the ocean floor started the precipitous rise that extended on to the land and up through the coastal cliffs of the Sierra Madre Mountains, he swept his left hand down his sweat-slick face

and scratched the dripping white stubble on his chin as he leaned
forward over the helm, squinting upwards through moss-brown
eyes. The sky was high and clear enough, in spite of a thin
scud of overcast reaching down from the north, in spite of
the heat-haze that threatened to warp the air as though it was
unseasoned wood. The stars which had guided him in from the
outer reaches of the Tres Marias Deep and across the Bahia
Banderas so far were still clear enough to rely on – unlike the
air conditioning on *Pilar*'s bridge. He nodded to himself and
stood back, lowering his gaze to the blaze of light dead ahead.
The trusty old Raymarine he had bought in La Paz in better days
was becoming increasingly unreliable now, as indeed was *Pilar*
herself and most of the equipment aboard, including the rusty
old Cummins KPA 1100 diesel.

The crew of twelve who had filled her crew quarters and filled
her freezer storage areas with blue-fin tuna, snapper and swordfish
ten years ago had begun to depart with the onset of federal
restrictions and the departure of the fish. Now *Pilar* was lucky
to carry half-a-dozen desperate and starving men in search of
sardines. Carlos took his sad and sorry vessel further and further
out, trailed finer and finer seined nets, tried longer and longer
lines – flirting with arrest and total ruin if he should be caught.
But tonight, as usual, he was bringing his boat and his crew
home empty, guiding them in by the stars because the equipment
was faulty. They were coming towards the harbour silently
because he could not rely on the ancient SEA222 HF transceiver
any more. He was confused and more hesitant than he cared to
admit, not only because of the cataracts darkening his vision
which he could not afford to have treated, but also because the
dazzle of all the new buildings along the Malecón beachfront
disorientated him, as though he had looked up into the heavens
and found half-a-dozen new galaxies suddenly appearing there.

But then he saw what he had been looking for. The white
house. Dahlia Blanca. The one new addition to Puerto Banderas
that earned his blessings instead of his curses. It sat high on the
jungle-dark cliff face, a still white beacon under the beams
of the three-quarter moon perched just above the starboard wing of
Pilar's flying bridge like a parrot on a pirate's shoulder. The
point of tranquil brightness was like a lighthouse to Carlos

Santiago. It shone out above the glare of new buildings like *la estrella pola;* it cut through the fog of his cataracts; it guided him across the approaches to the commercial dock beside the oldest beach of the burgeoning tourist venue that was now swamping the fishing village which had been his childhood home. The heart of what had been from time immemorial a *barrio mariner*, visited only by those wishing to hunt the big blue-fin tuna, the sail-fish and the swordfish, and to watch the migrating whales that populated the *bahia*. And the men in the old days – *los hombres machos*, the *Americanos* like the writer Hemingway, the filmmaker Huston and the actors Weathers and Schwarzenegger. The one place the effete, small-minded, modern tourists, the realtors, the speculators and the drug dealers hardly ever came to – Los Muertos.

'*Hola, Capitan,*' said Miguel-Angel Guerrero, the ship's boy, coming on to the bridge. 'It is hot tonight! *Verdad?*'

'*Verdad, hijo,*' answered Carlos. 'I have never known it so hot at this time of year in all my life.'

'Nor I,' agreed Miguel-Angel seriously.

Carlos smiled, but he did not laugh out loud. The boy was sixteen; a quarter of the age of his *capitan*. So of course he would never have experienced anything Carlos had not experienced. But Carlos was concerned that Miguel-Angel would be insulted if he laughed – even though he would be laughing at the situation, not at the lad, whom he treated as a son because the boy respected him like a father, though he always called him *Capitan*. Out of respect, of course, for his own father, who owned the dockside chandlery, and was, like Carlos, alone but for his child. Though, unlike Carlos, he had lost his woman not to childbirth but to the lure of California, north of the border. His woman and his elder son.

Lacking a son of his own, Carlos had been busily passing his knowledge of the coastal waters to Miguel-Angel. Earlier that night he had made the boy stand silently beside the open windows, listening to the voices of the Tres Marias Islands, each of whom sang her own song created as wind and water rushed through huge coastal caves which varied in size and depth. Together they had stood and listened to the northernmost voice, Isla Maria Madre, whose song was deep and unmistakable. Then, later, they had listened to the roaring of the waters as they rushed over the reefs beside Isla Saint Isabel, who, together with the Tres Marias, gave a measure of protection to the harbour at Puerto Banderas.

Miguel-Angel walked forward to stand by his *capitan* and follow the direction of his gaze towards the last of the features that guided them safely home. 'It is the Dahlia Blanca,' the boy said. 'It guides us home like a lighthouse.' But he used the word *faro*, which means 'beacon'.

'It is like a beacon to me, indeed,' agreed Carlos. 'And in more ways than one. It not only brings us home every night, but it ensures I have a home to go to, eh, Miguel-Angel?'

Miguel-Angel understood the old man's point, for they had discussed the situation often and in detail. Carlos's daughter, Pilar, had married a young man named Cesar, who had migrated here from Guadalajara and lacked any charm, skill or ambition that his father-in law could see. But Carlos, a fair man, admitted that few sons-in-law measured up to the dreams of their *suegros*. For some time the newly-weds relied on Carlos for housing and support while Pilar sought work in the villas and hotels being built on the outskirts of the old town. And Cesar had sought with little success to make the acquaintance of the most successful drug dealers in the *barrio*. It seemed for a while that Carlos would have to support them all for ever – or at least until he was called home to heaven by Nuestra Señora de Guadalupe.

But then *el Americano Señor Bosqueverde* – Greenbaum – came to Puerto Banderas, and this had led to Dahlia Blanca being constructed. Everything had changed. Pilar applied for a position there and was made a junior cook-housekeeper, earning a salary that seemed simply fabulous. Cesar most unexpectedly revealed a passion for plants and an ability to nurture them, an ability that might have recommended him to the local *jefes narcos* had they been interested in marijuana rather than cocaine and crystal meth. He too applied for work and was made junior groundsman, of equal standing in the gardens to Pilar in the house. And on an equal salary. They were able to afford a modest flat high on the hill slopes where the rent was cheap and the air was cool. A flat with a second bedroom for the baby they proposed to have soon. But in the meantime, Carlos occupied it, glad to get out of the two-roomed hovel behind Los Muertos in which he had been born and raised, with its veranda on which he had slept during the days – and nights – while Pilar and Cesar occupied the old bedroom and, indeed, the old bed in which she had been conceived. A veranda which was comfortable enough in the dry season and allowed the newly-weds some privacy, while being convenient to the outside lavatory which Carlos visited several time a night.

'I am pleased your home is so comfortable nowadays,' said Miguel-Angel wisely, 'because you will need to sleep well tonight. The tide will be against us in the morning, but nevertheless we will need to be out early if we wish to have better luck than we had today. I did not say, but this morning I heard Hernan, who runs the Cabo 32 Riviera sport fishing boat, say that these are the last good days. From tomorrow or the day after, we must expect a *Día del Diablo*. And he wasn't talking about *Día de los Inocentes*, such as we might have between *Navidad* and *Ano Nuevo*.'

'I know,' answered Carlos. 'It is something in the air. I have also smelt it. The heat, the humidity. There is something bad coming, and soon, I fear.'

'Do you believe,' asked the eternally hopeful young Miguel-Angel, 'that it will be enough, whatever it is, to make the *prestamistas,* the loan sharks, hesitate to collect everything that you owe them for keeping *Pilar*?'

The old man swung round to face the boy, unusually animated by sudden, frustrated rage. 'If you can say such things then I have indeed told you too much and treated you like a man, *un hombre*, when you are still a child, a *critura*. Perhaps it would be better if you helped your father, Shipschandler Guerrero, safely ashore in his chandlery if there are bad days coming and you cannot hold your tongue like a man.'

But the boy was used to the old man's temper. 'Not so, *Capitan*,' he answered gently. 'It is my place as your mate, your *primer official*, to carry some of your burden. My father is well able to look after the shop himself and has no need of me there. So I say all that I mean to say. If we are to work well tomorrow before the devil days arrive, and pay the loan sharks enough to keep them quiet for the moment, then no matter how late we dock tonight, we must be up before dawn tomorrow and out even before the tide. That way we will be first to sea, and have the best chance of filling the freezers with blue-fin or swordfish. Or even with sardines.'

'So long as they are full,' agreed Carlos. 'You are right, and I am sorry that I was angry. It is I who am the *critura*, the child. This is a thing which comes with age.'

'You are not so old,' said the boy with a smile. 'But if you wish to age any further, *Capitan*, you had best pay attention to your heading or we will collide with the pier and destroy the harbour as well as ourselves. Then we will, as likely as not, join *los muertos*, the dead, before our time.'

TWELVE

R obin woke next morning to the sound of distant thunder. That and the absence of her husband. Again. There was no hesitation this time, no bleary-eyed contemplation of their splendid accommodation, which was filled with sinister shadows today instead of yesterday's dazzling sunlight. Shadows that gave an ominous flicker before the threatening rumble echoed over the breathless air once more. And Robin was in action before the ominous sound faded back to silence, rolling out of bed and glancing around as she strode purposefully towards the en suite, muttering, 'Oh, you bloody man. I know where you will be. And I'd better get up and out PDQ myself . . .'

They had packed rather than fooled around last night, so she didn't even need to hesitate over her choice of costume. All she had left out were the toilet bag she shared with Richard and the outfit she proposed to wear aboard *Maxima* on her fast run south close behind *Katapult8*. Both were heading for Puerto Banderas a thousand miles away – and out from under whatever cataclysm the atmospheric river close above was preparing to hurl down upon California. Practical, almost indestructible, weatherproof clothing that was stylish, easy to wear and quick to get on and off. Much of it by Aquascutum of London, as she was going cruising aboard a state-of-the-art gin palace. Had she been joining Liberty aboard *Katapult8*, she would have preferred outfits by Helly Hansen or Gill Marine.

Her mood suddenly as dark as the dim, flickering daylight oozing coolly into her cabin, she shrugged off the confection by Janet Reger that had started their love-play off the night before last and padded into the bathroom where, prompted by the third distant snarl of thunder, she skipped her usual shower and brushed her hair and teeth with perfunctory thoughtlessness before getting dressed and going straight up on to the bridge without even checking Richard's cell phone for confirmation of his whereabouts.

Richard was standing at the portside window looking away westward, the rigid lines of his frowning face reminding Robin of Keats's verse as quoted by Nic yesterday . . . *like stout Cortez, when with eagle eyes he stared at the Pacific – and all his men . . . Silent, upon a peak in Darien . . .* Though to be fair she doubted whether the Spanish conquistador had been suited by Gieves and Hawkes or booted by John Lobb – like Aquascutum, the holder of many historic warrants for supplying the Royal family with clothes and shoes not least to the queen this vessel was named after and her husband, the king. The scar on Richard's cheekbone would have suited Keats's poetically heroic explorer well enough, however, she decided with a sudden rush of affection, if not the less politically correct conquistador thug of historical reality. She joined him silently, rose on tiptoe and kissed the buccaneer's scar before snuggling close beside him and following the bright blue dazzle of his brooding gaze.

The western sky was almost coal black, seeming to press down on to Long Beach with a terrible, physical weight. The bases of the huge dark clouds appeared to be writhing as though there were winds like the jet stream roaring through them at dreadful speeds. As Robin stood at Richard's shoulder, a great bolt of lightning struck down out of the black belly of the distant monster, seemingly straight into the invisible ocean. And still there was no wind, as yet, down here on the cowering earth. No rain. Just the rumble of distant thunder echoing in over the docks.

'I don't like the look of that at all,' she said.

'Me neither,' agreed Richard. 'If *mackerel skies and mares' tails make tall ships wear short sails*, as the saying goes, this lot to *Maxima* any moment now and I need to warn Captain Toro that we're inbound. He and Mr Greenbaum are very keen to get underway. *Katapult8* left at nine on the dot – though Liberty and her crew'll be fighting the tide for a while yet.'

'We haven't held everyone up, I hope?'

'No, Mrs Mariner. We're bang on schedule. It was Liberty who jumped the gun. I'll get on to *Sulu Queen* now . . .'

Richard was still blinking and rubbing his eyes when Biddy patched her conversation with *Sulu Queen* through on to the cabin's communications system. 'No!' spat Captain Sin's familiar voice, clearly partway through a conversation. 'No one aboard is hurt. Dazzled and deafened, perhaps. But not hurt. And yes, our control and communications systems are fine. Though I will, of course, be conducting a full inspection to make sure none of the navigating programmes or circuits have been damaged.'

'That put your mind at rest, Mrs Mariner?' asked Biddy.

'Yes, thank you. For the moment, at least.'

'Thank you for the information, *Sulu Queen*. I must break contact now. Your owners will be back in touch if they require any further information. Over and out. Hello, *Maxima*? *Maxima*, this is Biddy in the Bell, coming in for landing. Hello, *Maxima* . . .'

The Bell settled on to its landing pad minutes later. In the interim, Richard's eyes had cleared so that he was able to swing the luggage out into the hands of a waiting steward with enough speed to ensure the minimum possible soaking. Nic met them on the bridge as they hurried through the smoked-glass doors and past the silver-webbed fantasy of the lift shaft. 'Good,' he said, turning back from a conversation with Captain Toro. 'Now we can get underway and head out after *Katapult8*.'

'She left an hour ago, I understand,' said Richard.

'Yup. But she's fighting the tide and there's been precious little in the way of wind – down here, at least.' Nic looked up at the writhing clouds eerily close above, which came and went through the drizzle as it filled the air and smeared the clear views. 'This is one set of circumstances where *Maxima*'s big Caterpillar motors have the advantage. Especially as the tide's on the turn. We'll head out on the top of the water if nothing else. It'll be

would make any sane sailor run for safe haven with all the speed he can.'

'We need to get off this ship and on to *Maxima* as fast as humanly possible. It's only a short hop across the docks.'

He nodded. 'And we need to get Nic and Liberty running south before whatever is actually up there starts coming down in earnest.'

'Damn right.' She was in motion as she spoke.

'You get things organized in the cabin and I'll settle the bill. Meet you at the gangway,' he said decisively, following in her footsteps. 'And while I'm doing that I'll check how things aboard *Sulu Queen* are proceeding. I don't want Captain Sin to have to face this particular storm tiger either if we can possibly avoid it. Maybe Antoine can get some cargo for him in Puerto Banderas.'

'If they have port facilities anywhere near big enough to handle her down there,' called Robin as she vanished downwards towards their cabin. 'I mean, I know she's not a Maersk Triple E super freighter, but even so . . .'

Richard was waiting at the top of the gangplank when Robin reappeared with a laden steward in tow fifteen minutes later. 'Captain Sin is not a happy bunny,' he called, then paused, distracted by the coincidence that made him refer to Sin's favourite Chinese insult. Unconscious association? he wondered. Then he speculated for a sidetracked instant who the outraged captain would be calling a *son of a rabbit* next. Richard himself, probably, for the cunning plan seemed to have backfired. The National Guard containers had been loaded aboard *Sulu Queen* by midnight, just as he had calculated – but they were still aboard, apparently, as were Antoine Prudhomme, Major Guerrero and his people. The freight yards were being cleared far more slowly than they had hoped. Guerrero's emergency containers looked as though they would need to stay in place for much of the rest of the day, at least. And, until they were unloaded and the rest of *Sulu Queen*'s cargo removed and replaced, the vessel was stuck in dock. But maybe she was safer there, Richard thought, looking for the bright side as ever, in spite of what the NOAA scientists believed was on its way.

'Penny for them?' asked Robin, breaking into his reverie.

'Nic's sending Biddy McKinney with the Bell to pick us up,' he answered with a swift mental gear change. 'But we'll need to take a cab over to the Island Express helipad. I don't want to get caught in whatever's coming down. Especially not on foot and laden with luggage.'

'That cab waiting at the foot of the gangplank, perhaps? I got the steward to call on our way up here.'

As the steward packed their cases into the cab's boot and they folded themselves into the back seat, the rain started. Fortunately it was not the kind of rain they had experienced outside the Sky Room last night. There were no drops the size of baseballs, tennis balls or cricket balls. Just a sudden, penetrating drizzle, almost as warm as blood, which blew in across the docks as though some new-fangled colossal shower attachment was hidden behind the low black clouds.

'Is this the start of the ARkStorm?' asked the cabbie of no one in particular as he pulled away without even bothering to switch on his windscreen wipers. 'This ain't so bad. Take the storms during Oscars season last year. Now they were something! The cops closed major roads and highways. The fire department rescued people from tree trunks floating in the Los Angeles River. Power outages hit 24,000 customers. Evacuation orders were issued for 1,000 homes in Glendora and Azusa that sit beneath steep mountain slopes. Hell, they even had to cover all the big Oscar statues outside the Dolby Theatre with plastic sheeting. I've never seen anything like it. I tell you, there's nothing you can do. You can't stop water when it comes down hard. But this ain't even in the same league. All this Noah's ark stuff is just so much hooey, if you ask me.'

The Bell was sitting waiting on the helipad and it was empty apart from Biddy, so Richard had no trouble slinging their luggage into the passenger cabin at Robin's feet and scrambling in himself. As he strapped in and settled the headphones in place, the chopper lifted off into the low overcast sky and was soon immersed in a fog that was just on the point of turning from vapour to liquid.

'Lord only knows what's in this foul stuff,' said Biddy. 'There's enough static electricity to interfere with some of my displays.'

Even as she spoke, a huge bolt of lightning slammed down all too close on their left. By chance, Richard was looking in that

direction, straining to get a glimpse of *Sulu Queen*. And, indeed, it seemed to him that the lightning bolt illuminated her as it dazzled him. The searing power of it was like a blow from a boxer. His head reared back. He closed his streaming eyes as tightly as he could and, as he did so, he seemed to see a picture that had been seared on to his retinas. His brain fought to comprehend the frenetic activity of what he had observed almost unconsciously with the still picture that seemed to be all that was left. And it was not helped in this by the overpowering crash of instantaneous thunder, loud enough to be disorientating on its own. The Bell jolted as the power of the strike hit it like the blast wall of an explosion. There was a powerful smell of ozone.

It seemed to Richard that the lightning bolt spread out as it tore down, out of the clouds, with lightning branches striking in white and gold at the speed of light through the streaming air. And, eerily, answering wisps of electricity grew from the tops of the tallest points in the picture revealed by the blinding cataclysm. Ghostly fingers reached upwards from the top of *Sulu Queen*'s guidance and communication display, from the crest of her one tall funnel, the tip of the loading crane reaching across her square piled cargo and the top of the crane itself. The downstrike of lightning met each of these, flickering between them as it discharged its unimaginable static power.

But the picture that seared itself immovably, unmoving, as still as a photograph, on to the backs of Richard's eyes was that of the most powerful contact – of the great column of power connecting the heart of the black clouds to the top of the crane beside *Sulu Queen*. The crane seemed to explode with sparks as its metal structure earthed billions of volts and tens of thousands of amps into the concrete beneath it. It seemed incredible to Richard that the structure had not melted or exploded. It seemed inevitable that every electric circuit in the crane – and possibly in his ship – must have been burned out. He rubbed his fingers over his eyes, dashing away the burning tears, suddenly fearing that there might be dead and wounded over there.

'Biddy, can you contact *Sulu Queen*?' asked Robin, her voice level, calm, controlled – seemingly distant in Richard's ringing head. 'See whether there's any damage to ship or crew?'

'Will do, but I'll have to be quick. We're starting our descent

like skiing downhill if not quite surfing into the ocean with the flood washing out behind us.'

As he spoke the massive motors came online, two soaking deckhands pulled the mooring lines aboard and *Maxima* headed out of the marina, swinging on to a southerly course and surging up to full power as she did so.

THIRTEEN

'There she is!' called Robin. But then she corrected herself automatically. 'No. My mistake. I think it's a whale . . .'

'Is *Katapult8* still showing on the radar, Captain?' Richard asked Captain Toro, calling across the bridge from the open area of the radio shack, where he had just broken contact with Captain Sin aboard *Sulu Queen*. He was concerned about *Katapult8* because her cutting-edge automatic identification system, or AIS, kept cutting out. The equipment on *Maxima* should have been able to track that, but they were having to rely on old-fashioned radar at the moment. Liberty knew about the malfunction, but in order to fix it she would have to heave to in a period of relative calm and send someone up to the top of the huge composite sail. And, quite frankly, Richard suspected that Liberty was happy with the relative freedom the fault was giving her to run ahead and play hide-and-seek with her father.

'Yes, she's registering,' answered Captain Toro, 'but right at the outer edge. I really don't believe Mrs Mariner will be able to see her, even with our most powerful field glasses. Even if conditions were perfect . . .' The captain let his voice fade away as he gave an infinitesimal shrug. The tone and the gesture said it all. Conditions were well short of perfect. Even though *Maxima* had been running south at full speed for a good eight hours now, she only just seemed to be breaking out of the overcast that was still smothering Long Beach more than one hundred and eighty miles astern. The whole of the northern sky behind them was a wall of low, black thunderheads that stretched

away west, apparently far enough to be raining thunderbolts on
Hawaii; perhaps even on Tokyo too.

Richard paused for a moment, looking out through the clear-
view windows surrounding the command bridge. There was
something slightly out of kilter here, he thought. Something not
quite right. The hairs on the back of his neck pricked as he tried
to pin down the cause of his sudden disquiet. Perhaps it was just
the view, he thought. Yes. That was probably it.

The view was enough to give anybody pause. Even those like
Richard, who half believed the sayings his grandmother and
great-grandmother might have set store by. Like *red sky at night,
sailor's delight.* There was definitely a red sky tonight, he thought.
Red sky and then some. The sun was setting just south of the
massive wall of charcoal cumulonimbus, sinking into the western
ocean like a huge bullet wound in the heavens, spattering crimson
light northwards on to the coalface cliff of the clouds and south
into the haze above the restless Pacific. A blood-red haze sucked
up by the unseasonable heat that swept over them as soon as
they sailed out from under the lingering cloud cover, and threatened to intensify the further south they went. There was a wind
which was powerful enough to raise a disorientating chop, but
not strong enough to move the haze, because the air whose motion
caused it was dangerously close to one hundred per cent humidity
– only slightly less humid than this morning's penetrating drizzle,
in fact. The whole restless vista was full of lines and angles,
surfaces and shadows which were easily able to conceal
Katapult8's sail – even if it was the size of jumbo jet's wing;
even if it was blacker than the roiling clouds.

The drizzle they left in Long Beach had intensified into a
proper downpour now, Captain Sin had informed Richard during
the contact he had just broken. A downpour heavy enough to be
interfering with the clearing of the docks but not, as yet, heavy
enough to trigger the governor's emergency plans. Except in
places like Glendora and Azusa, at the foot of dangerously steep
hill slopes, where the deluge might loosen the topsoil with tragic
effect. A danger that was in the forefront of many minds, especially after 2014's terrible mudslide in Oso, Washington.

Not that Major Guerrero and his containers full of supplies
would be joining either the governor's or the National Guard's

plans anytime soon by the look of things, mused Richard now as he observed the sharp, red-fanged chop, narrow-eyed against the glare of the blood-orange sun. The lightning strike which had dazzled him eight hours earlier may not have damaged *Sulu Queen* to any great extent, but it had, it now transpired, fried several vital electronic systems in the crane that towered beside her. Particularly the anti-sway system – the electrical arrangement designed to limit pendulum movement of the containers, especially at the lowest points of lifting and placing – the points where the ropes were at their longest. The points at which absolute precision was most vital. The anti-sway system would be crucial as the rain intensified and the wind strengthened towards gale force. And the earliest an engineer would likely be able to start work on the repair would probably be tomorrow.

As far as Captain Sin was concerned, the storm tiger that had pursued him across the Pacific had not only arrived above his command, but it had also brought with it a whole range of bad-luck spirits. Intensified, the captain let slip, by the fact that this was his fourth command. And that, with Antoine, Guerrero and his contingent aboard, the ship's complement was effectively forty-four. To most westerners these coincidences would have meant little, but Richard had spent enough time in Hong Kong and Shanghai to know that to the Chinese, the number four – which sounded unsettlingly close to the word 'death' in Mandarin – was the unluckiest number of all. And forty-four – 'death-death' – ranked up with seating thirteen for dinner, walking under ladders and kicking black cats out of your path in Western superstitions. Richard glanced down at the radio link through which he had just finished speaking to his superstitious and apoplectic captain, and shook his head. Then he turned to more immediate matters – though he had no more control over these than he had over what was happening in the Long Beach docks.

The super-competitive Liberty was teasing her father and his friends in the face of Richard's wager, using the thick wind to drive *Katapult8* relentlessly at more than the twenty knots *Maxima* was cruising at, and using the fault on her AIS, the congealing, clotting haze, the ruby dazzle and the gathering shadows of sunset to play a game of hide-and-seek with the watch-keepers. The huge composite mainsail was too good a target ever to escape the radar, though, and, when full dark came, she would have to switch on her riding lights – which included one bright star right at the tip of the massive sail itself. Unless that, like the automatic identification system transmitter right beside it, was also faulty. It was for this sail that Robin, lacking a sense of distance and scale, had mistaken the tall black fluke of a local humpback whale as it rolled over and over among the white horses. He looked at the back of his preoccupied wife, feeling he could almost read her thoughts, then he was in motion across the bridge.

Twenty knots was fast for *Maxima*, Robin reckoned, but not for *Katapult8*. The multihull's crew was being tested, but by no means pushed to their limits. At twenty knots, they wouldn't even be up on the J hooks that lifted her long hulls right out of the water and allowed her to fly up towards her top speeds in excess of forty knots. Were Robin in Liberty's place, she would be running easy with two crewmembers on watch and the other two in the tiny little cabin below, heating up one of their pre-packed meals in the microwave, no doubt. And she would plan to ease back still further after sunset and dinner unless the wind got up and tempted them into something more challenging – or shifted, causing a change in the basic requirements of yacht handling.

Lowering the binoculars, she checked *Maxima*'s anemometer, which was adjusted for the ship's own speed, and read the wind speed as though *Maxima* was dead in the water. The thick, hazy wind out there was moving at fifteen knots. Force four on the Beaufort scale. A moderate breeze which she could have estimated from the one-metre waves and the pink, foaming whitecaps. The state-of-the-art weather predictor suggested that the wind would strengthen in the early hours of the night, sometime during the first watch, she thought; strengthen and swing round to come down from the north. It was information that might have rung alarm bells had she not been so fully focused on Liberty's probable problems with helming *Katapult8* most efficiently. A brisk northerly would help *Maxima* as it would settle in right behind her. But a northerly would likely hinder *Katapult8*, for Liberty would have to stop playing hide-and-seek and start to tack from side to side – reach to reach – across the following wind if she was going to get the best out of her command as she ran due south. *Katapult8* could run south at twenty knots across a fifteen-knot north-easterly wind forever, she reckoned, even with two on watch and two more making something hot to eat and drink. But once the wind went dead north, things would become more difficult.

Robin crossed to join Richard, who had come over from the radio and was now towering at the helmsman's shoulder for a closer look at the navigational display. *Maxima* had come the better part of one hundred and eighty five miles south since setting sail. *Katapult8* was an hour ahead, but she had made a slow start and was only fifteen miles distant, according to the radar. The instrumentation made it clear that if Robin looked away eastwards to port instead south-westwards on the starboard forequarter, which is where *Katapult8* seemed to be, she would catch the first glimpse of the lighthouse on Cape San Quintin on the west coast of the Baja California, that long peninsula running parallel to the west coast of Mexico, separated from the mainland by the Gulf of California. And even as she realized this, the beam of the light itself gleamed white against the darkening mass of the land. Dragging Richard with her, she crossed to the port side of the bridge for a closer look.

In the distance, beyond the light which was already beaming out of blue-black velvety shadows, the tops of the Baja's central mountain chain flamed as though they were erupting volcanoes as they picked up the last rays of the setting sun. And, above them, catching the light like a cross between a star and a ruby burning against the darkening vault of the sky, there was something else that caught her eye. At first she thought it was an aeroplane, but then she realized that it was lower and slower than a plane. And, even in the shapeless dazzle of the sunlight, it was the wrong shape – too fat and squat.

'What is that?' she breathed.

'Thunderbird Two by the look of it,' rumbled Richard.

And she saw at once that he was right. There, above the jagged peaks of the mountains, the airship Dragon Dream which they had seen yesterday above Los Angeles was heading southwards towards its destination in Mexico City. Robin smiled as though the distant gleam of the state-of-the-art dirigible was the face of an old friend, then she looked down at the peaks above which

it was passing. Those would be the Cordillera running through
Ensenada and Mexicali, she thought. The Sierra Juarez and the
Sierra San Pedro Martir. The high points of the long backbone
of the peninsula that rose to ten thousand feet here at one or two
peaks. But only one or two. It faded into much lower elevations
for most of the length of the peninsula before gathering again at
the tip into the Sierra La Laguna.

The mountains of the Baja formed a watershed which trans-
formed itself – after a valley filled by the mouth of the Gulf
of California – into the much more massive coastal mountain
system she had seen in Nic's film of Puerto Banderas: the solid
wall of the Sierra Madre mountains which began behind
Mazatlán and ran on down the coast towards Puerto Vallarta
and Acapulco, reaching heights of more than ten thousand feet
consistently and repeatedly within a very few miles inland from
the Pacific coast.

And no sooner had she thought of Nic than the man himself
appeared. 'Come on, you two,' he called from the doorway at
the aft of the bridge. 'Sundown. Time for some drinks before we
settle into supper. Alcohol-free, I'm afraid, Robin. But I think I
can promise you something to eat that will be the equal of the
last two meals we've shared.'

They lingered over their fruit-juice cocktails then ate, taking
their time over a dinner that was every bit as delicious as any
they had enjoyed so far. Captain Enrique Toro and chopper pilot
Biddy McKinney joined them and proved witty and amusing
companions, even though Nic ran a dry ship and the most powerful
stimulant available was the after-dinner coffee. After coffee, they
retired to *Maxima*'s cinema and Nic showed them the full film
of his new Puerto Banderas home, inside as well as outside – a
process further enlivened by Biddy's wry commentary on the
hair-raising things she had to do with the Bell in order to get
most of the pictures.

Captain Toro broke things up just before midnight as he went
up on to the bridge to oversee the change from the first to the
middle watch. Impressed by the professionalism of the captain
and his crew, Richard and Robin retired to their suite and fortunately decided not to christen the vast new king-sized bed that
occupied a good deal of it. Not tonight, at any rate.

So they were decently dressed in night clothes and contentedly asleep a little under two hours later when Nic tapped on their door with a worried frown and some disturbing news. The radio officer had been roused some ten minutes earlier by the officer on watch. He had taken an urgent radio contact from Long Beach, then he had roused the captain, who had woken the owner in turn. And the owner bore the bad tidings to Richard at once. 'Major Guerrero has been in contact from *Sulu Queen*. He needs to speak with you urgently. Apparently Captain Sin has suffered some kind of stroke or seizure. He's on his way to hospital and the first officer is in charge of *Sulu Queen* at the moment. Major Guerrero wants to know what they should do.'

Five minutes later, Richard, clad in dressing gown, was in the open section of the bridge they referred to as the radio room. A minute after that, he was talking to Guerrero. 'I don't know what triggered it,' explained the major on a tenuous link that sounded as though an ARkStorm was fighting for possession of the airwaves. 'I wasn't on the bridge when he collapsed but I was called immediately. His face was sagging on the left side; he had limited strength in his left arm and I couldn't understand what he was trying to say, though at first I thought that may have been because he was speaking in Chinese. But then the first officer couldn't understand him either, and he speaks Mandarin, of course – though his English is limited and I'm not sure I understood what he was saying either.'

'Sounds like a stroke,' said Richard. 'He's on his way to hospital, you say?'

'Long Beach Memorial on Atlantic Avenue.'

'Good. Is the first officer there? Put him on, would you?'

There was a sort of shuffling, which just managed to rise above the crackling downpour on the line, then a surprisingly youthful voice said, '*Nin hao?*'

'*Zushang hao,*' answered Richard, slipping into Mandarin as though he were back in Hong Kong. 'Can you please update me as to the current state of the ship and crew?'

'*Sulu Queen* remains in dock. We cannot load or unload until the crane is repaired. *Shushu* Sin was trying to get permission to move to another dock with a functioning crane when he fell down with whatever illness has overtaken him. Permission has been refused. No other dock can be made immediately available. So we are stuck, unless we wish to sail to another port altogether. The captain has not wasted his time in the interim. The ship is fuelled and our supplies have been replenished. We are ready for sea as soon as there is somewhere to go. The crew apart from the captain are well. Well rested. Well fed too, as the captain has given permission for the full use of kitchen equipment.'

Including the deep-fat fryer, thought Richard.

'. . . Except for one thing . . .' the first officer continued.

Richard frowned. 'What?'

'My Master's papers are not recognized here. It would be illegal for me to take the vessel out of dock. Perhaps even for me to be in command in harbour.'

That one word, *shushu*, made more sense then. It was Mandarin for 'uncle', although the relationship sometimes went well beyond 'parent's brother' which defined it in the West. Captain Sin had clearly taken the young first officer under his wing and had planned to give him the experience he needed to earn his International Master's certificate to command freighters and container vessels.

'Where did you get your papers from?' Richard searched through his memory for anything at all about the first officer, but he could recall neither face nor name nor – crucially – personnel record.

'Dalian Maritime University.'

'That course can only be completed with on-the-job experience and further certification, then final certification as Ship's Master. You're getting the experience but haven't qualified for the further certification. Or the final International Master's certification. Is that what you're saying?'

'Yes, sir.'

'What about the other navigating officers?'

'I am the senior officer, sir. I am the best qualified.'

God give me strength, thought Richard. 'Engineering officers?' he asked.

'The chief is extremely experienced, but he does not hold any Master's papers.'

Richard paused for a moment, breathing heavily through his nose, then turned to Nic. 'I have to get back. Can I borrow Biddy and the Bell?'

'If it's OK with Biddy, it's OK with me.'

Richard turned to Robin. 'You see I don't have any real choice here?'

'You could call Crewfinders. You set the company up so you know better than most that they could get someone with the correct papers to take command aboard *Sulu Queen* within twenty-four hours . . .' But even as she spoke, the certainty drained out of her voice. She knew she was wasting her breath.

'I can be aboard within two and a half . . .'

'Only if Biddy is willing . . .'

'And,' observed Nic, 'only if she thinks the Bell is up to handling whatever weather there is between here and Long Beach.'

The story went that someone had once gone into Biddy's cabin unannounced and had suffered several broken bones as a result. Richard, therefore, volunteered to wake her, and was circumspect as to how he did so. But, in fact, Biddy had taken a shine to him, so he probably could have survived a more direct approach. As things were, he dressed, tapped on her door and waited for an invitation before he went in and began to explain the situation.

'Where exactly are we?' was her first question. Unlike Robin, she was wide awake and raring to go the moment her eyes opened. Also unlike Robin, she did not sleep in a Stella McCartney camisole but an olive-coloured military T-shirt which had clearly been designed for a far larger frame than hers.

Richard had come prepared. 'We're three hundred and sixty miles south of Long Beach. That's five hundred and eighty kilometres. I'd give you the name of the nearest settlement on the Baja California but there aren't any. We're past the Arrecife Sacramento, the Sacramento Reef, but short of giving you the precise lat-long readings, that's about it.'

'That's OK. The Bell's got a range of four hundred and fifty miles, more than seven hundred kliks, so we'd have elbow room if we need to skirt round anything. And she can get up to two hundred and seventy kliks per hour if push comes to shove, so a couple of hours should get us there with the better part of an hour in hand. I'll get dressed and take a quick walk round her, but I'm willing if you're able.'

'Right,' said Richard. 'Let's get to it, then.'

FOURTEEN

While Richard packed a few necessities, Biddy dressed and walked around the Bell, checking it just as carefully as she would have done if she hadn't checked it from nose to tail soon after landing sixteen hours earlier. They met on the floodlit helideck half an hour later, with *Maxima* still powering southward at twenty knots, her speed enhanced by a brisk following northerly wind, her radar still observing *Katapult8* as Liberty tacked from one reach to another, hoping to pull further ahead by the time day dawned in three and a half hours. Richard slung his case into the side door then walked sternwards to join Robin, who had placed herself beneath the chopper's slim tail and was looking back along *Maxima*'s glittering phosphorescent wake into the world-wide cavern of utter darkness they had so recently escaped. Even though they were heading downwind at twenty knots, the gale was blowing past them forcibly enough to make her golden curls dance. It could have been coming from a hairdryer or an oven, except it was so thick with moisture that breathing was by no means easy. 'It's like being waterboarded in a hot bath,' she said as he joined her.

'Don't worry. Whatever's going on back there, Biddy'll keep on top of it.'

'You'd sure as hell better not get underneath it. Or anywhere near the middle of it.'

He slid an arm round her waist and gave her a reassuring hug as she snuggled her head against his shoulder.

'Take care, sailor,' she said. 'Take very special care.'

'You would never, ever believe,' he growled, 'how careful Biddy, the Bell and I are going to be.'

It never occurred to him that he should warn her to be careful too. *Maxima* was so sleek, solid, stable; so outstandingly designed, so painstakingly constructed, so well maintained, so excellently crewed. Everything, in fact, that the *Titanic* had been on her maiden voyage.

Five minutes later, he was buckling himself into the co-pilot's seat while Biddy went through the pre-flight instrument checks. 'You ready?' she asked as she completed the shortest possible formalities.

'Ready,' he said. The Bell elevated gently, almost imperceptibly, and reversed off the deck as he spoke. Then, nose down with her flood-lit launch pad already falling away upwind of her, she swung round to face the northerly wind head on. Richard turned in his seat and looked back as the brightness of *Maxima* passed beneath them and became blurred by a writhing haze almost at once as it fell away into distance and darkness surprisingly swiftly. Biddy began to power the suddenly frail-seeming Bell upwards and forwards, into the enormous darkness ahead.

It became obvious within the first fifteen minutes that the game little chopper did not like the conditions through which she was flying. The thick wind battered her with unexpected force and solidity, making the windscreen in front of them vibrate and seem to flex, while the doors on either side of them rattled as though invisible giants were trying to break in. Biddy ran out of conversation almost at once, and a glance at her closed face, lit by multicoloured brightness from the displays, frowning in concentration, made Richard decide against disturbing her. It seemed incredible how rapidly the storm swept over them. Fair enough, Biddy had pushed the engine controls to maximum and the Bell was doing a very respectable one hundred and fifty knots – say two hundred and fifty kilometres per hour – into a wind that seemed to be coming against them at the better part of fifty knots. 'How much flying time do we have?' he asked casually after the longest silence he could bear.

'Three hours or so, like I said. Plenty to get us there if I can shake this headwind,' she grated. 'I have a practical ceiling of about eleven thousand feet, and we're fully fuelled but otherwise unladen, so that'll help. Let's go up and see how far we get.'

'You won't get over the top of the ARkStorm,' Richard warned her, thinking back to Dr Jones's briefing yesterday morning. 'There are likely to be cumulonimbus thunderheads peaking above twenty thousand feet somewhere quite close ahead. Certainly between us and Long Beach. Think of the Himalayas.'

'Hunh,' she grunted. 'Like the weather predictor on *Maxima* didn't already tell me all I wanted to know about that. Well, maybe we can go round whatever's there. The top of my ceiling will put us a thousand feet above the highest peaks of the Sierra Juarez, so maybe we'll just take a little detour . . .' As she spoke she twisted her controls and the Bell swung to the right as it continued to climb. The wind continued to push back against her at first, but then Richard began to suspect that, in among the northerly gusts, there were occasional squalls coming in from the east. These had a beneficial effect to begin with, pushing them over the thin ribbon of land that was the Baja California.

After a while, Richard began to make out the jewel-bright lights of major highways winding like necklaces from north to south and, as the flight proceeded towards the end of its first forty-five minutes, the wider webs of brightness that denoted villages and towns. While the battering from the thick black northerly continued to intensify, he thought grimly, the sight of solid ground and civilization – even if it was sparse – was reassuring. Or it was so to begin with. After three-quarters of an hour or so of an unsettling flight, the Bell swooped eastwards and the ground began to rise towards the peaks of the Cerro Picacho del Diabolo towering above the National Park of Sierra de San Pedro Martir, their bright red warning lights designed to inform such aircraft that might want to venture nearby that these were mountains more than ten thousand feet high. The colour and the elevation of the red warning lights put Richard in mind of the glimpse Robin and he had shared that evening of the silver-skinned Dragon Dream airship burning low in the sunset sky. The bright red gleams were far ahead on what Richard would have called the starboard forequarter on a ship. In at two o'clock on a clock face.

But even as Richard fixed on the bright beacons that functioned as lighthouses for aircraft, their ruby brilliance was abruptly swept away. Or, he realized, as he narrowed his eyes and strained for a clearer view, they were simply washed away.

'What the hell . . .' snarled Biddy.

'What?' asked Richard.

'Easterly squall like a boot in the ribs,' she answered tersely. 'Now where the hell did that come from?' No sooner had

Biddy said this than the Bell was hurled further to the right by something more than the wind. A pounding deluge swept in over her, thundering against the canopy and smashing into the windows like a hailstorm. Richard swung round to look past Biddy into the blackness west of them, his all-too-vivid memory full of the raindrops outside the Sky Room. Raindrops the size of baseballs. They were coming at the Bell now as though there were some kind of rail gun out there firing from high in the sky. No sooner did he do so than the familiar pyrotechnic display began. Great white bolts of lightning began to slam down out of the clouds, igniting their writhing bases in a series of instantaneous flashes that also seemed to give depth to the night and some kind of illumination to the wild seas close beneath the writhing thunderheads.

Another gust of water-laden wind battered in from the west, swinging the Bell's fuselage like a pendulum beneath the four whirling rotors that fought to grip its howling thickness and keep the sturdy machine aloft. The windows went opaque, while the old-fashioned dials and gauges on the video display screens beneath them seemed to spin out of all control. The thunder of rain and wind all but drowned out the roaring of the twin Pratt and Witney engines fighting to keep them aloft.

But no sooner had the blinding blast from the west obscured everything around them than another counter-blast from the north replaced it, scouring the panoramic windscreen just beyond their knees clear in an instant. The blood-red light of the Picacho del Diabolo returned – seemingly a little closer this time. Or it did so for a gleaming instant before the next vicious squall roared in from the west to obscure it once more. 'If it gets much worse than this I'll be putting down at Cielito Lindo airfield,' warned Biddy grimly. 'That's just across the bay to the east of the San Quintin light.'

Richard nodded but said nothing. He strained to see the San Quintin light, thinking back once more to the moment Robin and he had shared, looking eastward towards it from *Maxima*'s bridge at sunset. And there it was – the yellow-white finger of its beam given definition by the downpour. The circle of brightness it cast gave some hint of the wilderness of wild water beating in out of the Pacific against it. Richard was put in mind of the pictures he had seen of the south coast of England during the storms of 2014. Of apparently fragile lighthouses standing bravely against spring tides with storm surges on top of them and hurricane-force winds behind them. Slim fingers of brick and concrete pointed up from the hearts of great walls of spray. He swung round again, frowning, just in time to see the red beacon on top of Picacho del Diabolo vanish once again, drowned out by the deluge.

'I'd have a chat with whoever's up and about at Cielito Lindo before you come to any decisions,' he advised grimly. 'Things down there look even worse than things up here.'

'Good thinking. *Buena tarde*, Cielito Lindo. *Me escuchas?* This is Bell helicopter Maxima One. Can anyone hear me?'

'*Buenas tardes*, Maxima One,' came a faint reply. 'This is Cielito Lindo airstrip. What can we do for you?'

'Could you update me as to your current weather, Cielito Lindo?'

'Bad and getting worse. We've had nearly two inches of rainfall in the last hour. No sign of a let-up anytime soon. Wind speeds gusting to storm force – with some hurricane-force on the way. The guys at the San Quintin light ten kliks west of us say this is the worst weather they've ever experienced, and they're looking at a storm surge of twenty-five feet which may well wash in here sometime soon. The guys up at the San Quintin airbase twenty kliks north are getting ready for a flood coming down from the mountains of the national park just inland of them. They say they may have to evacuate. We have reports of serious flooding in arroyos that are usually dry this time of year. Our two nearest bridges on highway one are in danger of being swept away, according to the *federales*. Certainly the bridge over Arroyo Colonet north of here seems to have gone. Where are you bound for, Maxima One?'

'Long Beach.'

'If I were you, I'd swing in here and see can you get a visual on highway one – the bridges might be at risk but there's still traffic moving and lights along some lengths. You should be able to follow it easily enough up past San Quintin and Ensenada to Tijuana and San Diego. That way, if you have any trouble, at least you can put down on land.' The radio operator gave a bark of laughter. 'I almost said *dry* land. Not much chance of that tonight, Maxima One.'

'Thanks for the advice, Cielito Lindo. We'll give it a go.'
'Good luck, Maxima One.'
'And you, Cielito Lindo. Stay safe now.'

FIFTEEN

By the time Liberty and the crew of *Katapult8* snuck out
of Long Beach with the last of the incoming tide running
against them, leaving *Maxima* lying snugly in dock waiting
for the top of the water, as well as Richard and Robin, *Pilar* had
been heading west out of Puerto Banderas for the best part of
four hours. Her destination was the Pacific fishing grounds off
the west of the Baja California. She had aboard the usual crew,
together with the ship's boy, Miguel-Angel Guerrero. She had
passed south of the reef at Isla Santa Isabel, and Miguel-Angel
had listened to the distant roaring. They had passed south of the
smallest of the Tres Marias, Isla Maria Cleofas, and the boy,
once again, had listened to her unique song, feeling that he was
becoming a master of the seas like his *capitan*.

Carlos Santiago and Miguel-Angel had gone aboard together
at four thirty local time and the others had joined them half an
hour later, just before they eased out of harbour with a star-
spangled sky ahead of them magnified by the hot and heavy
humidity of the air – and the brightness of Dahlia Blanca high
above the breakwater with its towering hotels, Los Muertos
beach and the Malecón astern. The crew, below, had come aboard
suspiciously heavy laden and, although Miguel-Angel had asked
no questions, he assumed they were planning on a much longer
voyage than usual. He stood beside his *capitan* on the bridge
in the darkness of pre-dawn while the rest of the crew sleepily
prepared for a long day's fishing – maybe two or even three,
thought the boy, with a prickle of excitement at the novelty, the
adventure. However long they were coming out for, it would be
their last trip if they came home empty once again.

Under the brightness of the dawn gathering behind them after
the coast – and even the mountaintops of the Sierra Madre – had

fallen below the horizon, the old man was unusually grim-faced, Miguel-Angel observed, though he made no remark. And taciturn. There was none of the wisdom, the inconsequential chat or the banter that usually enlivened their hours together. His lips and eyes were narrow; his nostrils flared in thought – something that he did unconsciously when his forehead was at its most creased. Miguel-Angel had known *Capitan* Carlos his whole life and understood his moods as well as he understood the moods of the sea and the sky. At first, the boy wondered whether *Capitan* Carlos was worried about the weather, for after four hours heading due west at full speed he had suddenly swung the helm round forty-five degrees to starboard and *Pilar* had turned on to a new course dead north, still with the throttles as wide as they would go.

It was clear that *Pilar* would be heading up towards a considerable tempest if she stayed on this course. The preparations in California for the threatened ARkStorm were a lead item in the news down here. But then, on closer inspection, Miguel-Angel had realized that the old man was not afraid of the sea. The *capitan* was wrestling with his conscience. And that explained why no one aboard seemed keen to tell Miguel-Angel anything. He was as much their good-luck mascot as he was a crewmember, and they would never willingly make him complicit in anything illegal. And they were clearly planning something desperately illegal, the boy thought grimly.

Miguel-Angel knew enough about fishing – and, indeed, about life – to understand that legality was hard. Illegality was too easy. Especially for desperate men staring ruin, destitution and starvation in the face. The commercial fishing licenses that lay folded into the log books on the chart table were specific about what types of fish *Pilar*, her master and his crew could take from the ocean. About the requirements – such as VMS transmitters – that the vessel should be carrying to give their location at all times when at sea. About the areas that were open to them – and those that were closed. About what methods of fishing they were allowed to use – and which were absolutely forbidden. As soon as Miguel-Angel saw the new course he realized that Carlos was heading north into the danger of inclement weather on purpose. Fishery protection vessels would not be likely to stay out if conditions got worse, as the Americans seemed certain they would do. And, under the quiet *capitan*'s steady hand, *Pilar* was heading not only into the possibility of foul weather but also into a closed area that stretched up the Pacific coast of the Baja California, where the great whales went to breed, where no one but whale-watchers and tourists were permitted. And where fish – especially skipjack, blue-fin and albacore – were consequently plentiful.

That explained why the VMS tracking equipment was turned off, observed Miguel-Angel, and also the limited clearance proce-dures that had been made with the harbourmaster at Puerto Banderas. A quick tour of inspection under cover of fetching a mug of coffee and a breakfast burrito for Carlos further revealed that the crew – as desperate as their *capitan* – had laid aside the long lines with which they could legally catch tuna and had instead brought up the last of the utterly illegal drift nets which they had hidden in a false bottom below the main freezer – and which now looked like their only chance of survival. They had found the nets floating at the end of last season while the boat that had deployed them was taken north to US waters by the coastguards and fisheries inspection officers, under close arrest. Drift nets made of the new polymers that had no smell or sonar signal, utterly invisible to every creature in the ocean. Drift nets so strong and yet so tightly woven that every marine life form from the greatest whales to the smallest tuna would get trapped within them.

Throughout the day, *Pilar* pushed north at her maximum speed of twelve knots – just under fifteen miles per hour. But that speed was on top of the north-running counter-current that ran up the coast inside the more powerful California current that was carrying *Katapult8* and *Maxima* southward out in the deep Pacific. Twenty miles per hour might have flattered the old girl, but that was her effective speed all day. Or it was until she found herself vanishing into a blood-red sunset with a black wall of cloud along the far northern horizon fourteen hours – and nearly three hundred miles – out. *Capitan* Carlos gave the order to ready the nets and attach them to the big winch over the stern.

'We will fish all night,' he ordered, 'as we run on north into the closed area off San Quintin. It will take many more hours to reach the San Quintin light, but when we do we will check the nets, begin to fill the freezers and ease out into the California current which will bring us home again – still with the nets out – and, through the grace of God, with the freezers full at last.'

As the night closed in and the wall of cloud in the north obscured more and more of the stars, *Pilar* sailed more slowly northward towards the restricted area south and west of San Quintin. Miguel-Angel went with the crew on to the aft deck to see how they jury-rigged the main winch there to ease out – and pull back – the long net. 'It will be hard to bring that back aboard if you net a big haul,' he observed. '*Pilar* is not designed for this sort of work.'

'She is not,' agreed the busy crewmen. 'But we will find a way.'

'Keeping control of the net will be a difficult task on its own,' said the boy. 'We will know where the near end is because it will be attached to the winch. But what about the far end? I could curl round on a rogue current and foul our propellers and we would never know until it was too late.'

'The *capitan* has thought of that,' said Hernan, one of the crewmen and ship's cook. 'Look. Here at the far end of the net, on the first float we will put into the water, we have secured a beacon. It will give a signal both by light and radio, telling us its location and the location of the end of the net.'

'That is very clever,' said the boy. 'But still, if the catch is a large one you will have great difficulty in getting the net back in.'

'We will bring it in a fish at a time if we have to,' Hernan answered. 'But things are not that bad. A section of the transom opens.'

No sooner had he said this than two of the crew did indeed unclip a section of the low transom. As they did so, the northern darkness flickered and the thick, hot wind brought a whisper of distant thunder. But the sound was almost immediately drowned in the wheezing rattle of the winch as the net went over the stern, feeding out through the open section with the beacon lashed tightly to its end.

The net was the better part of a kilometre in length, though it was only a part of the original. It was ten metres deep with its top attached to floats and its bottom tied to weights. It was designed to hang like an invisible wall across the upper reaches of the ocean where the great shoals of tuna ran, between the stern of *Pilar* and the little beacon flashing at the far end. As they eased it out, the crew debated whether it would be better to hang it parallel to the distant coast, along the north-flowing current in the hope of catching the tuna as they headed into the shallows to feed. Or whether it might be better to move *Pilar* out to the deeper water on the outer edge where the north-flowing current met its south-flowing parent, and hang the net from side to side across the northward current to catch the fish running up towards the US or down towards Puerto Banderas.

Miguel-Angel took this debate up to the wheelhouse and asked the *capitan* what he proposed to do. 'I will hang it along the current to begin with, at least,' decided Carlos. 'I trust my instincts more than the fish-finder, which has never worked properly. And my instinct suggests that fish run towards their feeding grounds in the turbulent waters beneath the surf at the shore, then out into the depths to rest and play. It is not something I would normally discuss with the crew, but they would understand the logic in that. However, the decision is made simple for me in any case, Miguel-Angel, because of what I must do to keep control of the net. *Pilar* is not a proper trawler – as you have no doubt seen as the net went out through the transom. Even with the little beacon telling me where the far end of the net is – you see it flashing on the radar there? – in order to keep control of such a great length, which will act like a sea anchor, I must run fast enough to keep it streaming tightly out astern, a little like a kite in a strong wind. I can only do this if I run faster than the current. So we will ease out to sea a little until the California current is running southwards against us like a strong wind helping to keep my kite aloft, then we will sail north, and maintain the fastest speed the drag of the net will allow.'

'But then we may miss the fish that are running with the current.'

'True. Then let us pray that most of the fish in these waters are running across the current tonight. Now, I am hungry. Go below. When the men have finished putting the net out they will prepare food. Hernan has brought *gorditas*. Bring me two. One stuffed with egg and the other with fish. And coffee, though I will have to relieve myself soon if I drink too much. Then I will let you take the helm while I eat and work the stiffness from my bones.'

Miguel-Angel took the helm for the first hour of night while the old man ate his *gorditas*, drank his coffee and exercised in a series of squats and stretches. The wheelhouse became a place of low light and massive shadows, especially after Carlos decided that switching on the running lights would only invite trouble. Just as the disconnected VMS kept them invisible to the GPS tracking systems designed to alert the fisheries protection officers to the very thing they were in fact doing, remaining invisible to everything except the chance of radar or sonar contact seemed the best idea under the current circumstances, especially as someone official might yet pick up the signal from the little beacon behind them and grow suspicious enough to come looking.

Then Miguel-Angel went below and consumed his own *gorditas* – hungrily, for he was young, growing still, and had eaten little so far today. And in truth, Hernan made exceptionally good *gorditas*. Especially when he filled them with hard-boiled egg mashed through with finely chopped red jalapenos and served them with a salad of *cilantro*, spring onions and green peppers. The crew teased the boy over the matter of coffee when he requested a mug-full, asking whether he was old enough to drink such a powerful brew. But he did not mind. The teasing was good-natured, and was a sign that the crew were beginning to relax. Now, he thought sleepily, if he could get the *capitan* to relax as well . . .

Exhausted, the boy fell asleep at the table and Hernan carried him through into the tiny cabin and laid him on one of the two bunks there, tucking him in just like his mother used to before she went north across the border with his elder brother, Juan Jose. Then the ship's cook went up on to the bridge to report, and relieved *Capitan* Carlos at the wheel while *Pilar*'s master went down on to the aft deck and relieved himself over the half-open transom, with the hot wind strong against his back, before checking the winch and the lines that stretched away into the darkness where the net flared like a banner just beneath the increasingly choppy waves of the wake.

Carlos Santiago went up to the forecastle before returning to the bridge. He stood on the forepeak, looking along the course

Pilar was following, smelling the wind and straining to see into the sinister blackness ahead. The unseasonably oppressive heat, the presence of whales that ought to have been up in the Arctic feeding grounds, the constant flickering of light just below the far horizon – as though there was some unimaginable battle raging in the north with salvo after salvo of great guns spitting fire and explosive shells – all made him regret the position that fate had placed him in. And which he in consequence had placed his ship and crew in. And the boy. Most of all, he regretted the boy. Suddenly he looked away to starboard. There was nothing to see – they were far out on a benighted ocean now, in the grip of the south-flowing California current, and the land was below the horizon there. But he knew well enough where they were in relation to the Baja. If things became too dangerous, he decided, he would run for the safe haven of Puerto San Carlos. He half laughed, making a sound that was almost a cough. He'd likely end up saving them all – while ruining himself – just because he was worried about the boy.

Miguel-Angel was woken four hours later when his head hit the side of the bunk. He sat up, banging his head again with disorientating force. His whole world reeled and heaved so powerfully he thought he must be on the verge of passing out. Then the door of the cabin opened and he recognized the figure of Hernan hanging in the doorway, keeping himself erect by spread-eagling himself against the doorframe. 'It's getting rough out there,' said the ship's cook. 'The *capitan* asked me to check on you.'

'I'm fine,' said Miguel-Angel. 'Shall I come up on to the bridge?'

'If you can. It'd give the old man something less to worry about.'

'OK. Is there anything you want me to take up with me?'

'Coffee. And try not to spill it.'

Five minutes later, Miguel-Angel was staggering up the bridge-house companionway, concentrating fiercely on the steaming black surface of a mug of coffee that was doing its best to emulate the steaming black water outside. At least the top few steps were illuminated slightly by the green glow of the instruments that filled the bridge house with eerie light.

'I brought coffee, *Capitan*,' he said.

Then he realized the *capitan* wasn't going to be able to hear him, for they were seemingly in the middle of a storm. The heaving of the deck was matched by the roar of the wind, the battering blasts of rain and spray and the mercifully distant flashes of lightning and the rumbles of thunder they generated – sounds so deep and powerful that they made everything on the bridge seem to shake.

And there, unmoving in the midst of it, *Capitan* Carlos stood at the helm like an anthracite statue. Apparently unconcerned by what the night was throwing at him, holding *Pilar* on course, dead into the very jaws of the thing. Miguel-Angel staggered over towards him, fiercely focused on the lurching, slopping coffee once again. This time he waited until he was almost at the *capitan*'s shoulder. 'I brought coffee, *Capitan*!' he shouted. The old man looked round and nodded, then gestured with his white-stubbled chin towards the cup-holder on the console.

The boy hesitated, frozen with surprise. He had seen his *capitan* under every circumstance he could readily imagine, but he had never seen him like this. The angular old face seemed to have lost ten years in age. The pale brown eyes burned with exhilaration as though there was some kind of a light behind them. The usually narrow mouth was wide in a grin of fierce elation. The big white teeth were clenched, squaring the stubbled jaw. And it was only this, thought Miguel-Angel, awed, that stopped him from laughing aloud with simple, fearsome joy.

'Come here, boy,' ordered this strange new creature in a deep, booming voice that rode over the thunder and the wind. He lifted his left hand from the helm and spread his arm wide in invitation, taking a firm half-step back to leave room for one slim boy to go in front of him. 'Take the helm for a moment and feel her! Feel the life in old *Pilar*. She was born for this! *We* were born for this!'

With his heart suddenly pulsing at fever pitch, half with excitement and half with terror, Miguel-Angel stepped forward into the space between the *capitan* and the helm. As soon as he entered it, the arm came down again and he found his left hand folded in the *capitan*'s, wrapped around the curve of the wheel. The old man's right hand grabbed his and for a moment both pairs of hands were on the wheel, with Miguel-Angel feeling the disorientating thrill of the life coursing through the battling boat. Then the *capitan*'s right hand was gone, reaching over to push the throttles further forward still. The boy at the helm blinked as a set of waves charged in at them, each one taller than the last. *Pilar* threw up her head and kicked up her heels, pitching and heaving through the water like the most powerful Azteca filly jumping over hedges and arroyos at the hunt.

But then, in a heartbeat, everything changed. *Pilar* gave a terrible lurch. The boy and the man behind him were thrown forward so forcefully that Miguel-Angel was winded. 'Have we collided?' he gasped. 'But there is nothing there! Have we run aground? Will we sink?'

'I don't know,' gasped Carlos. Even before the brief conversation was done, Hernan was at the top of the companionway, hanging in the opening there as he had hung in the cabin doorway. '*Capitan!*' he bellowed. 'The net! The winch! You must come.'

'Hold her steady, boy,' ordered the *capitan*. 'Head to the wind, bow to the waves and throttle at full ahead. I won't be long!' As he spoke, *Pilar* gave another lurch, as though she had been struck on the aft starboard quarter. Miguel-Angel held on to the wheel for grim death, fighting to make her forequarters behave no matter what was happening to her stern. He only released his death grip on the little wheel to reach across and push the throttle levers as far forward as they would go, which was what he believed Carlos had ordered him to do. He was so frightened that he didn't even notice that the green light which had dully illuminated the bridge so far had changed to red.

Out on the heaving after deck in the middle of the storm, Carlos Santiago stood beside the winch, scarcely able to believe his eyes. The whole thing was threatening to tear off its mountings. The steel cables running down to the net were writhing and twisting. The whole lot was fighting to pull itself back into the black depths even as the screaming motors were trying to tear *Pilar* forward.

'What is it?' bellowed Hernan, spokesman for the panicking crew. 'Have we snagged a submarine? Are we tangled round the propellers of some massive cruise liner? What is it, *Capitan?*'

'It must be a whale,' said Carlos, shaken.

'A *whale*? What sort of whale could do *that*?

'Humpbacks,' shouted Carlos, his voice breaking as his throat began to tear. 'We must have netted a pod of humpbacks!'

But as he realized this, two things happened in such swift succession that none of them was able to decide which happened first and which second.

The cable parted, causing the whole back section of the boat to leap out of the water, propeller screaming as it found nothing to bite on but thin air.

And the screaming engine coughed and died.

SIXTEEN

At dawn the wind suddenly died. *Katapult8* slowed to a dead stop and all four crewmembers stood side by side in the cockpit and looked around at the gathering brightness. Never one to sit on her hands and complain, Liberty decided, 'Right. This is a good opportunity to fix some food. Emma and Maya, could you do the honours there? Coffee and bacon rolls. And Florence, can you shin up the sail and see what's up with the running light and the AIS?'

As the off-watch team of Emma and Maya went below to heat up some food and coffee, the tall Australian redhead stepped up out of the cockpit and strode down the central hull, past the huge black wing of the sail, trailing her fingers along its surface like a proud owner petting a thoroughbred. The sail was a perfect aerofoil shape. The rear edge was a little thicker than a knife blade, but the leading edge was as wide as a mast. As she reached this edge, she paused, unclipped her safety harness from the deck lines and clipped it to a toggle set into the sheer composite cliff, then paused, looking up. The toggle she was connected to was set in a shallow groove running right up to the tip of the sail. Just beside it was a ladder of indented foot and hand-holds, designed to make it easy to climb the sail itself. With no further hesitation – as she had done countless times before – she set her toecap into the lowest rung and heaved herself up off the deck. The toggle slid up easily as she climbed nimbly upward. But should she slip and fall, it was designed to hold her safe like an inertia-reel seatbelt. There was no chance of Flo falling, even though the pitching of the hull in the restless early-morning chop was magnified up here.

Five minutes of vigorous climbing took Flo to the top of the sail and she stopped there, twisting the toggle so her harness held her safe as her hands came free. There was a little compartment up here which contained the VMS locator beacon and the electrical wiring that allowed the main battery below to power that and the signal light on the topmost tip. A moment's inspection showed that the fault was simple – and easy to fix. A connection had come unfastened and the main power wire hung loose. Florence pushed the connection together, snapped the cover home and glanced up at the signal light which was now shining brightly and steadily just above her. 'Good job, girl,' she said to herself, and paused to look around.

The sky behind *Katapult8* remained low, black and threatening but, for the moment, the heavens immediately above her were blue and clear, as though she was sailing through the eye of a storm. The ocean beneath her triple keel was choppy and unsettled – on the rougher side of moderate and rising force five on the Beaufort scale. And for every degree of movement at surface level, the top of the mast swung ten or more degrees. But Florence was used to the movement and luxuriated for a little longer in the privacy. The day dead ahead looked bright and welcoming, she thought, even if the threatening clouds covering half of it behind were repeated in the far distance, forming a thick charcoal line right across the southern horizon.

Even as Florence, frowning, took all this in, a wind stirred against her cheek and set her red curls dancing. A new wind, from a new direction. It puffed again, feeling somehow determined, promising. Florence knew what this meant. Liberty would want to be off at once. She checked the cover over the little electrical compartment once again and started back down the sail as fast as her safety line allowed. By the time she reached the cockpit and grabbed the mug of coffee and the huge bacon roll Emma and Maya had heated in the vessel's tiny microwave, the wind that had kissed her cheek up aloft had swung round to the north-west and settled into a steady twenty knots.

As far as Liberty was concerned, after a night of hard sailing and tacking from reach to reach across a dead northerly, the new wind meant freedom and a renewed chance to win her bet with Richard. During the hours of darkness the sleek multihull had covered many miles at a steady twenty knots. But most of those miles had been along courses to the south-west or the south-east as she tacked across the following breeze – far too few for comfort had been dead south. But the crew pulled together, working through fatigue to that plateau where a mixture of exhaustion and adrenaline worked on their systems like a potent drug. This was the level they wanted to attain for their most testing competitions. Every woman there felt utterly at one with the sea, the wind, the multihull and her crewmates. The fact that they had hardly slept in twenty-four hours, that they had loosened their watertight clothing only to relieve themselves, that nothing chafed any longer – not even the long emergency blade that each one wore down her right calf or the safety harness they all wore beneath the life preservers – all became nothing in comparison to the possibilities unleashed by the clear dawn sky, the steady new wind and the broad blue ocean ahead. Not to mention the enhancing effect as mugs of coffee strong enough to dissolve coffee spoons and thick, hot bacon rolls hit their systems. The fiercely competitive Liberty had begun to suspect that her father in *Maxima*, powered by those two big Caterpillar motors, must be breathing down her neck. Especially now that the AIS was back online and he would be able to pinpoint their precise location every moment of every day and night during the next twenty hours or so it would take them to reach Puerto Banderas. 'Right,' she ordered, 'let's do some serious sailing while we can.'

If Florence, Emma or Maya had had any second thoughts about the height of the waves, the reliability of the wind, the weather surrounding them or the wisdom of pushing their vessel to the limit when they were further from land than they had planned – for dawn broke and the wind shifted at the outer jibe point of a south-western reach – it never occurred to them to say anything. They were a widely experienced team, used to working together, at that euphoric pitch which comes only once or twice in a lifetime. And although they planned to split up soon and each go their individual ways, preparing to battle the others during the waterborne heats of the Tokyo Olympics – they knew better than to question Liberty. In matters such as mutiny, she made Bligh of the *Bounty* look like Anne of Green Gables. Without a second thought, therefore, they drained their coffee, stuffed the last of the food in their mouths and fell to working their beautiful multihull. Under Liberty's steady hand, the huge black composite sail soon grabbed the wind and the multiple hulls sat up on the surface and were skimming from wave-top to wave-top as *Katapult8* pulled twenty-five, then thirty knots on a south-south-easterly course across the wind towards Puerto Banderas.

This was exhilarating sailing, and the whole crew was as entranced as their breathless captain, for it was exactly what the cutting-edge machine was designed for. And one of *Katapult8*'s more wonderful attributes came into play. The hand and foot holes down each surface of the huge wing of her sail designed to allow crewmembers, like Florence, access to the electronics and lights at the very top had a strange effect. When the wind was right, these indentations would begin to make sounds like an Aeolian harp – and the sail would sing. The sail was singing now and the wind was working its magic against it most powerfully. But all of them knew *Katapult8* could do better still.

'Flo,' bellowed Liberty over the rush of the wind, the hiss of the foam, the thunder of the hulls through the surf and the keening song of the sail, 'do you think we can risk the J's?' On either side of the multihull's outer hulls were tall walls of black composite, like the sail, that stood perhaps a third as high as it did. Each outrigger boasted a pair of them – with anchor points in-between so that *Katapult8*'s crew could still swing out on their safety lines and hold her down against the wind. And equally tall, lean blades of rudders stood high behind Liberty's shoulders. The bottom section of each sidewall curled round into the shape of a capital J. The uprights were robust, thick, made of composite and polymer stronger than steel. The hook sections, equally robust, were the same thickness as the uprights at the after edge, but the leading edges were razor-sharp so that they could – literally – cut through the water at amazing speeds. Each hook bedded into a cavity that made the whole hull perfectly aquadynamic. But the walls were designed to slide down once *Katapult8* reached a certain speed. The hook sections on the bottom were so perfectly designed and placed that when this was done the whole multihull rose out of the water and aquaplaned.

With her J hooks deployed, *Katapult8* was capable of another ten knots – perhaps more under the right circumstances – controlled by the tall rudders that were designed to lower themselves in unison until only the hooks and slim rudder-blades were in the water and all resistance was effectively gone. So that *Katapult8* not only sang like a bird, she flew like one as well. It was a system designed by 'Doc' Weary, Flo's father, and she knew more than any others on Liberty's crew about what stresses the J hooks and the rudder blades could withstand. 'Go for it,' she advised. 'Let's see what she can do.'

'Right!' ordered Liberty. 'Get ready to deploy J hooks and rudder blades.'

Five minutes later, *Katapult8* was running across the wind at forty knots. Her whole hull was more than a metre clear of the choppy water, balanced perfectly on the pairs of J hooks that seemed merely to kiss the surface as it sped beneath at breathtaking speed. The rudder, too, seemed only just to reach deep enough to keep the whole thing under control. Liberty had never experienced anything like it. She had ridden up on the J hooks before, but always in placid harbours or calm seas. This was the difference between boating on Central Park Lake and rafting the Colorado. She was so overcome that there were tears mixed with the spray whipping into her face. When she called to Florence, who was on the radio, her voice didn't work at first.

'F-F-FLO! Call up *Maxima* on the radio and tell my dad "goodbye", would you? And tell him and Richard Mariner that we'll see them in Puerto Banderas this time tomorrow!'

'Aye, aye, Captain,' answered Florence.

Ninety minutes after Florence broke contact with Liberty's father, *Katapult8* hit the humpback whale.

SEVENTEEN

The weather got worse between Ensenada and Tijuana. Biddy took the Bell down as low as she dared and loudly considered setting down on at least three occasions. Richard kept quiet – never one to try and outguess the captain of a vessel or the pilot of an aircraft. He craned sideways instead so he could keep the line of highway one in as clear view as possible beneath the worsening downpour and the battering wind. He could see why the bridges might be at risk, though the ones up here seemed to be holding on more successfully than the man at Cielito Lindo airfield had supposed or than the guys at San Quintin had warned. The highway ran as straight as a Roman road through Molino Viejo, Lazaro Gardinas and San Quintin itself, all of which showed as webs of blurry brightness on the ground and as names on Biddy's rolling locator map. Then, after twenty or so kilometres of occasionally lit highway with precious few vehicles coming or going through the deluge, they arrived over Vicente Guerrero, which looked to be a much larger settlement. But the brightness of the streetlights and the ant-like scurrying of all sorts of vehicles soon made it clear that the warnings from their friends at Cielito Lindo and San Quintin had not been exaggerated after all. The town was built astride a sizeable arroyo. In summer – and most recent winters, Richard supposed – this was little more than a dry valley bridged by a single span. But the arroyo was anything but dry now. Even under the current conditions of darkness, wind and rain, Richard could see the raging torrent that was pouring down from the western slopes of the San Pedro Martir mountains. The centre of the town had been torn away by the violent flow, and where there had been a bridge – as suggested by the disposition of the highway – there was now the kind of cataract that Richard remembered seeing where the Colorado River rushed through the Grand Canyon.

The next town, Camalu, seemed to be faring a little better, but the bridge over the Arroyo Colonet, twenty kliks further north again was down as well, just as the men from San Quintin Airfield had feared. Biddy swooped down over the raging wreck, then followed the roadway inland. Almost immediately the mountains of the Cordillera loomed, their presence mostly subliminal – just a massive threat of deep darkness on Richard's right. It was an unsettling conjunction of rising ground and falling water, where the north-westerly flow of the saturated air was forced up so violently that it bled its precipitation in great pulses, as though it was a throat passing over a razor blade.

During the next half hour, however, things began to quieten, especially after they eased back towards the coast once more, and by the time the Bell was powering over Ensenada the wind had fallen lighter and the rain was beginning to ease. 'I think we're going to make it,' observed Biddy. 'Looks like things are easier up here after all.' Richard didn't answer, because he agreed. And he suddenly realized that that was worrying. Biddy took them out over All Saints Bay and followed the coastal highway up past San Miguel Bay and Salsipuedes Bay. Within the hour they were over Rosario, immediately to the south-west of Tijuana, then over the western outskirts of Tijuana itself, and suddenly Biddy was negotiating them into US airspace as the bright bustle of the border swept beneath them, looking like a treasure trove of yellow diamonds in the brightness of the downpour. Then San Diego appeared, and in less than an hour they had followed the brightness of the coastal highway along the one hundred and eighty kliks or so that separated San Diego from Long Beach.

'Made it,' announced Biddy with enormous satisfaction as she began her short descent into the Island Express landing area.

'And I can't thank you enough,' said Richard. 'What will you do now?'

'Drop you off, refuel and fly out to the Greenbaum International helipad up in Glendale. There's accommodation there. I'll grab some food and some shut-eye then wait for further orders, as they say.'

Richard ran up the gangplank and went back aboard *Sulu Queen* halfway through the morning watch, just as a sullen, stormy dawn was beginning to threaten. He ran round the foot of the great square gantry immediately in front of the bridge with only the briefest pang of frustration that the massive mechanism could not lower containers on to the dockside – merely rearrange them on the deck. Then he swung through the A-deck door into the bridge house and pounded straight up to the command bridge, where he found the youthful first officer keeping watch himself. The young man turned round as Richard strode on to the bridge, and Richard recognized the badges of rank on his uniform before he registered the almost elfin youthfulness of the face above them. 'I am Cheng, Captain,' said the young man. 'I am the first officer. Welcome aboard.'

'Thank you, Mr Cheng. Tell me, are the National Guard soldiers and Mr Prudhomme still aboard?'

'Yes, Captain. They went back to bed after you informed us that you planned to take command yourself. I can have them woken . . .'

'Not yet. Any updates on Captain Sin's condition?'

'He is resting comfortably.'

'Good. You said he had toured the ship, checked for damage after the lightning strike yesterday morning and everything was OK?'

'Yes, Captain. And he had also ensured that our supplies and bunkerage were full, as I said. Apart from the situation with the cargo and the National Guard containers, we are ready to sail at a moment's notice.'

'The crew?'

'All ready, too . . .' There was some hesitation in Cheng's voice, as though he could not see the purpose of the question.

'No one demanding shore leave?' Richard elaborated.

'No, Captain. No shore leave. There was never any question of that.'

'Very well. Are the logs up to date?'

'Yes, Captain.'

'Then I am happy to relieve you until the end of the morning watch. It will give me an opportunity to read the logs and make my plans. Then at change of watch, eight o'clock sharp, I will conduct my own inspection. I will want yourself and the chief engineer available as I do so.'

'Yes, Captain.' The young man hesitated, looked around the bridge and then – literally – bowed himself out.

Richard walked to the forward section – the area that had been forbidden aboard *Queen Mary* – and looked moodily out through the clear view over the square top of the gantry and along the grey-black Rubik's cube of the cargo as the dull brightness of the leaden dawn began to reveal it. He noted precisely where Major Guerrero's National Guard containers stood, estimating that there must be between seventy-five and a hundred of them in all.

Then, deep in thought, he crossed to the little side table beside the pilot's chair and shook the kettle standing there. It gave a satisfying slopping sound, and the weight of it told him it was almost full. He switched it on and made himself the strongest, blackest cup of coffee he had ever sipped. At the very least it was going to be a long day, and three hours' sleep followed by a hair-raising helicopter ride were not the best possible preparation for it.

He crossed to the chart table and opened the old-fashioned log book there. Punctilious in this as in everything, Captain Sin had clearly insisted that the log be kept in both Chinese and English, and that every detail of shipboard life be entered. The last entry in the English section – and, probably, in the Chinese – was the report of the captain's illness, the arrival of the paramedics and the address and contact number of the hospital he had been taken to. Richard flipped back and began with the entries for the last few days, focusing on the way the weather had behaved as the storm tiger chased poor old Sin across the Pacific and finally cornered him here.

The detailed description of the air pressures, the cloud forms, the wind speeds, the states of sea and sky soon filled his head like a pattern, and he went through them almost like Sherlock Holmes looking for clues to a puzzle he wasn't even certain existed. But he did see a pattern beginning to emerge – and one at variance with what Dr Jones of NOAA had been saying the best part of three days ago. He was so immersed in his detective work that it came as a shock when he turned over the last page to find he was back at the report of Captain Sin's illness – there were no further meteorological observations at all.

Richard looked up, blinking a little blearily. Dawn was gathering more forcefully now. The ship's chronometer above the binnacle told him it was coming up to seven thirty a.m. local time, which to be fair, he reckoned, was probably the time everywhere from Alaska to Tierra Del Fuego – Pacific Standard Time. It certainly reached up as far as Alaska and the coast of Canada, and down as far as the parts of Mexico he was most deeply concerned with at any rate. He rubbed his eyes and sat back, scanning the bridge once more. On one corner of the chart table someone had placed a portable TV. It was probably a recent addition to the bridge equipment – Richard couldn't see Captain Sin being too happy with the thought of his watch officers being offered such a potent distraction, even in harbour. And he couldn't remember having seen it here on his earlier visits. But he switched it on now and the little screen was filled at once by the logo of KTLA5, the local TV station. Then, immediately, by the face of the woman he had just been thinking about.

'So, Doctor Jones,' said an interviewer currently out of shot. 'Your ARkStorm seems to be less cataclysmic than you feared.' A bit of an anticlimax, the interviewer's tone implied. Richard was reminded of the taxi driver and his dismissive opinions.

'We certainly seem to have been lucky so far,' allowed the climatologist warily. 'Though, as you know, there have been dangerous mud slides in Glendora and Azusa. Both of those neighbourhoods have been evacuated and we're looking at moving more folks out of houses on the western slopes of the Sierras. Things will continue to worsen here if the rain continues like this. The Los Angeles River is on flood alert too, of course. An inch an hour is still a dangerous level of precipitation.'

'But,' purred the invisible interviewer, 'we were informed you were predicting amounts in excess of *two* inches an hour. There have been no reports of that level of intensity.'

'Yes, there have,' Richard informed the television. 'Down in Cielito Lindo and San Quintin and on down the Baja California there have . . .'

Then he stopped talking and sat silently for a moment as the most obvious truth of all hit him and the pattern he had been seeking in the log books became clear. 'It's gone south,' he said. 'Your ARkStorm's not going to hit the coast of California, Doctor Jones, because it's already hitting Mexico! It's heading on south. Bloody *hell*!'

No sooner come to that conclusion than his cell phone started ringing. He pulled it out of his pocket and saw Robin's face on the screen. Where in heaven's name did she get a signal way out there? he wondered. Perhaps there were cell phone satellites as well as the NOAA weather sats in low orbit over the Pacific just at that moment.

'Hi, darling. What can I do for you?'

'We have a bad problem here, darling. We've lost *Katapult8*.'

'Lost her how?' He stopped wool-gathering and focused on what Robin was saying.

'Well, you remember we had her on radar all last night, even though her AIS locator wasn't working?'

'I do . . .' Richard thought he could see where this was going.

'Well, they fixed the locator nearly two hours ago so we had them on both radar and the AIS equipment. They called in, and Florence issued another of their challenges. Really, darling, what *have* you started! Well, then *Katapult8* took off like a bat out of hell. We lost her on radar but we still had her on locator. Then, suddenly, she vanished. Even the locator signal vanished.'

'Maybe it just went offline again. Same problem as before.'

'Maybe. That's what I said, but Nic's worried.'

'Fair enough. You know what to do – it's partly why you're there, after all. Take no risks. Head for their last location as fast as you can.'

'We are doing.'

'Good. And watch out yourselves . . .'

'Why?'

'It looks as though this ARkStorm everyone's been so worried about isn't going to hit Long Beach and LA after all. It's going to hit Mexico. Everywhere from Tijuana to Puerto Banderas and on down south. Wherever *Katapult8* and the girls are, they're likely to be right in the worst of it.'

EIGHTEEN

Katapult8 had topped forty-four knots soon after contact with *Maxima* ended. When she'd hit the whale she'd been sailing faster than she'd ever sailed before. The only parts of her that broke the surface were the J hooks and the long rudders. Under normal circumstances, the whale would have heard her coming and dived. Even had she not, the leading J hook would hardly have touched her and both yacht and cetacean would have survived the collision undamaged. But the whale was one of a hunting pod of nine powerful fifty-footers that had become wrapped in *Pilar*'s nets away south in the middle of last night. They were lucky to have survived so far – many of the other ocean-dwellers caught in the nets around them had failed to do so. But, working together, the bull, the cow and the near-grown calf of the main family group and the half-dozen others that swam and hunted with them had kept at the surface, still able to breathe as the polymer mesh billowed around them like a gigantic, undulating spider's web the best part of a kilometre long.

Katapult8's J hook bounced off the humpback's head, doing only a little damage to the whale. But it snagged on *Pilar*'s illegal drift net wrapped around its massive face. The leading edge of the hook was razor-sharp and it sliced through the net easily, cutting a hole large enough to let the family pod of whales swim free and offer the other six huge creatures a chance of escape as well. But even the slightest resistance interfered with the physical laws that *Katapult8* relied on to keep moving in this manner at these speeds. The starboard hooks sank deeper. The net slid up the uprights away from the sharpest section. It began to bunch up and to offer more resistance. The hull sank further. The port-side hooks became involved. At first they too cut the net. But then they also began to sink and the net entrapped them.

One second *Katapult8* was hurling across the wind at forty-five knots; little more than a second later her J hooks were enmeshed. A second later still, her rudders were trapped. The hull itself, under the pressure of that massive sail, strove to keep moving at forty-five knots. The hooks in the net were forced to come almost to a dead stop as they pulled the deadweight sea anchor of the drift net, made heavier still by the corpses of *Pilar*'s enormous final catch of hundreds of dead and dying tuna – and the energetic attempts of six fifty-foot humpbacks to follow their friends to freedom.

Before Liberty or any of her crew had the faintest idea of what was happening, *Katapult8* pitchpoled. The J hooks snapped, pulling her bows downward. The three sharp forecastles punched into the back of a wave all at once. They stopped moving forward, as though they had hit a wall. But the sail did not. It pulled the stern and the women in the cockpit there out of the water as the rudders, still caught in the net, shattered, letting the poop leap up off the surface and high into the air like a rocket lifting off. *Katapult8* stood on her nose for a nanosecond, with the sail and the stumps of the J hooks parallel to the water. The three hulls between them pointed their bows towards the bottom of the ocean and their sterns towards the top of the sky. Liberty, Flo, Emma and Maya were hurled out of the hull, flying through the air until their safety lines snapped taut.

Katapult8 flipped over. The top of the sail slammed into the water at a speed which made the surface seem as hard as rock. The sail snapped free of the central hull which somersaulted over it and crashed upside down into the water beside it with an impact hard enough to smash all three hulls open. The composite of which the hulls were made was as light as it was strong, but it was not as buoyant as the sail or the J hooks. Burst open, they were still weighed down with kit: microwaves, tackle which included their emergency equipment, distress signals, radio and supplies. The instant the air exploded out of them the three hulls immediately began to sink, dragging the crew, still secured by their safety lines, down into the depths. Even though their top-flight Gill ocean-going lifejackets began to inflate automatically, the stunned and disorientated women would all have died then. But the net that had put them in this terrible danger saved them – for the moment, at least. The sinking hulls became trapped in it just as the J hooks and the tall rudders had. A kilometre of net, with most of its floats intact, was more than enough to slow its descent. And, ironically, the net stopped the ruined hull from sinking, while there was still just enough length on the lifelines to allow Liberty, Flo and the others to reach the restless, choppy surface.

Liberty's head burst through the surface and she pulled in a great shuddering breath in spite of the fact that her ribs complained agonizingly and part of the air going into her was compromised by saltwater foam. The sharp-edged chop which had seemed so trivial from *Katapult8*'s cockpit now seemed dangerously overwhelming. And, in spite of her deep-water clothing, it felt icily cold. Her field of vision was reduced from the furthest horizon to the nearest wave-top. She was still looking wildly around and preparing to call out when the next wave surged under her. Her head jerked back under water because the line still secured to *Katapult8* was a foot too short to keep her above the wave crests. Cold pierced her eyes. Brine hit her adenoids like acid.

Liberty's brain kicked fully alive and the adrenaline of shock and fear joined the cocktail of elation and exhaustion, coffee and protein in her blood. She began to look around for her friends. But the water was thick and salty. Her vision was limited. She could see vague shapes; some movement, and nothing more. The billowing net formed a lumpy, disturbing background to what little she could make out. She did not know it, but at least the whales had gone. It occurred to her that she should use this moment underwater to curl over, grab the handle of her safety knife and cut her line before she was dragged further down. It wouldn't take much: two more feet and she would be a mermaid.

Fighting to ignore the pains in her chest and back, momentarily irritated by the fact that her buoyant PFD was fighting her every inch of the way, Liberty used the tension on the lifeline to pull herself down until she could reach the knife sheathed against her right calf. She slid it free and cut the line in one blessedly swift and fluid motion. At once she exploded to the top, seeming to burst out of the water until half her length was above the surface like a breaching whale. But then she settled back in, gasping, choking, blinking. It took her a moment to realize two extremely worrying things: she had dropped the knife as she exploded upwards. And as soon as she reached the surface, she started drifting, taken by the wind and the current.

Her next thought, once again, was for the others. 'Hey!' she called. 'Can anybody hear me? Flo? Emma? Maya? *Flo?*' A wave slapped her in the face and filled her mouth. She choked into silence, then remembered her basic first-aid training. You can't help others until you are safe yourself. Kicking her legs wildly, waving her arms and wrenching her body, she managed to swing herself round in the water. And there, immediately behind her, sitting high on the wave-tops, was the solid composite sail. Lighter and less encumbered than the hulls, it was buoyant and steady. She kicked towards it desperately, fearing that the wind which had powered it so far would blow it beyond her reach. But no. After a moment or two's exhausting effort, she found she had forced her unwilling body and recalcitrant personal flotation device through the restless water until she could touch it. The next problem was the sail's height. Even lying on its side, it formed a disturbingly substantial wall. The thick leading edge rather than the slim aft blade was closest to her. Even flat on the surface, this section of the sail was more than a metre sheer. After a couple of convulsive attempts to get up on to it, she discovered that although she could reach up over its rounded black circumference, she couldn't get a grip secure enough to allow her to pull herself aboard.

Such was her concentration on this dilemma amid the splashing restlessness of the icy water that she didn't hear the first of her crewmates approaching until Florence appeared at her shoulder. 'Feel for the footholds,' bellowed the Australian. And as she advised this, Liberty's fingers found a foothold. She closed her fingers to a fist, though they felt like sausages by now, and heaved herself upwards. Florence shoved a shoulder beneath her backside, risking a bruise or two from her thrashing legs, and shoved. Liberty slid up on to the flat surface. Spread-eagled herself at once and scrabbled herself round. Thrust her head and shoulders back over the edge. Held on like grim death with her left hand as she reached down with her right. A moment of frenetic activity later, Florence was lying beside her. 'You seen the others?' gasped Liberty.

'Nope.'

Liberty gingerly gathered herself on to all fours, then slowly and carefully pulled herself upright on her knees. The sail beneath her heaved as she moved, but it was a surprisingly solid platform. It was the best part of twenty-five metres long with a surface area of several hundred square metres. It was light, but incredibly strong and solid. Even so, she didn't want to risk standing upright, for the surface was so perfectly aerodynamic that it was also as slippery as ice – especially at the moment, when it was awash. She knelt there, looking back at the vacancy of choppy water, trying to work out exactly where the triple hull had gone down. Quite apart from anything else, if there was a chance of getting down to it, she might take the risk. Somewhere in the wreck was a proper life raft equipped with all sorts of signalling devices. But, unlike the Gill Marine lifejackets, it would only inflate if someone got down to it and pulled the emergency cord – a preference she regretted now, but one born of a panic aboard an earlier racing yacht where the life raft had inflated mid-race because some water had flooded into the cabin. That incident had cost her the race, a good deal of precious kit and very nearly her life. And in any case, Liberty was the sort of person who liked to be in control as well as on top and in the lead. So it looked as though the life raft was on its way to the bottom of the Pacific, along with everything else aboard. In the meantime, they only had the sail. And the AIS signaller on that would be out of commission once again.

At first she thought there was nothing left to mark the passing of her command and everything it contained. But then she noticed something that she hadn't even considered. At first she thought it was a massive shark's fin sticking up out of the water, and her heart gave a terrible lurch at the sight. But then she realized that it was the base of one of the J sections from *Katapult8*'s side. Like the sail, it was solid and buoyant. As she focused on it, she realized that there were two bedraggled women clinging to it. Her heart gave another lurch and her eyes filled with tears once more. 'Emma!' she bellowed. 'Emma! Maya! Can you hear me?'

A wearily waved arm was answer enough. Liberty looked around. The sail she was kneeling on seemed far too large to try to control – even if they'd had anything other than their hands to paddle with. If the four of them were going to get back together, Emma and Maya were going to have to propel the J hook over this way, or abandon it and swim. The distance between them was not great, but for some reason beyond Liberty's immediate understanding, it was widening. They were going to have to make the decision soon and take action immediately after that.

'Can you get to us?' shouted Liberty. 'The sail seems safe for the time being. It'll keep us out of the water, at least.'

Once again, a weary arm waved to show that the others had understood. And immediately the J hook started to move determinedly towards the sail as Maya and Emma started kicking in unison. Satisfied that there was nothing else she could do for them for the moment, Liberty began to look around. Her kneeling position on the sail gave her a view over the tops of the waves, though she couldn't see all that far. The set of the steep-sided chop all around them was disturbed by what looked like a ring of bright orange basketballs. They curled around almost in a circle, then wandered away downwind into the distance. And right in the shadowy heart of that distance, every now and then, something shone with the same jewel brightness as the rescue lights on their Gills. It was only when she saw the bright orange balls and recognized them as net floats that Liberty began to understand what had happened to them.

'Flo,' she said to her companion, 'it looks as though we got tangled up in some kind of drift net. But I can't see a trawler. It must have come free.'

'Really?' Florence answered, her voice flat with exhaustion and depression. 'Better hope whoever left some kind of drift net drifting out here hadn't caught much in it, then.'

'Why?'

'Scavengers. Sharks. They'll be around as soon as they smell death. And they won't care whether they're eating dead tuna or a living yachtswomen.'

'OK,' allowed Liberty bracingly, narrowing her eyes automatically and looking out for Maya and Emma, only to realize at once that the waves which surrounded them all looked like sharks fins anyway. 'But on the other hand, whoever lost the net might well look for it. Especially if the catch was good.'

'I suppose.' Florence's tone made it clear she supposed nothing of the sort.

'And in any case, my dad'll be coming after us as fast as he can the moment he realizes he's lost radar and AIS contact.'

'Maybe it wasn't such a good idea to get so far ahead of him after all.'

Liberty bit back a retort. Then she took a deep breath, thinking that *Katapult8* must have meant so much more to the daughter of the man who designed and built her – who designed and built a fair bit of her herself – than it did to the woman who'd merely bought her and sailed her. 'You think?' she said instead. But as she spoke, the float nearest to them jerked under the surface, as though something pretty big had become caught in the net. Or as though something pretty big was eating something that was caught in the net. 'Come on, Emma,' she called. 'Give it all you've got, girl!'

A few moments later, the shark fin of the J hook was bumping against the metre-high wall of the sail's edge. Liberty reached down and caught Emma's raised hand, hanging on tightly to one of the toeholds, just as she had done with Florence, and pulled the Japanese Olympic sailor aboard. Flo shook herself out of her depressed inactivity and pulled Maya on to the sail as well, using the grab handle on the lifejacket. The sail was so massive and so buoyant that it hardly registered the added weight or activity. It just sat on the water like a huge black raft. Then the four of them lay spread out like starfish and gasped at the humid air, waiting for their pulses to slow down.

But not for long. 'This won't do,' said Liberty, rolling over and kneeling up again. 'Did any of you see anything of *Katapult8*? If she's still tangled in the net I'm game to get my lifejacket off and go down after the life raft.'

'She's gone,' said Maya. 'I saw her going as I cut my lifeline. I was pretty damn lucky not to go down with her.'

'Don't get ideas above your station,' said Liberty. 'That's the captain's job. But *Katapult8*'s gone, you're sure?'

'Deep six,' said Maya. 'Davy Jones. Full fathom five. Gone.'

'Right. Then what I suggest is this, just for the time being. Flo, you snap your harness on to the inertia-reel toggle and you two tie the ends of your lifelines to Flo's harness. I'll do the same in a moment and that way we'll all be secured. In the meantime, while things are relatively settled, I'll stand up and take one good look around.'

While the other three were doing as she suggested, Liberty slowly and carefully pulled herself erect. In actual fact, the sail was pretty steady. Her footing on the black composite was quite secure. And yet Liberty felt as though she was on a tightrope.

The situation went straight into her unconscious – the difference between walking along a metre-wide pavement on Knight Way outside her alma mater in Stanford and crossing a metre-wide ledge high in the Himalayas. Even erect, on the stable platform of the sail, her calf and thigh muscles jumped and her torso felt dangerously top-heavy, making her wave her arms for balance. The wind didn't help, blowing steadily from the north-west. But after a few moments she straightened and her eyes cleared.

She saw the serpentine pattern of bright orange floats more clearly and followed the bobbing tail of the things across the restless ocean until they ended in that bright, flashing light made more vivid by the gathering darkness out there. It was a phenomenon she found acutely disturbing, given that it was early morning and ought to have been getting brighter – not darker. But then, right in the very distance, far beyond that flashing light, she saw something else. A shape back there in the shadows that looked to her like some kind of vessel. A small one, running without lights, that seemed to come and go like a ghost ship. It was so vague and fleeting that she wondered whether it was anything more than a coincidence of shadows and wishful thinking.

And Liberty was still trying to focus on this, to get some kind of idea exactly what and where the mysterious vision was, when something hit her on the back of the head. She staggered, her imagination conjuring everything from attacking seagulls to flying fish. She began to turn and was hit again – on the ear this time. An ear that was instantly full of water. She looked down. The composite at her feet seemed to explode as though a little bomb had detonated there. One the size of a baseball. She turned further still and looked up. The blue of the morning sky had vanished. In its place there was a low scud of rapidly moving overcast. And beneath it trailed grey veils of rain, sweeping across the agitated ocean towards her. Another rain-drop hit her, square on the forehead with enough force to make her stagger. It was the size of a baseball – and felt as hard as one into the bargain. Within a heartbeat, the four women marooned on the sail, unprotected in the middle of the ocean, found themselves at the heart of a deluge that would have done credit to Angel Falls.

NINETEEN

'Look, Nic,' said Robin, keeping her voice at its calmest and most reasonable, 'the chances are that *Katapult8*'s AIS has just gone offline again. That's all. If anything more serious had happened, we'd know about it, wouldn't we? I mean, if *Katapult8* was in trouble the girls would radio for help.'

'That's all very well, but *I've* radioed *them* and they're not replying.'

'Nic, you *know* that's Liberty playing her mind games with you. She was sneaking around and hiding yesterday evening. Now she's probably got a wind that we haven't caught yet and is making such good time she doesn't want to give anything away. That was the last message, wasn't it? They were coming up past forty knots and due in Puerto Banderas by sometime tonight? That's probably what's happening, then. If there was anything serious enough to put the yacht at immediate risk, especially if this rain has started wherever she is, they'd go into their life raft, and that has EPIRB emergency beacons which would alert us automatically – alert everyone from Canada to Costa Rica. *Really*. Think about it. They are four of the most competent sailors in the world, in one of the best-designed vessels afloat. Face it, Nic. In this case no news really *is* good news.'

Nic didn't look convinced, though he nodded in courteous agreement.

But Robin could see why he was worried. She had never come across rain like this. Huge drops were smashing down out of the low sky with astonishing force. The wipers on *Maxima*'s clear-view windscreen had given up the fight and seemed just to be sliding an inch of solid water back and forth across opaque glass. Even Robin's most reasonable tones had to be projected in her quarterdeck voice as though calling down half the length of a super tanker instead of across *Maxima*'s command bridge. Water thundered on to the deckhead above them as though they were trapped beneath a waterfall. The decks outside were inches deep in seething water, even though they were open, with nothing but deck rails surrounding them. Robin had visions of paint and varnish being stripped from metal and wood, as though the downpour was as powerful as a sandblaster.

Nic had ordered the automatic cover to be slid into place over the pool, which was just as well, Robin thought, or it would have been overflowing. Not that it made much difference to the amount of water cascading off the lower deck – just in its temperature and quality. What little could be seen of the sea that they were sailing in seemed to be boiling fiercely. Indeed, the surface was so completely shattered by the downpour that it formed a low mist which looked disturbingly like steam.

And yet there was almost no wind. That was part of what made this such a strange experience. That the sky could be vomiting down gallon after gallon of water hour after hour on to *Maxima*, but without a storm or even a squall. Robin had a mental image of a wedge of air trapped against the Baja California, backed hard up against the Cordillera's ten-thousand-foot peaks while the ARkStorm was forced to rise high above it. Forced up fast enough to be losing some of its massive weight of water, even out here. It would have to be a wedge of hot air rather than cold, which tested even her meteorological understanding to its limit. Yet there was something. Right at the back of her mind. What did they call it? A temperature inversion? Was that it? But whether this *inversion* was real or something she was making up, it was all she could envisage that made any kind of sense of the weather they were experiencing now. If *Katapult8* was caught in this, whether she was becalmed or running at forty knots before a friendly wind, then Nic would be getting a radio call, no matter how much pride and humble pie his over-competitive daughter would have to swallow.

And then she thought of Richard's all-too accurate words: 'This ARkStorm everyone's been so worried about isn't going to hit Long Beach and LA after all. It's going to hit Mexico. Everywhere from Tijuana to Puerto Banderas and on down south. Wherever *Katapult8* and the girls are, they're likely to be right

in the worst of it.' The only thing he had missed out was that
Maxima would find herself in the way of it as well, particularly
as she was going at full speed south after the girls like a blind
man running across a motorway.

But then she realized that this might not, in fact, be *the worst
of it.*

Humming thoughtlessly and nearly silently as she crossed to
the forward section of the command bridge, she was surprised
to find she was unconsciously partway through an old Bob Dylan
song about dead oceans and hard rain falling down. That's all I
need, she thought. Both Bob Dylan and my bloody husband
screwing up my head.

'What's that?' demanded Nic suddenly, his voice pitched loud
to overcome the roaring rain, his tone rising with tension. 'Looks
like some kind of emergency beacon ten or so miles dead ahead
of us.'

Robin and Captain Toro crossed to stand beside him at once.
The three of them crowded together in silence, looking into the
ship's state-of-the-art electronic display. There were screens
showing readings from the big navigation and communications
systems in the white domes on the communications masts high
up above them. Sonar, radar and satellite feeds, each with their
own display. Then there was a big central screen where all the
information came together. And, just as Nic said, this screen
showed, somewhere way out ahead, a tiny signal. An electronic
contact registered by something in low orbit over their heads
and rebroadcast to their displays down here. Matched with the
sonar feed and the collision alarm radar, then put on to the
electronic chart that reflected their immediate environs above
and below the surface. And that little point of electronically
generated brightness could only mean one thing. Maybe twelve
miles up ahead of *Maxima*, someone was probably having quite
a serious emergency.

Robin wondered whether either of the men beside her saw
the irony of the fact that the emergency signal was in all likeli-
hood being picked up and broadcast to them by the same
NOAA satellites that were watching the ARkStorm which was
making their current predicament so risky. But even she
remained ignorant of the fact that the downpour was limiting

the range of their radar, so that although the pre-programmed bands reached outwards promising to see contacts as far away as one, five, ten, fifteen and twenty miles, the radar could actually scarcely see less than five with any accuracy. Had *Pilar*, which was in fact twenty miles south-east of them and easing north-west on a reciprocal course, had her location system switched on, the NOAA satellites would have displayed her position accurately in spite of the torrential rain. But she did not, and so, although the bright emergency beacon blinked on the read-outs clearly enough some twelve miles ahead, the fishing boat remained invisible to *Maxima*.

'It's too small to be a lifeboat beacon,' said Robin after a moment. 'They tend to be emergency position indicating radio beacons: EPIRBs. Like I said, the ones on *Katapult8*'s life raft certainly are. This may be something smaller, maybe a personal locator beacon or PLB. Like you might find on a lifebelt.'

'On a *lifebelt*!' said Nic, horrified at the thought of someone actually in the water under these conditions.

'Not one of ours,' said Robin. 'Didn't you tell me the girls' Gill Marine lifejackets didn't have individual beacons? Just lights, whistles and grab handles. Basic standard issue with no fancy bits to get in the way and slow them down. Lean and mean. If they're in trouble, they'll activate the life raft and their big, bright, in-your-face EPIRBS satellite locator beacons.'

'It's what they've planned and practised.' Nic nodded, a measure of relief creeping into his voice.

'Still, *Señor* Greenbaum,' said Captain Toro quietly, 'we should go to this beacon. It may be your daughter or it may not. But it is somebody. And it looks as though they may need help.'

'If they're out on the water in this,' said Robin, 'they will certainly need help. And we are likely to be the only vessel in the immediate area not running for safe haven. The only vessel about legitimate business, at any rate. If we don't go and check it out then it's a fair bet no one else is going to.'

'Yeah,' agreed Nic grimly. 'It's on our way. And anyone out on the water in this will need all the help they can get. Especially if, as you say, there's no one else likely to be out there except pirates, smugglers or drug runners.'

TWENTY

'Have you ever known rain like this, *Capitan*?' asked Miguel-Angel, simply awed as he stood and looked over Carlos Santiago's shoulder out at the watery nothingness cascading blindingly down the windows of *Pilar*'s bridge.

Carlos grunted his customary paternal 'don't bother me now, boy' reply. Given an edge, if the truth be told, by the fact that it had been Miguel-Angel at the helm when everything went so catastrophically wrong. But, in spite of the fact that he was little more than a metre away, Miguel-Angel didn't hear it over the relentless roaring of the downpour.

Pilar was feeling her way gingerly forward through the blinding deluge as her *capitan* nursed her badly damaged engine into turning the twisted shaft that made her dented and misaligned propeller spin. The loss of the net, the inexperienced helmsman's unthinking demand for full power at the worst possible moment and the way the propeller had leaped right out of the water while this was all going on had done more damage than even Carlos Santiago could have imagined. But, he told himself, he blamed himself, and then his bad luck, long before he blamed Miguel-Angel. Besides, now that the damage had been assessed and some basic repairs put in place, *Pilar* had come back to life.

Carlos had long since stopped worrying about the torrential rain, for, once the wind had fallen away, the hull and upper works were well enough maintained to keep most of the weather out. The unsettling, sharp-sided chop was even easing back into the familiar sets of long Pacific rollers he and *Pilar* knew so well. Besides, he had a simple, unalterable mission: to follow the faint signal of the beacon he had providentially attached to the end of the net. To find it and to pull it aboard no matter what the heavens were throwing down at them. To fill his freezer holds with the biggest catch *Pilar* had ever brought home in all her life, if the nets were as full as he hoped and prayed they were. If San Telmo, patron saint of sailors, would intervene for them. If San Andreas, patron of fishermen, looked kindly down. If Hernan and the others had fixed the winch by the time Carlos found the net. If the propeller maintained them on a true course and kept turning. If the twisted shaft did not warp any further or jump out of its bed along the keel or – heaven forbid – break altogether. If the motor that kept both of them turning and also worked the winch continued to do so until Hernan and the others pulled the catch aboard and *Pilar* brought them safely – and richly – back to her dock by Los Muertos.

The fact that his equipment saw so little – for it was hardly even comparable to that aboard *Maxima* twenty miles north-west of him and racing blindly south-east towards that same faint beacon – meant that he had to rely on his instincts. And, although his experience was wide enough to give him almost god-like status in the boy's eyes, the fact was that age was beginning to dull them. And desperation, in any case, was driving him more powerfully than his usual care and caution. It was as though the act of letting that net go out over the transom had changed him from a model citizen to a desperate *pirata*.

Straining forward over the wheel, able to see no more than the boy whose reflection filled the windscreen from behind his right shoulder, Carlos eased the throttles another couple of centimetres forward. The engine responded without complaint. The twisted shaft remained in its bed. The battered propeller turned faster. The faint signal on his battered old screen seemed to approach more rapidly. He allowed a little hope to trickle in among the prayers. 'Go down and see how work is coming on the winch, Miguel-Angel,' he ordered. The reflection of the boy sitting like a good angel on his right shoulder deepened the guilt the old man was feeling at what he was doing and deadened the hope as it threatened the effi-cacy of the prayers. He half expected to find a devil reflected on his left shoulder prompting him to run faster down the wide, welcoming road to hell, like in the Sunday-school stories of his youth. But when he looked up again the screen was empty of all reflections except for his own. And he wondered

for a fleeting, bitter moment whether he was becoming a devil
himself.

Miguel-Angel came out of the bridge house and ran down the
five steps on to the after deck. At once he found himself wading,
almost up to his knees in frothing, writhing water. For a moment
he panicked, thinking *Pilar* must be sinking after all. But then
he realized: the rain was coming down so hard that the scuppers
and pumps could not get it overboard quickly enough to keep
the well of the after deck dry. Especially because, now the net
was gone, they had closed the gap in the transom once again.
The only thing that stood above the foaming little lake, apart
from the main winch which stood beside the five steps down
from the wheel house at the forward end of the aft deck, was
the top of the main hatch which opened down to the freezers
below. Miguel-Angel walked to this and perched on the very
edge of it for a moment, watching and waiting for his pulse to
slow. He had seen the winch used in long lining before and knew
it was designed to pull lines in through the open transom at the
rear of the boat, allowing the hooked fish to slide aboard on to
the deck area between the side and the raised hatch he was sitting
on. He had seen men working there, unhooking the sleek, solid
tuna and throwing them into the open hatchway down into the
freezers. But he had never seen the equivalent process performed
on a net.

Hernan and the others working on the winch at the near end
of the little lake of icy rainwater did not seem to be unduly
worried by the fact that the surface of rainwater in the low
deck area was higher than the tops of their boots. The light
Capitan Carlos had grudgingly allowed them – in spite of the
fact that it was mid-morning and ought to have been bright
enough by now – showed them bent over the winch like so
many jaundiced hunchbacks, the yellow brightness gleaming
strangely off their yellow oilskins. Miguel-Angel did not have
oilskins, though his father's chandlery on the Malecón had sets
of them to spare. And, he thought, pulling himself upright
beneath the stunning deluge and wading carefully across
towards them, he would not have wasted his time on them in
any case. For when he reached Hernan it was clear that the

cook was no dryer than Miguel-Angel, in spite of his cumbersome coverings. He had even put on a sou'wester from which the water cascaded like a mask made of golden chains. '*El capitan* wants to know how work on the winch is going,' he said.

Hernan dragged his hand down over his streaming face and whipped the drops off his finger ends. But no sooner had he done so than rivulets of rain wound down across his forehead once again, pulling locks of thick black hair into his eyes. 'Tell him it is done,' he answered. 'We are just about to put the cover back on. Tell him to thank both San Telmo and San Andreas that it is worked by *Pilar*'s engine and not by electricity, for nothing electrical would stay alive out here in this. Have you ever seen such rain?'

'There has never been such rain,' called one of the crew. 'If Jesucristo came walking on the water to tell us the world is ending I wouldn't be surprised.'

'We don't need Jesucristo,' called another. 'We need *el arco de Noa!*'

Miguel-Angel chose to disregard the blasphemous byplay which would certainly be bringing the worst of bad luck down on *Pilar*. 'Very well. I will tell him,' he said stiffly. 'What will you do next? *El capitan* will want to know.'

'I will get as dry as I can, then I will prepare the last of the food and coffee. Things will become very busy after we find the net, and we will need to have mustered all our strength.'

'The *capitan* will want *gorditas*, I am sure. Egg and fish. And coffee. I will come down for them.'

Hernan looked over his shoulder at the team of labouring crewmen. They represented about three-quarters of those aboard. Pablo the engineer and his little team were down below, nursing the engine along. For the engine was the heart of the vessel – indeed, of the whole enterprise. If it stopped then all was lost. Hernan and the deck hands would never be able to get the nets aboard without the winch. And even if they did so, the freezers in the holds beneath the raised hatchway would not stay cold for long without power. And *Pilar*, in any case, would just go drifting helplessly and impotently through the storm. But in the meantime all those busy and hardworking men, above deck and below, would be hungry. 'You had better be quick, then,' said Hernan, 'or there will be nothing left – for *Capitan* Carlos or for you.'

TWENTY-ONE

Liberty had never before had to consider the weight of water. She had considered its fluidity – its habit of forming currents, tides, waves and races. She had considered its depths and shallows, especially as these affected wave-sets and, consequently, sailing speeds. She had also considered its solidity – even before that very characteristic smashed her pitchpoling multihull to pieces. But she had never considered its simple weight. Even when stocking holiday sail boats with supplies as a girl, she had never really thought about the mass of the one-gallon plastic jugs of fresh drinking water she used to haul aboard her grandfather's yacht in Hyannis Port. She never really considered the heaviness of a kettle or a teapot filled to overflowing. Of a cup or mug of tea or coffee full to the brim.

But now the weight of water was something of immediate concern to Liberty and to the others as well. Because she felt that – even through her sailing gear – she was being bruised by the weight and clout of the rain cascading relentlessly down on to her. Had she not lashed the cut end of her lifeline to Florence's harness, which was in turn clipped to the safety toggle attached to the inertia reel system in the groove beside the footholds on the sail, she would have been even more worried, for the water not only had weight that was beating down on her with stunning power, it also had force that was trying to wash her off the slick surface.

Liberty was lying face down, as securely spread as the closeness of the other three would allow. The inflated Gill Marine lifejacket kept her face above the water level, for there was a good solid inch of water on the surface of the sail. The back of it mercifully protected the back of her neck. The hood of her Helly Hansen sailing jacket helped to protect the back of her head. But nothing, it seemed, could protect her shoulders, back or ribs, which felt as though she had just survived a lively boxing bout. And for some reason she could not get out of her head the strange idea that her buttocks, thighs and calves were being tenderized for a cannibalistic feast. Or as toothsome morsels for the sharks she was sure were circling in the depths immediately below.

And yet, she did not give up hope. Bad as things were – and every now and then she considered the possibility that they might get even worse – she never really doubted that she and her crew would survive this. Her father was an hour or so behind, she assured herself – maybe two hours given *Katapult8*'s phenomenal run earlier. But he was coming, alerted as he had to be by the fact that his daughter's command must have simply vanished off his radar and his satellite monitoring system in the blink of an eye. He had to realize that something cataclysmic had overcome her. So he would come looking – at full speed, even through this fearsome downpour. And he would find her. With Robin Mariner at his shoulder, how could he fail to find her?

Unless, of course, the ghost ship she thought she might have seen in the shadowy distance south east of the bright little beacon found them first. Whichever one got them out of this weather soonest would earn her undying gratitude. In the meantime, thank God for the bacon sandwich and the coffee, the memory of which was all that was keeping her warm. The immediate personal consequences for her and, she suspected, for the others, were covered by the fact that they were all running with so much liquid that a little more would hardly make any difference. Wearily, she pulled her head up for another look round. It hurt and seemed, frankly, pointless. But she found she could only stare at a perfectly black, utterly featureless surface for so long without feeling that her mind – her will, her very soul – was draining relentlessly out through her eyes and into the void. Instead, she found herself looking eagerly beyond the edge of the sail, which at a metre, was just high enough to give her a little elevation, especially now that the steep-sided chop was settling into sets of long rollers washing in from west to east. But there was precious little to see. Beyond the rounded black edge of the sail there was the surface of the ocean, the smooth green backs of the Pacific rollers boiling with a rash of massive raindrops.

Liberty's train of thought was abruptly interrupted. Something

strange seemed to be happening. The bright orange basketball
floats that had been lazily bobbing in a rough open-sided circle
round the sail since the nets they supported had destroyed her
command, seemed suddenly to be taking on a life of their own.
A life filled with sluggish but quickening purpose. As Liberty
watched uncomprehendingly, almost mindlessly, the nearest float
stirred and began to slide through the water. And the one behind
it suddenly sprang to life as well, following in its fellow's wake
– such as it was. And a third . . .

Had Liberty been less shocked, battered and disoriented, she
might have thought this odd. Had she been able to communicate
with the others, she might well have called their attention to it.
But she was so worn out as to be incapable of much more than
childlike observation. And she had given up trying to talk to the
others some time ago. So she just held herself above the spitting
surface of the sail and watched the floats all come to life. And
even when the next few in that long, swirling tail actually gathered round the sail itself and began to pull it gently across the
ocean, all she did was lower her head again and lie there, almost
comatose, unquestioningly awaiting events.

TWENTY-TWO

'It's gone!' said Nic, his voice rising angrily.

'What's gone?' asked Robin.

'The signal. It was there, just over five miles ahead, and
now it's gone.'

'Maybe someone's picked up whoever was wearing it.'

'That's not likely,' said Captain Toro. 'If there was a ship out
there we'd see it on the radar. But there's nothing showing.'

The three of them looked at each other. They were all thinking
the same thing: *sharks*. There was not an emergency beacon in
the world that would transmit from the belly of a Great White,
a Bull or a Tiger. There were mortal dangers here that came from
below the surface as well as above it.

'Looks like we're too late, then,' said Nic.

'Let's get there, even so,' said Robin. 'We know exactly where the signal was coming from. The quicker we're there the sooner we'll have a clear idea of what was going on.'

'Can we go any faster, Captain?' asked Nic.

'*Si, señor.* We just take less care, is all.'

'Go for it,' decided Nic. 'In the meantime, I need a coffee. Robin?'

'Me too.'

'I have Blue Mountain high roast Arabica. It's Richard's favourite. Captain Toro, shall I send some up?'

'That would be very kind,' answered Toro, his voice preoccupied.

'What?' asked Robin.

'Nothing,' answered Toro, his tone unusually uncertain. 'I thought I saw something on the radar this instant, just inside the five-mile line. But it's gone now. It was nothing. A ghost.' He looked out through the opaque side window. 'It's this rain. I think it's even more intense . . .'

'Coffee it is, then,' said Nic bracingly, taking Robin by the elbow and leading her back towards the lift. 'Blue Mountain high roast for all.'

As they sat in *Maxima*'s huge lounge, cocooned at last from the pounding downpour, sipping the fragrant black coffee, Nic said, 'Maybe we should contact Richard? Update him on what's going on down here?'

'I'd leave well alone for the time being,' she said. 'If I know Richard, he'll be up to his elbows in something: getting those National Guard containers off *Sulu Queen*, arranging for the rest of the cargo to be unloaded – whatever. It'll depend on what the weather up in Long Beach is doing.'

'Well, at least we can find that out easily enough,' said Nic, and he pointed a handset at the massive TV on the wall, which was currently in mirror mode. At once, the screen sprang to life. Biddy's film of the aerial approach to Dahlia Blanca suddenly filled the screen – wave after wave of steep-sided green mountains rising step by step from the white-sand beach on Los Muertos to the ten-thousand-foot peaks of the Sierra Madre ten miles or so inland.

'That's not what I want,' said Nic. 'Where's Channel Five? It was preset in Long Beach and we should still be able to pick it up.' He pushed buttons on the handset. The pictures of Puerto Banderas were replaced by the logo of the Los Angeles local TV channel, KTLA5. They had obviously tuned in partway through a news broadcast. Footage of the Los Angeles River in flood filled the screen an instant later. Disturbingly, the sound on the footage matched the sounds from outside exactly. 'Several more areas have been evacuated,' the announcer was saying, 'including the notoriously flood-prone neighbourhood of Lytle Creek in San Bernadino. There has been a storm surge reported, which has put some sections of the Long Beach dock facility at risk of flooding. Work in the docks has been suspended until the area is declared safe.'

'Richard won't like that,' observed Robin.

'You think?' agreed Nic wryly.

'He'll up sticks and move out at the drop of a hat if they're not careful,' she said. 'Looks like the National Guard and their containers won't be required in Los Angeles after all.'

Nic just grunted by way of reply, focusing on the news report once more.

'Officers in the San Gabriel Valley foothill community of Glendora have also reported a serious mudflow at North Ben Lomond Avenue and Hicrest Road, just below a hillside that caught fire in January, burning off all the vegetation, including the tree cover, leaving the topsoil unprotected. Mud flowed down from Yucca Ridge to Hicrest, a city engineer said. More than one hundred homes that were fortunate to survive the fire have now been destroyed, though there are no reports of any lives being lost.

'Nearly six inches of rain fell in the area over a twenty-four-hour period that ended at midday yesterday. But the governor's office has informed KTLA5 that the worst of the weather is over. NOAA scientists have confirmed that, according to the latest data from their satellites, the ARkStorm may in fact move south. The governors of the districts along the Pacific coast of Mexico from Sonora to Jalisco, including Baja California *Norte* and *Sud*, are all preparing to declare states of emergency, and our President has promised the *presidente* of Mexico all the assistance at our disposal should the need arise.'

'Looks like Richard called it right,' said Nic. 'I think that guy is psychic.'

Before Robin could come up with a suitable riposte, she was distracted by the continuing new briefing. The footage of the Los Angeles River was replaced by a serious-faced blonde newsreader. 'The scientists from the United States Geological Survey confirmed within the last hour that the storm they predicted would deposit millions of tons of water on California will certainly now do the same along the west coast of Mexico.'

'It's currently doing so on top of *us*,' said Robin. 'In spades! In fact, now I come to think of it . . .'

Nic never found out what Robin thought because the ship's tannoy interrupted her. 'This is the captain. Would *Señor* Greenbaum come to the bridge at once, please?'

Nic grunted as he rose. 'I don't like the sound of that.'

'Me neither,' said Robin, standing at his shoulder with a worried frown.

TWENTY-THREE

*P*ilar was a long liner. The paperwork in her log book was quite specific as to what she was licensed to do as well as where and when she was allowed to do it – far to the south and west of here. Long lining was what she was designed and fitted to do, so it was going to require all of her desperate crew's ingenuity to deal with the better part of a kilometre of fish-laden net which she had never handled before and which she was in no way designed to control. Miguel-Angel had never been on a trawler, never seen a drift net like the illegal net they had put out come aboard. He was at once, therefore, completely ignorant about what ought to be happening and only imperfectly aware of what was actually happening. But he found the whole adventure absolutely fascinating. To begin with, at least.

As Capitan Carlos brought *Pilar* gingerly up to the flashing red of the beacon, Hernan advised and guided him on the one portable two-way that the battered old boat had aboard. And the instant they were close enough to that light for Hernan to use the long boathook to snag it, he told his captain to stop engines before the propellers became enmeshed in the nets floating all too close behind them. Before he did anything else, however, as *Pilar* idled with her stern to that one lone dot of red brightness in the huge, shadowy storm-bound noon, he and one of the others went to the low transom at the back, loosened a series of safety clips and lifted the removable section free once more. The open section comprised about a third of the boat's rear wall, immediately aft of the main winch on the starboard side and the length of the after deck away from it. Much of the knee-deep water trapped in the well of the deck immediately began to cascade out through the opening, so that even Hernan, who was big and very powerful, had a problem standing beside it as he wielded the three-metre boathook with its strong wooden shaft. It took several tries before he snagged the beacon and dragged it aboard. This was not too difficult to do because it was attached to a long section of the float line, and he did not have to deal with the weight of the net itself to begin with.

Hernan pulled the beacon and the first float aboard, dextrously freed the beacon and switched it off before throwing it to Miguel-Angel. 'Stow that safely away,' he shouted over the rumble of falling water. 'If this keeps on we'll need all the emergency gear we can get. When you've done that, make yourself useful by checking all the scuppers are clear and stay clear no matter what comes aboard with the net in the way of weed and rubbish. *Pilar*'s scuppers were designed to keep a long liner's decks clear, remember, not a trawler's. They will clog up very quickly if we aren't careful, especially the starboard side ones, for that is the side the nets come on to. I want this water off the deck as fast as it comes aboard, because once the net comes in it will block up the opening in the transom as well as bringing in a great deal more water, along with the fish we want and the rubbish we do not want. And, boy!' he called as Miguel-Angel turned to go, 'get yourself some heavy-duty gloves. And a jacket. Jeans and a T-shirt will not be anywhere near enough protection.'

Then he and one of the others staggered up to the winch and wound the float line round it while Miguel-Angel ran obediently below, thinking in his innocence that Hernan just wanted him protected against the freezing downpour and the icy outwash from the nets. In the meantime, Hernan took charge of the winch, though Captain Carlos came and stood on the top step, nominally in charge of the deck now that he could no longer risk using the propellers, and therefore had nothing immediate to do on the bridge, which was, for the moment, unmanned. Hernan engaged the mechanism. The barrel spun wildly for a moment, then the rope caught. *Pilar* eased backwards as more line came aboard. 'Go!' shouted Hernan, and the others went to the opening on the transom. One of them took the long boathook and two others took the shorter two-metre ones with strong metal shafts. Together the three of them manoeuvred the first section of the net aboard, snagging the weighted footrope and pulling that on to the deck. The crewman with the long boathook ran it back towards the winch, then stowed his hook and opened the hatch cover, which tilted up to an angle of forty-five degrees, leaving space for the crew to throw fish in from the starboard side while still covering the hatchway itself and letting the rainwater run down on to the port side of the well deck and out through the scuppers there.

Down below, Miguel-Angel discovered Pablo the engineer and his team waiting to pack the fish in the freezer compartments now that the propellers had stopped and the motor was only running to power the winch. Pablo told him where there was a spare jacket and some gloves – both of which were far too big for him – and hurried him back aloft, knowing that Hernan was likely to need him as soon as the haul started coming aboard. Halfway back, he realized he was still holding the emergency beacon. In his excitement he had forgotten to stow it. He put it in the inside pocket of the jacket and ran on aloft, forgetting all about it.

As the net began to come in through the open transom, Miguel-Angel arrived back on deck, fully dressed and breathless. As he watched from the top of the steps beside his *capitan*, *Pilar*'s stern sank until the lip of the deck was almost level with the fizzing sea surface and the battered little vessel settled further backwards as the winch took the first section of the net itself and began to haul the rest aboard. The crewmen with the short boathooks stood either side of the transom's open section, heaving the net slowly upwards and inboard. The rest of the crew formed a long line along the starboard gunwale and fell to work as though they had been trawlermen all their lives. And they were soon hard at it, for, after a short length of empty net, there were suddenly plenty of fish. Most of them were tuna, as compact and heavy as cannon shells. Most of them were alive and flapping. Blue-fin, yellowfish, albacore and bonita – they all went into the hold. As did anything else of commercial value – dolphin fish, tilapia, snappers. But the commercially valuable fish were by no means everything that came aboard. There were barracuda and sharks – thankfully small at first. Then, after a while, there were suddenly more dangerous fish coming through the open transom in among the treasure trove of tuna: sailfish, marlin, the first of several turtles, the first big bull shark.

The men with the boathooks pulled them aboard carefully, checking as best they could that those which looked dangerous were dead before passing them on up the line as everybody else heaved and sorted and the winch span and rested. But it was simply impossible either to be certain that the big predators were as lifeless as they seemed to be, or to disentangle them from the net and separate them from the fish that the crew so desperately needed to throw into the fast-filling freezer holds. But fish were only part of what was coming on to *Pilar*'s streaming after deck. The nets dragged in great lengths of seaweed. Sheets of polystyrene. Disposable bottles. Plastic bags. Crisp packets. Styrofoam cups. Cut fishing tackle. Tangles of mooring rope and cordage. Rubbish of all sorts – much of it indestructible polymers. Suddenly Miguel-Angel was in business. As the smallest crew member there, it was he who crouched down behind the line of men freeing the fish from the net and either throwing them down the hatch or hurling them over their shoulders and back into the foaming sea. As soon as he got down he saw that the scuppers were partially blocked. He slid full length on to the deck beneath the seat, fighting to keep them clear. Behind him stood a wall of legs. In front, beneath a narrow bench seat scarcely more than a foot wide, lay the line of scupper holes at deck level designed to let water flow off the deck as fast as it came aboard. But the rubbish – flora, flotsam, jetsam and the rest – was blocking these even more rapidly than Hernan had feared. All the water coming aboard from the sky and the sea built up rapidly. Miguel-Angel slithered along the deck as lithe as any of the fish going into the hold. He used his thick-gloved hands to ease the mess of weed and rubbish back out into the ocean, glad of the jacket as the water washed past him increasingly forcefully.

But then he learned – the hard way – that Hernan's suggestion of jacket and gloves was to protect him from more than just the cold. He had fallen into a rhythm of sliding up and down the deck on his right shoulder, pushing and pulling the rubbish until he could shove it overboard. As he tired, he grew slower, until the surface of the outwash was up against his right ear and, occasionally, his right cheek. Suddenly his cheek was aflame and he felt as though he had been slapped very hard indeed. He jerked his head up fast enough to bang it hard on the underside of the seat. And as he did so, something large and slimy slid past. Its body was clear and glassily lucid. Its heart was a delicate tracery of purple. The whole of its bulk was more than a metre wide. It dragged a tangle of tentacles behind it that started as thick as string and ended as fine as thread. What sort of jellyfish it was, the boy never knew, but that one fiery lash across his tender cheek was more than enough warning to keep his head up and his senses alert. But the pain in his cheek was real and hard to bear. So he struggled out from beneath the seat once more and complained to Hernan, who was understanding. 'The pain will pass,' he said. 'We have nothing aboard that will ease it.'

'But there might be more,' said Miguel-Angel. 'And I cannot keep the scuppers clear if I am worried about keeping my face free of jellyfish.'

'A fair point,' allowed Hernan. He reached behind him and pulled a bright yellow bundle free of a fitting beside the winch. 'I tell you what. Here's one of the lifejackets. Put it on but do not inflate it. That will help keep your face up out of the water and away from jellyfish.'

So Miguel-Angel pulled the lifejacket on over the too-big oilskin, and found that it did indeed go round his neck tightly enough to keep his face above the water. Even uninflated, it was like a cushion. He went back beneath the long seat with more enthusiasm and stayed alert. Which was as well, for the next crisis arrived scarcely more than a minute after he went to work once more. In the distance, beyond the thunder of the rain, the sloshing of the boots, the flapping of the desperate fish and the relentless cascade of rubbish and water through the scuppers, he heard someone call, *'Tenes cuidado todos!* It's a big one. *Muy grande! Muy peligroso!'* Of course, he squirmed over to get a good look at the very big, very dangerous creature that was coming aboard. Through the gaps in the stockade of legs he saw the body of a shark come sliding up the deck. What sort of shark it was he had no idea. Nor at that stage did he particularly care. For, big though it was, and dangerous though it looked, it was clearly dead.

Until shockingly – terrifyingly – it wasn't.

The shark suddenly came to life. More than five metres of rock-hard muscle, sandpaper skin, white-tipped flippers, fins and tail were suddenly thrashing wildly about among the scattering crew. A head at least a metre wide slammed this way and that, its mouth, just as wide, snapping open and closed, the razor-sharp hooks of its numberless teeth coming out past the vivid pink edges of its lipless maw, scything this way and that, bouncing off the wall of the raised hatchway to come slithering through the suddenly empty air between the hatch and the scuppers, face-to-face with Miguel-Angel. The boy saw the flat yellow coin of its black-centred eye and realized that it was fastened on him. There was a shiver of communication. A flash of feral intelligence and deadly purpose that made him freeze with utter horror. He understood that the next lunge would bring that huge mouth, bristling with teeth, up against his head and chest. But he simply couldn't move. He gasped in a breath to scream, but chocked to silence with his stomach wrenching. He was overwhelmed by the stench of the thing – worse than any of the stinks that had accompanied the rubbish he had been pushing through the scuppers. And he knew that he would soon be dead.

But as the monster tensed itself for that fatal lunge, *Pilar*'s stern slammed round to port. The winch gave a protesting scream. The deck tilted as the port side sank beneath the strain. The net was jerked back out through the hole in the transom, as though another set of whales had run into it. And the shark was yanked back with it. For a moment, the great sleek body was jammed sideways across the opening in the transom, but then the relentless pressure of the net simply snapped the shark in half, and it was gone.

Pilar, powerless and drifting, answered the imperative of that sudden new tension on the float line and sluggishly swung round until her stern was pointing along the curve of the net towards something, perhaps half a kilometre distant, indistinct in the relentless downpour, that looked like a fairytale floating palace of light.

TWENTY-FOUR

'What is it, Captain?' asked Nic a couple of minutes after the summons over *Maxima*'s tannoy.

'My ghost contact has reappeared,' answered Toro. 'It suddenly came out of nowhere dead ahead and well inside the five-mile line. One second there was nothing, then there was a firm contact. It is the same vessel, I am sure, because it is in exactly the same place as the earlier insubstantial contact was, only this time it looks more solid. It is very disturbing. And there is another, much less substantial contact, too, perhaps a quarter of a mile north-east of it.'

'What do you think, Captain?'

'Obviously my first action was to contact the first by radio. It is not a large signal, you understand. It is most likely to be a fishing vessel of some sort. But all the legitimate fishermen down here should have a VMS system aboard and switched on at all times when they are at sea so the fisheries protection service can monitor where they are and what they are doing. This vessel has no such signal. When I radioed her I used all the usual bands, and they must have known I was addressing them as I gave their precise location. But, whoever they are, they aren't answering.'

'I see. So what do you suggest?'

'With your permission, *señor*, I will alter course to port. That will take us on a slightly more easterly heading. If we find nothing, we will be ready to run on along that course before swinging due east to Puerto Banderas – if you still wish to go there, though from the sound of things you may not wish to stay after we have caught up with *Señorita* Liberty and her crew. But in the meantime, such a move will ensure we do not collide with our silent ghost. And it will also take us between that and whatever is giving the fainter reading.'

'That sounds fine,' said Nic, nodding. 'Robin, have you any thoughts?'

'No.' Robin shook her head, frowning. 'I don't like the look of that ghost boat, though. In all sorts of ways.'

'Meaning?'

'Obviously the fact that it has no VMS and won't answer the radio makes me wonder what it's up to out here in all this.' A wide gesture of her hand encompassed the weather outside. 'But it's also worrying that it's coming and going on the radar. That means you either have a fault in the system or the range is being interfered with by the downpour. Neither of which is particularly healthy under the circumstances.'

'So,' said Nic, 'do you advise that we do something different to what Captain Toro plans to do?'

'No. Captain Toro's plan is the best we can do under the circumstances. Though I was just wondering: do you have an electrical engineer aboard who could check your sonar? It's crucial to know whether it's the conditions or some sort of malfunction that's affecting your readouts.'

'In this?' said Toro. 'You want me to send someone aloft in *this*?'

'We can wait for conditions to ease, I suppose, but I'd be happy to go with him,' said Robin. 'I've never seen the inside of one of those golf balls of yours and if someone's going up to check things out, I'd love to get the chance . . .'

Twenty minutes later, a flaw in the wind and rain gave them a realistic chance of going outside. Robin was following a less-than-happy electrical engineer up on to the top deck, immediately above the command bridge. The rain was much lighter and the wind had eased for the moment. Robin's vision was no longer blocked by streaming windows. After the interior of the bridge house, she felt she could see for miles. The engineer had told her his name was Manuel. He was easy enough to follow, however, as he sloshed forwards.

They were both carrying two-way radios and wearing safety harnesses. As soon as Manuel arrived at the bottom of the ladder up to the golf ball housing the radar, he stopped to clip his safety line on to the banister running up on the right. The wind and rain might have eased but *Maxima* was still pitching and rolling. Manuel's careful actions gave Robin a chance to look around. There was no doubt that in the easier conditions the view was better than the view from the bridge. As Manuel toiled up the steps to the big white sphere of the radar cover, Robin found herself walking forward until her hands were gripping the yacht-varnished teak of the safety rail. Pressing against the curved wood like an elevated figurehead, she strained to see forward. In spite of all her comforting words, she was worried about *Katapult8*. Even with her most competitive game face on, Liberty should have radioed in to assure her father that all was well. The only positive reason that she hadn't done so which Robin could think of was that she still had the good wind behind her and was sailing through the last of the calm weather, racing the ARkStorm down to Puerto Banderas. Every alternative to that scenario involved danger, disaster and perhaps death.

Straddling her legs and pressing herself hard up against the rail, Robin lifted both her hands to make a makeshift peak above her eyes, hoping to see a little further ahead. And, as she did so, the downpour hesitated in unexpected cooperation. Robin's view leaped forward and out to the sides. Like Richard with the lightning strike, the picture was there and gone so fast that it was only after her sight was snatched away that she was able to make sense of that instantaneous glimpse of what lay ahead of *Maxima*. Away on her right, perhaps half a kilometre distant, there was a fishing boat. It was facing away from *Maxima* so all she could see was the stern, over which draped a tangle of netting. Away on her right, low in the water, and so unexpected that she had trouble defining what it was she saw, there was the black wing of a jumbo jet, floating high on the waves, with a clump of figures on it almost as bright at Manuel's daffodil yellow. And, joining the two, a chain of bright orange basketballs.

'Oh, shit!' she said. She slammed the walkie-talkie to her mouth so fast she almost split her lip. 'Captain Toro! There's a net dead ahead!'

But she was too late. *Maxima*'s bow powered into the space between two of the orange floats. Her keel drove the fish-laden netting down, but the tension between *Katapult8*'s sail and *Pilar*'s winch pulled it up again, so that when the twin screws of the super yacht thrashed at full speed into the tangle of webbing, it wrapped itself around them.

Maxima was fitted with every modern essential. And this included a state-of-the-art Spurs Marine line-and-net-cutting system. But that was the system which the crew, distracted by *Katapult8*'s crew swimming like mermaids in the glass-sided pool, had not had a chance to check. And it wasn't working. The net wrapped itself round the racing propellers and jammed them in an instant. Like *Katapult8* before her, *Maxima* went from full speed to dead stop in a heartbeat. Even so, she jerked the net with far more power than even the pod of humpbacks had unleashed. The water in the pool ruptured the cover and broke through the inner wall, cascading into the living areas, pouring down into the engine areas, doing untold damage to much of the equipment and circuitry down there. Robin was very fortunate not to be pitched over the rail and down on to the foredeck. Manuel, up in the radar equipment, was not so lucky. He was thrown sideways and fell, still holding on to a good deal of the delicate equipment he was up here to check. It came away in his fists, effectively blinding the vessel altogether and doing a fair amount of damage to several other systems into the bargain. His life was saved by his safety line, which brought his tumbling body up with such a shock that he cracked several ribs. As though the whole disaster was part of a cunning plan devised by the weather gods, the rain returned, heavier than ever.

Under the circumstances, Manuel had to be Robin's first concern. She freed him from his harness and helped him down on to the bridge, where there was a kind of ordered chaos. Captain Toro, very much in charge, was issuing terse orders in a mixture of English and Spanish both face-to-face and over his walkie-talkie. *Maxima* needed checking from stem to stern at once. All damage was to be assessed and reported to him. The chief engineer was to update him as soon as possible on the state of the Caterpillar engines and the main drive shafts. If possible, he should assess and report on the state of the

propellers. Anyone in need of medical assistance was to report
to the medical facility. Robin registered all of this as she brought
the wounded engineer into the dry. Then she to dispatched him
to the ship's medical centre and caught Nic's eye.

Nic strode over to her at once. 'This is a disaster,' he said, his
voice shaking. '*Maxima* seems to be crippled. Heaven knows
what we'll do now. I'd like to radio for assistance at once but
Captain Toro wants to check the boat over first so he knows
exactly where we stand. Jesus, this is a mess.'

'You have a point, Nic. It seems pretty bad.' She looked her
old friend straight in the eye, willing him to calm down. 'But
things could be worse. She's crippled, maybe, but she doesn't
seem to be sinking. And there's a silver lining.'

'A silver lining! A *silver lining*! I have to tell you, Robin, I'm
damned if I can see one. Where in hell's name is the silver lining
in all this mess?'

'Well,' answered Robin. 'For a start, I think we've found
Liberty . . .'

But as she spoke her bracing words, they were lost under the
jangling of the fire alarm as all the lights went out.

TWENTY-FIVE

The sudden wrenching of the float line when *Maxima* became
entangled was enough at one end to jerk five metres of
the net and the shark off *Pilar*'s deck and to swing her
right round. At the other end it was enough to flip *Katapult8*'s
sail right over. The four women attached to each other and to the
toggle beside the hand-holds were tossed from relative safety to
deadly danger in an instant. Had it been any of the others secured
to the toggle they might well have drowned there and then, but
Florence Weary was quick-thinking and given a blessed extra dose
of the grit with which Antipodeans count themselves blessed. She
disregarded the desperate floundering of the three bodies tied to
her harness, therefore, and felt for the simple carabineer clip that
had them all fastened to the underside of the sail. Her face was

hard up against the slick, black surface, her body was bent agonis-
ingly at the waist and her back and legs were getting the crap
kicked out of them, but all her focus was on that little metal hook.
Blindly but unerringly, she felt for the tiny column of the catch.
Disregarding the growing pain in her oxygen-starved lungs, she
unscrewed the safety and pulled the spring clip wide. But there
she stopped. The combination of her relentlessly buoyant life vest
and increasingly vigorous movements of the others simply made
it impossible for her to angle herself so as to slip that last couple
of inches out of the toggle. For the first time since *Katapult8*
pitchpoled, it occurred to Flo that they might actually die here.
Killed, for the most part, by their survival gear. She wondered
whether to laugh or cry. But she did not panic. She simply focused
on working out how to retrieve the situation. Then she felt something unexpected. Someone was feeling down her leg. At first,
she thought that it was one of the others, tangled and panicking,
and she kicked, trying to heave her body upwards that final inch
or two. But the grasp on her thigh tightened; she felt a steady
hand exploring the outside of her calf, and she understood.
Someone was reaching for the knife strapped to her leg. It had
to be Liberty, who had lost her own knife as she cut herself free
after the wreck. Florence stayed still – in spite of the overpowering
need to breathe – willing her friend and skipper to work more
quickly. Because getting the knife would only be the first step.
Liberty would have to use it accurately, carefully and quickly to
cut them all free.

Flo did not feel the knife come out, for her consciousness
was beginning to come and go. Only her Australian grit kept
her mouth shut and what little was left of good air firmly in her
lungs. But abruptly the grip on her leg loosened. The next thing
she knew, her PFD exploded into a fury of bubbles and her
harness sprang free. She felt herself falling out of it, weighed
down by what she was wearing now that her lifebelt was punc-
tured. But a firm hand caught her deflated lifejacket's grab handle
and dragged her back to the surface. 'Shit,' she heard as her
head burst into the blessed air. 'Now I've dropped that one too!
What is it with these bloody knives?'

'Look on the bright side,' gulped Florence, still fighting for breath.
'You only tend to lose them when you're saving someone's life.'

'Enough of the byplay already,' called Maya. 'Let's climb back aboard the sail before we get tangled in that fucking net or bitten by whatever's eating the poor bastard fish that are caught in it.'

This time the four women found themselves at the narrower side of the sail, so it was possible for them to help each other flounder aboard and scrabble their way up the slick surface to the thick part. Emma clipped on and the others hung on to her because their lines, cut by Liberty, were too short to tie again. And in any case, Florence's whole harness was gone, while her lifejacket looked as though Jack the Ripper had been playing with it.

The only one who did not spread-eagle herself and hold on for dear life was Liberty. The near-death experience had galvanized her. No longer listless and comatose, she knelt up, holding Florence's right hand with her left, and used her own right to shade her eyes as she looked along the float-line towards a vague, distant brightness. She couldn't see it clearly, but it had substance. It was there. She was certain. Seventy-five per cent certain. 'It's some kind of boat!' she yelled down to Florence, hoping her voice would carry over the rumble of the rain.

'Do you think its *Maxima*?' asked Florence.

'I don't know. I hope it *is* because she has to be here looking for us. And I hope it's *not* because I think she must be tangled in the net like *Katapult8*.'

'Not quite like *Katapult8*,' countered Flo bracingly. 'At least she's still afloat, whoever she is. Have we got any way of signalling to her?'

'Shouting and waving and that's about it. All the flares and stuff went down with *Katapult8*.'

'Then if they haven't seen us already we're screwed,' said Florence roundly. 'No one's going to see us waving or hear us shouting in this.'

Liberty agreed. She knelt there, staring hopefully along the line of floats, cudgelling her brain for any sort of an idea to help them attract the attention of whoever was out there when suddenly the brightness vanished. Through the overpowering roar of the rain there was a strange, keening wail. Her heart gave a horrified lurch and she gasped in shock and actual pain. She felt as though she had been stabbed in the chest – and suddenly registered how much hope that vague, distant brightness had given her. And now it was gone. Her mind whirled. Had it moved off? Had it sunk as suddenly as *Katapult8*?

She abruptly realized that she was shouting. Screaming. 'Hey! Hey! We're here! *Over here!*' There were tears streaming down her face, distinguished from the rain on her chilled cheeks only by the fact that they seemed scaldingly hot. Her right arm seemed to take on a life of its own, waving so wildly that her left hand tore out of Florence's grip. Then she was waving with both hands and Florence was up on her knees beside her, screaming and waving madly as well. Then Maya joined in. Leaning against each other for support and stability, the three of them pushed themselves erect, still shouting, screaming and waving wildly. They stood there unsteadily, making so much noise and movement that even the huge sail began to rock. Only Emma was left, spread-eagled, attached to the toggle and too sensible to risk uncoupling herself, just in case her apparently hysterical crewmates still needed a secure anchor.

So it was Emma, flat on her face and ready to grab any of the others who might lose her footing, but looking in the opposite direction to them, who saw it first. It was so silent and so unexpected that she doubted her eyes; doubted her sanity for a moment. Initially Emma saw a darker shadow in the restless grey veils of the downpour. A shadow that coalesced into a vague shape as it approached through curtain after curtain of rain. It gradually became a fat, black, inverted capital T. The crosspiece on the water looked to be a couple of metres wide and the upright rising above it a couple of metres tall. And it approached silently – whatever noise it was making lost behind the sound of the rain as its precise shape disappeared behind its relentless thickness.

But then, as though emerging from a fog bank or a wall of smoke, the fat bow of a RIB inflatable came clear. And standing in it was a tall figure dressed in yellow oilskins. Emma scrabbled round, looking up. The others, facing the other way, still had no idea that anything was approaching. Suddenly the Japanese yachtswoman's usually calm eyes filled with tears. Her steady, sensible hands were scrabbling at the carabineer clip almost as wildly as Florence's had done when all of them were trapped and drowning. Then, free, she pulled herself on to her hands and knees. She put her right arm around Liberty's thigh and began to pull herself erect.

When Liberty felt the movement, she looked down. When she saw what Emma was doing, she turned and looked the way Emma was looking – and found herself almost face-to-face with her father. She stood there, stunned into silence. The fat black bow of the inflatable kissed the thick edge of the sail. Robin Mariner appeared at father's shoulder and everything seemed to freeze.

Then Nic reached out to his daughter and Liberty led the way off *Katapult8*'s sail and into *Maxima*'s twelve-seater RIB. It was incredibly easy. The sail was steady and still, and the RIB remained hard up against it. Liberty, with her right hand in her father's, stepped down into the RIB like a princess alighting from her coach in a fairy tale. The others followed in her footsteps as though in a trance. They were all so stunned that there was a dream-like quality to the whole rescue. Even questions such as, *How did you find us? What on earth went wrong? Are you all right?* got put on hold. Not that Liberty, Florence, Emma or Maya had much of their voices left. And Nic suddenly discovered a lump in his throat that effectively gagged him, while tears streamed down his cheeks along with the rain as he slipped his arm round the oil-skinned bulk of his daughter's slim waist, hugging her to him as hard as he could. So they sat in silence to begin with, while the crewman holding the controls of the outboard guided them on the long, circuitous course back towards *Maxima*, once again avoiding all contact with the fatal nets.

Until Robin, never one to sit silent for long, said, 'Welcome aboard, ladies. I hope we aren't taking you from the frying pan into the fire.'

Liberty found enough voice to answer. 'It would have to be one hell of a fire to be worse than that particular pan.'

TWENTY-SIX

'*esus Christ*,' said Liberty a few minutes later. 'I didn't think you meant it *literally*!'

The crewman brought the RIB round *Maxima*'s stern, well clear of the line of floats, passing beneath a disturbingly heavy plume of smoke that was belching out of the engine areas past the ruins of the swimming pool. Maya and Emma glanced up then returned to the vital work of bailing, for the rain was beginning to swamp the RIB with unsettling speed and *Maxima* was still a good way distant, especially as she sat on the far side of the maze of tangled net.

'The engineers say it was a combination of electrical short and water damage,' Nic informed them grimly. 'But the way we were brought to a halt so suddenly may have caused some fuel lines to rupture as well as breaking the pool's cover and causing it to overflow, which is what they reckon may have caused the electrics to short out and start sparking. But they think they can contain it. At least, that's what they told me as I was coming aboard the RIB. Sometime in the near future, though,' he added darkly, 'I'm going to find out whose job it was to make sure the Spurs net-cutting equipment was working properly. Then I'm going to find out exactly whose nets these are and make them rue the day they were born.'

'Come on, Dad,' teased Liberty gently. 'Who says *rue the day?* I mean . . .'

He laughed a little ruefully, but his expression didn't really lighten.

'We've shut off the main electric circuits except for the basic emergency systems, power to the davits and so forth, as you can see,' added Robin, gesturing to *Maxima*'s dark windows. 'Because if the fire is electrical, they'll just reignite it time after time while there's enough power to cause a spark. But without electricity we're finding things a little difficult, especially as the sonar, the radar and some of the communications equipment were damaged as well. At least the fire-fighting equipment is on an independent circuit and seems to be working. I just wish more of the lighting and *any* of the heating was, too. The only warm place aboard is the burning engine room.'

'But if we can't radio for help at the moment, we have emergency beacons. We'll deploy those before we let anyone freeze to death,' promised Nic. 'That will alert everyone nearby that we're in trouble.'

'If the ones nearest to us take any notice,' said Robin bitterly.

'Who's nearest?' asked Liberty.

'There's a vessel about half a kilometre south of us, but they're maintaining radio silence and seem to be running without lights. Up to no good,' Nic explained, his expression darkening once again.

'Illegal drift netting, I'd guess,' added Robin. 'And they've sure as hell caught more than they bargained for.'

'We could take the RIB, pack it with the heftiest men aboard then go across and talk to them,' suggested Liberty, her voice suddenly shaking, going from elated to enraged in a heartbeat, delayed shock making her almost bi-polar. 'I mean, I know how you feel about *Maxima*, Dad, and I must admit, all joking aside, I'm pretty pissed at what they've done to *Katapult8*. Perhaps we do want to make them *rue the day* sooner rather than later . . .'

'Not a good idea,' said Robin. 'I don't want to leap to conclusions or indulge in stereotypes here, but all of the Mexican pirates and bandits I've ever heard of are usually armed to the teeth and then some. Besides, we have other stuff to plan and try to do once we've had a chance to settle.'

'Like what?' asked Liberty.

'Like getting some sort of control over *Katapult8*'s sail, which is a shipping hazard itself in its present state. But until the fire's out and we have some sort of secure, well-lit and warm base to work from, getting *Maxima* fixed and functioning has to be our main priority.' She looked up suddenly, her eyelids flickering helplessly as the rain beat against her face. 'I wish poor Manuel hadn't managed to do so much damage to the communications and so forth. If that report from KTLA5 was in any way accurate then this downpour is going to be followed south by one long son of a *bitch* of a storm . . .'

This conversation was enough to take them through the maze of nets to *Maxima*'s stern, where the bathing and boating section was folded down to sit a foot or so above the waterline. Behind it, the glass wall of the pool showed the sad state of things. The pool was half empty, its surface boiling in the downpour, which now had access past the ruined cover. The smoke which formed a big black plume immediately above them was oozing up on either side of it and through the vents from the engineering sections below. But Robin was pleased to see that it was no thicker than when she and Nic had climbed aboard the RIB half an hour or so earlier. And the gangway from the boating section to the main deck house was still clear and smoke-free. If things were no better aboard the incapacitated gin palace, at least it seemed that they were no worse. The CO_2 fire control systems were working well. Maybe it was a flash in the pan after all. And they had Liberty and her crew back. That was a huge step forward.

Or it would be if they could restore enough power to keep them warm and dry pretty quickly, and *Maxima* remained safely afloat – and as long as someone could be tempted into the biblical deluge to rescue them sometime soon. Ideally before the meteorological Armageddon that was scheduled to follow it arrived with its massive seas and its hurricane-force winds. It was with these dark thoughts in mind that Robin climbed back aboard the crippled *Maxima*. She followed the others across the lowered bathing deck with hardly a glance towards the sad spectacle of the pool, though she did wonder how they were going to raise the bathing deck back into place if the electrics were dead for any length of time. And she thought – briefly, because she simply squashed the speculation – how *Maxima* would fare in a hurricane with no power, no propulsion, the pool in the state it was and the bathing deck still down. Then, like the others, she hurried up the narrow, smoke-free gangway to the accommodation areas.

As Robin stepped in out of the rain, however, her expression grew more worried. Things hadn't looked any worse from outside in the RIB but they certainly smelt worse in here. Even if the fire down below was out, the smoke damage up here was quite noticeable. The fumes made her cough, bringing tears to her eyes. Her normally buoyant mood darkened. The worries she had squashed earlier were not so easy to overcome now. *Maxima* was in no shape to offer refuge to anyone as things stood. If things grew worse they'd find themselves in real trouble. And if things got as bad as the USGS predicted for California, they were all as good as dead.

Robin pushed past the others as they staggered, exhausted, towards the cabins they had shared before going aboard *Katapult8*. She slipped past Nic, who was seeing to their comfort, very much the caring *paterfamilias*, and ran up the companionway to the bridge. Captain Toro was there, but there was little for him to do other than oversee the varying attempts to repair his vessel and the various areas aboard that had been damaged, seemingly almost everywhere, from the golf balls high aloft to the engines far below.

'How's the radio?' she asked breathlessly. 'Have we had any contacts?'

'Like the automatic CO_2 fire-fighting equipment it is on an isolated circuit that is battery powered,' he said. 'If Manuel did not do too much damage aloft it should still be working. I have to insist that you do not put out a general distress call yet, however, if that's what you were considering. Especially as the engineers say the fire came under control almost immediately. Lots of smoke but limited damage.'

'I wasn't,' she answered. 'It's not my place to do so. I'm a passenger. You're in command and Mr Greenbaum is the owner. I'm not about to second guess either of you. I just want to reach my husband if I can.'

'Very well. But please understand I am not questioning your experience or your competence to take such decisions. My priority, too, is the safety of the passengers and crew. But it is also my duty to try and retrieve this situation without handing *Maxima* over to salvage under Lloyds Open Form, which is what will happen if we call for help because we cannot sail to safe haven ourselves.'

'I'm aware of that. But on the other hand, I suspect that if your weather predictors were working they would warn you that what we are experiencing is only the first stage of one of the worst storms to hit the West Coast of America in more than a century. Unless we can arrange for some sort of Plan B to be in place we will simply be another set of statistics on the missing, presumed drowned list in the aftermath of whatever this thing turns out to be.'

'I understand your concern. Do you wish me to summon the radio operator? He is, of course, with the other electrical specialists and the engineers fighting the fire.'

'No. I know how the radio works and I know the wavelength and call sign of the man I want to speak to.'

Just as she said this, Captain Toro's walkie-talkie buzzed and he answered it. 'You're wanted below,' he said after a moment.

'Miss Liberty and her friends need a check-up and are reluctant to let our medic do it because he's a man.'

'OK,' answered Robin. 'But I'll be back to try to use the radio as soon as I've finished. If I can't get through then no one can. If I do get through then I think we have a good chance. If I can't for any reason, then I suggest that everyone aboard starts praying for a miracle.'

TWENTY-SEVEN

'It was a miracle,' gasped Miguel-Angel. 'I have thanked San Andreas, who must have been watching over me; and when we return home I will light a candle in the cathedral to his name. I was never so frightened in all my life. When that *tiburon* looked me in the eye and I could see he had decided to kill me, *Madre de Dios!*'

Some of the crew were impatient with the boy, for while he stood there on top of the net, gabbling out his terror, they could not retrieve the length they had lost and proceed with loading their fabulous catch. Hernan and the captain, however, were more indulgent.

'Yes, indeed,' said Hernan gently. 'It was a *galano. Galanos* are the worst. Everyone knows this. San Andreas was smiling down on you today, Miguel-Angel. And so was San Telmo.'

'But you showed no fear,' added the captain from the top step by the bridge-house door, staring down the rest of the crew as they grew restless. 'I know many men who would have cried out in fear at such a time. But not you. You looked the *galano* straight in the eye and dared him to do his worst, eh?'

The boy was not so innocent that he would risk the respect of such men by admitting that he had actually been too terrified to scream. But the little deception broke the moment. He stopped jabbering and stepped off the net. The crew went back to work. This time, when the shark came back aboard there was no doubt that it was dead, for it was folded in half and its belly had burst. Miguel-Angel made a point of spitting on

the broad grey shovel of its head before he slid back under the
seat and continued keeping the scuppers clear as the broken
body rolled overboard and splashed into the sea beside *Pilar*.

As time passed, the rain began to ease. The men in general
conversation agreed that this was a thoroughly good thing.
Without the downpour to distract them, they began to work faster,
forcing Miguel-Angel to work faster too as the volume of weed
and rubbish that came aboard with the nets grew in proportion
to the speed with which Hernan winched them in. The increasing
drag, however, pulled the stern down further so that, although
the rain eased, the larger waves began breaking in over the open
transom, spewing across the deck and draining out through the
scuppers. Miguel-Angel didn't get much benefit from the fact
that the rain clouds were relenting, therefore. But the others did,
and soon felt confident enough to open the hatch cover altogether,
which in turn made it easier for them to throw the fish in, which
allowed them to work faster, which made Hernan winch the nets
in more rapidly still.

Miguel-Angel soon lost track of time, but he was certain that
several hours must have passed. His work became a series of
flashes that punctuated a dream of near exhaustion like the jellyfish and the shark had done. But the seat above, the side in front
with the openings of the scuppers at its base, and the restless
legs behind kept the boy cocooned. The others, hard at work,
fiercely focused on making the most of this one last chance to
mend their fortunes, did not really notice the slow changes in
the weather around them, other than those which continued to
make their work easier.

When, a good deal later, Miguel-Angel was at last given the
chance of a toilet break and a cup of coffee, he noticed the
changes as soon as he pulled himself out from under the seat.
The rain had fallen light, though there was still no hint of blue
sky above the clouds, and in place of the blinding downpour was
an impenetrable mist of drizzle. The wind had shifted and
strengthened. The set of the sea had swung round too – the rollers
seemed bigger. They were coming from the north-east now and
they were breaking in through the gap in the transom more
regularly, sometimes heaving lengths of net in with them before
Hernan winched them aboard. Miguel-Angel did not like the look

of the new weather. But the exhausted men all around him raised no concerns. So the boy who had looked a *galano* in the eye and not screamed could hardly say he was worried by improving conditions. Not even to his *capitan*.

Captain Carlos was on the bridge when the boy found him. 'I am going below for coffee, *Capitan*. Would you like some? There is no food left, though of course we can eat some of the catch, if you like. There are several tuna that we cannot put in the freezer because they have been half-eaten by sharks or barracudas, but they are still fat and would be tasty enough.'

'No,' said the *capitan*, preoccupied. Then he changed the subject altogether. 'Your eyes are better than mine. Can you see something to the north of us? Another vessel?'

Miguel-Angel crossed to the rear-facing window and rubbed the foggy glass with his sleeve. He peered into the drizzling mist to the north, but he could see nothing distinct. 'If there is anything there I cannot make it out,' he said after a while.

'I am concerned that it might be a fisheries protection vessel sneaking up on us,' said Carlos. 'Take the *prismaticos* and go aloft. Take a good long look from up there.' As he spoke, the old man handed over the battered binoculars. Although the boy was bursting to use the toilet, he took the binoculars and obeyed. He slung them round his neck and swarmed up the ladder to the cluttered little deck on top of the bridge house. He stood tall, straddling his legs against *Pilar*'s rhythmic pitching. The change in the weather was even more obvious up here. But he disregarded this. He put one arm round the slim communications mast which fed the radio *Capitan* Carlos kept switched off because he wanted no contact with anyone at the moment. He steadied himself and brought the binoculars to his eyes. He looked back down the length of *Pilar*, over the open hatch, over the line of exhausted men sitting on the portside bench on his left, past the open transom and the net still spewing apparently endlessly out of it. And he looked into the drizzling mist to the north.

There was nothing distinct. Just a fog of grey, as though the air was filled with dusty spiders' webs. Then he began to notice that the dullness was occasionally lit by flickers of brightness. Not the sort of brightness that might come from a nearby vessel, but something brighter, vaster, more distant. Miguel-Angel held his breath, willed his thumping heart to quieten. He disregarded the creaking of the pitching boat and the hissing whisper of the passing waves. Far away, there was a continuous rumbling. It was like thunder, he thought. No, it *was* thunder. He frowned, and suddenly his heart seemed to be making even more noise than before. Almost as much, in fact, as when the shark's yellow eye had met his. But he had no idea why he should suddenly be so terrified.

And yet, he was.

TWENTY-EIGHT

'Hello, *Sulu Queen*, this is Robin Mariner aboard *Maxima*. Is Captain Mariner available? Hello, *Sulu Queen*?'

'Any luck?' asked Captain Toro.

'Nothing yet. I have the right wavelength and *Sulu Queen*'s call sign. She should be able to hear me as long as there's someone on radio duty. And I can't imagine that there isn't, not with Richard in charge. Not under these conditions. And it's less than a thousand miles. She's not on the moon! God, I got through on my cell phone a little while ago! Signal's gone on that now too!'

It was the better part of an hour since Robin and Nic had brought Liberty and her crew aboard. At Nic's request, Robin, first-aid trained and careful to keep her certificates up to date, had checked them all over one at a time in preference to *Maxima*'s perfectly capable but masculine medic. After a thorough examination, she declared them surprisingly fit under the circumstances but battered, bruised, exhausted and suffering from mild exposure. She prescribed a stiff drink and eight hours' sleep. Then she tucked them into bed. Nic was in the lounge immediately outside their accommodation in case they needed anything. The lounge was no longer so glorious, though. The TV had fallen off the wall and the carpets were soaking with water from the damaged pool. There was, as yet, no power, light or heat. Robin left him to his vigil and came up to try to contact Richard – so far with a spectacular lack of success. After a while, Toro had returned from the engine room with the news that the fire was safely out and repairs were well in hand. Robin could not meet his good news with good news of her own. The only positive she had to offer was that the weather immediately around them was moderating once again. But the clearer air did not mean a stronger radio signal.

'Perhaps Manuel did more damage than we thought when he fell,' suggested the captain.

'Possibly. I've been thinking, though. If I can't get through I'll have to borrow another electrical engineer, if you have one, and go back aloft. The weather's eased enough to make it fairly safe even if we still have high seas running. See if we can make some repairs.'

Toro shook his head. 'Only Manuel. Electrical officer and radio officer. What you would call "Sparks", I believe . . .'

'Well, he'll have to do, no matter what state his ribs are in. And the quicker the better. It's all hands to the pump.'

'Literally, if we aren't careful,' said Toro grimly. 'I'm going back below to get an assessment as to when we can restore power. Will you hold the bridge? I'll be on the end of a walkie-talkie if you need to call me back.'

'Fine. I'll keep trying for a bit longer then; if I can't raise *Sulu Queen* I'll ask you to send Manuel back up and we'll take it from there.'

'OK.' Toro went through the rear door of the bridge and vanished into the shadowy, smoke-smelling corridor.

Robin looked down at the recalcitrant radio with a frown. 'I don't know,' she told it. 'If you can't reach *Sulu Queen* then you probably aren't going to reach the emergency services either when Captain Toro or Nic decides the situation is bad enough to start calling for help – no matter what it's going to cost. We really need you fixed as the next priority after putting the fire out and restoring power. I truly do not want to find us just relying on the emergency beacons.'

The radio did not answer. She made herself comfortable in the radio officer's seat and put on the headphones. She pulled the stick microphone towards her, checked the digital readout and started again. '*Sulu Queen*? Hello, *Sulu Queen*, this is yacht *Maxima* . . .'

Half an hour later she admitted defeat. She threw herself back in the chair and pulled the headphones off. She picked up the walkie-talkie, which was lying on the table beside the useless radio, and put it to her bruised lip. 'Captain Toro,' she said, 'could you please send up Manuel with whatever equipment he needs to test the communications system?' She looked out of the bridge windows and raised her eyebrows in pleased surprise. 'It looks like the rain's moderating even further. If we shake a leg we should be able to do some good before things close in again.'

Manuel came up ten minutes later looking less than happy. And Robin could see why. In spite of his sore ribs he was carrying a case on a shoulder strap that looked pretty big and heavy. 'Give that to me,' she ordered abruptly, and he did so without hesitation. Then the pair of them returned to the topmost deck. They stood for a moment at the bottom of the ladder leading up to the damaged communications equipment. 'The main priority has to be the radio,' Robin said, putting the heavy shoulder bag down. 'Sonar, radar and so forth would be important if we were going anywhere. But we aren't. Next, after the radio, we need the weather predictor back online.' She looked around. The rain had eased back to a clinging grey mist. Something seemed to flash in the corner of her eye and she wondered whether she should get her sight checked when she got home. But then, in the furthest distance, just audible above the waves, she heard a whisper of thunder. 'Yes,' she said decisively. 'The weather predictor could be very useful indeed.'

'That'll all be through the satellite feed,' said Manuel. 'It's what I was holding when I fell. But I'll go back up and see what I can do.'

He opened the case and started rummaging around in it. Robin watched him for a moment then drifted away, her senses expanding as she began to take stock of the changes in the weather since she'd brought *Katapult8*'s crew back aboard. Even though the drizzling mist remained disturbingly thick, it was just possible to see a broad black line in the distance, which she assumed was the northern horizon. And even as she established this in her mind, the flickering in the corner of her eye was repeated. She held her breath, counting. Until, once again, that almost subliminal rumbling was repeated, seeming to come from the sky, the sea – everywhere around. And, seemingly born of that disturbing rumble, a wind sprang up. One minute there was a chilly dead calm, the next there was a wind that Liberty might have been able to make *Katapult8* run across fast enough to make her sail start singing. Her thoughts were interrupted by the walkie-talkie. 'How are things going?' asked the captain.

Robin looked up at the communications mast. Manuel was up there connecting a couple of wires that led back down to his box to something deep inside the golf ball. 'Hard to say,' she answered. 'How are things down there?'

'The fire's burned out, as you know. But so are the bearings, the engineer informs me. There was a colossal engine overload when we hit the net. I've got a couple of divers kitted up ready to go over and cut us free as the weather seems to have moderated, as you say. Then we'll take it from there. But even if we can't move, at least we'll be able to restore power to the lighting and heating.'

'Fine. Better hurry with those divers, though. I don't like the look of things up here. We seem to be fine at the moment but I think our friend Noah is just about to arrive with his ark.'

'What?'

'The storm Richard flew through on his way back with Biddy. I think it's just about to catch up with us.'

'OK. I'll tell them to hurry. Out.'

'*Señora?*' called Manuel as Robin broke contact with Toro. 'Yes?'

'I have made a connection. Please contact your husband. The portable in the shoulder bag should get the best signal – I have wired it in directly.'

Robin crossed to the foot of the ladder and found that half of the bulk of the shoulder bag was taken up with what looked like a radio-telephone. There was a handset and a touchscreen with a series of icons that adjusted the wavelength, call identification, volume and so forth with a simple tap. Squatting beside it, Robin pulled the handset free and pushed it to her ear, listening to the whisper of the open channel. Then she tapped in the wavelength that *Sulu Queen* was on and followed it with her call sign. 'Hello, *Sulu Queen*, this is Robin Mariner aboard *Maxima*. Is Captain Mariner available? Hello, *Sulu Queen*?'

There was a hissing whisper in reply.

'Hello, *Sulu Queen*, this is Robin Mariner aboard *Maxima*,' she repeated. 'Is Captain Mariner available? Hello, *Sulu Queen*?'

Then, as though from the bottom of a very distant tomb, she heard, 'Hello, *Maxima*? This is *Sulu Queen*. You are very faint. No, I am very sorry. Captain Mariner is not aboard. I repeat, not aboard this afternoon . . .' There was more, but she couldn't make it out. Desperately, as though the action would improve the signal, she stood up. Her concentration on what she was hearing was so fierce that she did not at first register what she was seeing.

A sudden gust of wind just managed to part the clouds of grey mist for an instant. Robin found herself looking up a grey hill of water. Wave seemed to be piled upon wave. Long before she registered what was happening, her unconscious was in action, listing things she had seen and experienced that could explain this new phenomenon: what she had seen on the video of the Indian Ocean in 2004 and Japan in 2011. What she had experienced herself on Tiger Island. But this couldn't be a tsunami, she thought numbly. Her hand fell to her side, still gripping the handset, unaware that the channel to *Sulu Queen* was still open. 'Manuel!' she shouted. 'Get down here *now*!'

She felt in her pocket for the walkie-talkie and jammed it, left-handed, to her mouth. 'Captain Toro! There's a series of large waves approaching. The biggest rogue waves I've ever seen. You'd better tell your men to brace. And pray. There's nothing else to do.'

As she finished speaking, Manuel stumbled off the bottom rung and staggered to her side. *Maxima*'s stern swooped down into the trough in front of the first waves. 'Get down,' Robin advised, following her own advice at once. 'Get down and lie flat. This is going to be a rollercoaster ride . . .'

TWENTY-NINE

With increasing desperation, Miguel-Angel searched the northern mist astern of *Pilar*. He didn't really know what he was looking for. And when he saw the danger approaching, he didn't recognize it for what it was or understand the menace that it represented. For it seemed simply to be a bigger wave than most. It was approaching from the same direction as the other waves. It might have just been a seventh wave – traditionally taller than the rest. But it kept growing until it threatened to touch the top of the circles of clarity that the binoculars presented. Miguel-Angel lowered them, looking back at the approaching wall of water, frowning. The leading edge was steep. The top few metres were capped with foam, though the wave itself was nowhere near breaking into surf. But it had brought a wind with it, the boy realized suddenly. A steady wind that was building with astonishing rapidity. The wave and the wind seemed somehow very dangerous. But the boy who had faced down a shark laughed at his fears. *Pilar* was a boat, and boats rode over waves. Even waves such as this one.

But then the crew on the deck saw it. They started shouting and milling around. The winch sprang into life and it seemed as though the men who had pulled the nets aboard were suddenly pushing them overboard again. One of them grabbed the section of the transom that would close off the open section, but he could not put it in place until the nets were out of the way. Someone reached over and grabbed the hatch cover, fighting to pull it shut, but it was old and stiff. Then the wind snatched the mist away and Miguel-Angel was distracted by the sight of the boat he had been sent up here to look for. She was too expensive-looking to be a fisheries protection vessel. But she was dark, dead. She seemed battered. Damaged. In danger. Especially as she was tipping helplessly backwards over the crest of the wave that was just about to hit *Pilar*.

This thought, in turn, was overwhelmed by more immediate

concerns as *Pilar*'s stern slid back and down into the trough
immediately before the big wave – a trough which the inexperienced young seaman had entirely failed to notice in his fascination
with the white-topped wall that followed it. He staggered forward
and, had he not been hanging on to the radio mast, he would
have fallen. He found himself looking down on to the deck once
more. Both of the boathook men were trying to get the transom
section in place now, in spite of the fact that the net was still in
the way. Two more were fighting to get the hatch cover closed,
but the harder they tugged, the more firmly it seemed to be stuck.
It was only when Hernan joined them and glanced up so that
Miguel-Angel could see the expression on his face that some
idea of the true danger registered with the boy.

With a sick fascination that mounted second by second, and
held him statue-still, the youngster watched events unfold. *Pilar*
settled into the bottom of the trough. The wind that had been
blowing so powerfully in Miguel-Angel's face faltered. It occurred
to him that this was because he was in the wind shadow of the
wave. The roaring of the waters seemed to stop as well, replaced
by a sinister, all-pervasive hissing. *Pilar*'s stern bit into the face
of the oncoming wave and she began to rise like the thoroughly
seaworthy vessel she was. But the nets did not want to rise as
fast as she did, for they were heavy, laden and caught in the
undertow. Still *Pilar* struggled gamely up the watery slope of
the huge roller, pulling the protesting weight of the drift net with
her. It seemed to Miguel-Angel for a moment of dizzying hope
that *Pilar*, like the strange vessel half a kilometre north, would
ride sedately over the wave.

But even as he thought this, green water slid over the bundle
of net and flooded sinisterly across the deck. The water level
rose and rose until Hernan's boots were filled once more. And
still the boy did not quite comprehend the danger. For the deck
had been awash before. The scuppers he had kept so clear would
surely let even this amount of water wash away.

Suddenly the wind hit him in the face again and he staggered
back, still hanging on to the radio mast. He found himself looking
over the top of the white wall of surf that crested the wave. He
saw the other boat in the near distance, settling into the trough
in front of the next great wave, bleeding smoke from her stern

up into the torrent of air. Beyond her, the ocean was grey and ridged with more waves that looked even bigger than this, each one part of a much more powerful movement of water that the boy did not recognize as a rogue wave. Above the grey of the surge there was a low, grey sky and, as Miguel-Angel watched, the two were joined by a massive bolt of lightning.

Then *Pilar* gave a kind of lurch. Miguel-Angel looked down and understood at last. As though she had used up all her strength, *Pilar* stopped rising and was slowed to a stop by the drag of the nets. So the crest of the wave had killed her. Miguel-Angel understood that even had the transom been closed, the nets would still have pulled her down. Had the hatch closed beneath the desperate hands of Hernan and the others she might have stood a chance. But the hold was stuck open wide to receive the catch from the nets. And that was the end of it all.

The last two metres of the wave came straight aboard, topped with another metre of foam. The weight of the water washed the men with the boathooks helplessly back and drowned them. Then it reached the open deck hatch. Not only was the top of the wave two metres high, it was twenty metres wide. And, for the time it took those twenty metres to wash over *Pilar*, untold tons of water thundered down into the hold, so that the catch, like the net, was suddenly pulling her down. The water exploded out of the freezer hold into the lower decks and killed the engine – as well as those men tending it. The crest of the wave smashed through the bridge house immediately below Miguel-Angel and burst out of the front, taking the windscreen with it while flooding down the forward companionways into the crews' quarters. As well as the windscreen and much of the bridge equipment, it vomited out *Capitan* Carlos Santiago, dead already, his body as broken as that of the shark as he was forced through the narrow metal frame of *Pilar*'s windscreen.

One moment Miguel-Angel was standing on the top of the bridge, elevated high above the surface. The next, a wash of foam exploded over his boots with such force that he lost his footing and fell. He fell forward off the bridge house into water that was already knee-deep. It was only at this instant that he realized that not only had the wave been rising but that *Pilar* had been sinking too. The roiling surface closed over his head and icy brine filled his eyes. He floundered helplessly for a moment. The too-big gloves and boots slid off his hands and feet. The too-big jacket, full of air, buoyed him up until his head broke the surface and he found himself in the middle of a vicious squall, surrounded by steep grey rollers that seemed enormous in size and force. And he was alone. Absolutely and utterly alone.

Stunned, he trod water, looking around for *Pilar*, still unable to comprehend that she and all aboard her were gone. '*Capitan?*' he called. 'Hernan? *Hernan?*' But there was no reply. As he fought to keep his head above water, the air began to leak out of his oilskin and he was jerked beneath the surface once again. The shock kicked his mind alive and he remembered that Hernan had given him a lifejacket to help keep his face out of the water and away from jellyfish. His fingers scrabbled at the front of it. Found a handle. Pulled. The jacket sprang to life, inflating with incredible rapidity. His head and shoulders exploded out of the water once more and he twisted round, looking for the other boat. She hadn't looked much like a safe haven, but if *Pilar* and her crew were really gone, she was the only hope there was.

But although she had looked to be nearby from the top of *Pilar*'s bridge house, from down here she was invisible. And probably unreachable. Certainly, he thought, he would never be able to swim to her through the storm that seemed to have sprung, like the wave, out of nowhere. But if he could attract her attention, he thought, then she might come to him.

The lifebelt had a whistle attached to it, but that would never sound loud enough in this. It had a grab handle that would let someone pull him aboard, but only if someone came close enough to reach it. And it had a light that flashed like a beacon, activated automatically by the water. If he turned his head, he could see the light flashing red. But it was tiny. A pinprick in the massive storm that was relentlessly overwhelming him. And what use was a single light in the middle of the vast ocean? He needed something that would broadcast more than a simple flash of light. And then he realized that he had just such a thing. With some difficulty, Miguel-Angel reached in past the inflated lifebelt and through the front of the oilskin. In the inner pocket there was the beacon that *Capitan* Carlos had put on the end of the float line and which Hernan had told him to stow safely away. Thanks to both San Andreas and San Telmo he had not obeyed that one fatal order. Its signal on *Pilar*'s electrical equipment had guided *Capitan* Carlos unerringly to the net. Perhaps it would guide the other boat to him.

He took it out, switched it on and started praying.

THIRTY

'Hello, *Maxima*? This is *Sulu Queen*. You are very faint. No, I am very sorry. Captain Mariner is not aboard. I repeat, not aboard this afternoon. He has visited Captain Sin in hospital and should currently be at the port authority office with Major Guerrero and Mr Prudhomme. They are due back at the beginning of the first dog watch. May I take a message? Please speak slowly and clearly. I am afraid we have a very weak signal here and you keep breaking up. Hello? . . . Hello, *Maxima*? Are you there, *Maxima*? *Sulu Queen* calling *Maxima*. Hello, *Maxima*, can you hear me?'

Sulu Queen's radio officer turned to face First Officer Cheng, who was in command of the bridge. 'It was a very weak signal,' he said. 'I have recorded it, of course. I will play it back to the captain as soon as he returns at sixteen hundred hours. It is mostly static and the message seems very garbled to me. But he may be able to make out more than I could. And he may recognize the voice of the woman. Do you want me to try again?'

'Yes,' said Cheng. 'The captain's wife is aboard *Maxima*. It must have been her. The vessel is en route to Puerto Banderas on the Pacific coast of Mexico and may well be in the path of the ARkStorm that the USGS and NOAA have been warning California about ever since we berthed here – the storm which is apparently heading south at speed. There have been reports of a storm surge and rapidly worsening conditions all along the coast of Baja California *Norte*, beyond even the report that Captain Mariner brought back himself after the helicopter flight. Did you get the impression that this was a courtesy call, a domestic matter, or something more serious? The weather down there is likely to be deteriorating quite rapidly according to the weather predictors. There are danger signals out all the way down the coast as far as Acapulco.'

'I have no idea,' answered the radio operator. 'But it seems to me that matters may be getting serious. There was something in the background – someone she may have been talking to. I could make no sense of it. Also something in her tone before we lost contact, especially as she was coming and going. It is worrying. From what I understand of *Maxima*, everything aboard is state of the art. Mrs Mariner should be able to communicate with Shanghai or Beijing, yet she cannot get a signal across a thousand miles of empty ocean.'

'If the weather is bad, could that interfere with the signal?' asked Cheng. 'The captain reported that his helicopter flight up was a very rough one.'

'Unlikely. I know we have been dealing with peculiarly powerful electrics in this storm, but even so . . .'

'Then it is probable that the equipment on *Maxima* is malfunctioning,' concluded Cheng. 'Did your contact give any hint of damage or danger?'

The radio operator shrugged. 'Who can tell?'

'Captain Mariner will want to know as soon as he returns, which, with luck will be at any minute now at change of watch. Try and contact *Maxima* again.'

Cheng was waiting at the top of the companionway ten minutes later at four p.m. when Richard, punctual to a fault, led Guerrero and Antoine back aboard. The solicitous first officer had brought an umbrella as well as hard hats and hi-viz jackets, but the rain had eased about five minutes before their taxi drew up and the four of them were able to walk the length of the deck in the dry. 'I have some news which might concern you, Captain,' said Cheng as he almost jogged to keep up with his Richard's long strides.

'Yes? What is that?'

'A radio message from *Maxima*, sir. It was incomplete and garbled. The contact was very bad and comprised mostly of static. But it was almost certainly from Captain Mrs Mariner. The radio operator and I are concerned that the vessel may be in some kind of trouble, sir. We have recorded the contact of course. You may want to listen to it as a matter of some urgency.'

'I do indeed, Mr Cheng. You and the radio operator have done well.' Richard stepped through the bulkhead door into the A-deck corridor, shrugging off his vest and hanging it with his hard hat on the wall hook labelled 'Captain' without a second thought, already very much in charge.

Ten minutes later, Richard was seated in the radio officer's chair with a pair of headphones clapped to his ears. His eyes were closed as he concentrated absolutely on the recording the usual occupant of the chair had made. Richard was not only listening to the words; he was listening for the tone. He was trying to make out from the background noise what was static and what was actual sound broadcast from *Maxima* herself as Robin vainly attempted to make contact with him. His normally open, cheerful face was closed and grim. His lips, which normally turned up at their ends, were turned down. The knuckles of the hands that controlled volume, pitch and tone were white.

'Hello, *Sulu Queen*, this is Robin Mariner aboard *Maxima*,' the recording began. 'Is Captain Mariner available? Hello, *Sulu Queen*?' There was a hissing whisper in reply. Richard strove to hear what was going on in the background. Was there wind? There was nothing that sounded like the torrential downpour she had reported on their last contact. But the timbre was strange. Flat, lacking in echo. And there was that whisper of wind or waves. Was she outside? What on earth was she doing radioing from outside on the deck?

'Hello, *Sulu Queen*, this is Robin Mariner aboard *Maxima*,' she repeated. 'Is Captain Mariner available? Hello, *Sulu Queen*?' Richard skipped through the radio officer's recording of his own lengthy reply and focused once again on the incoming signal, such as it was. And his frown deepened at once. The downturned lips thinned. The nostrils on that aquiline nose flared. The blue eyes flashed open for a moment then closed again as Richard leaned forward, his concentration redoubled. For everything had changed abruptly. Robin had stopped talking to *Sulu Queen*, but she had not stopped talking. 'Manuel!' she shouted. He could tell she was shouting from the tenor of the voice but not the volume – her words were scarcely more than a scratchy whisper.

'Get down here *now!*' The voice suddenly became even more distant. A hissing roar filled the airwaves. No wonder the radio officer had given up on it, he thought. Nothing he did with the sound controls shifted it. Was it static or was it real? he wondered. The agitated voice continued distantly, only just audible above the mounting noise. 'Captain Toro! There's a series of large waves approaching. The biggest rogue waves I've ever seen. You'd better tell your men to brace. And pray. There's nothing else to do.' The roaring gathered. Then there was a sudden silence, broken only by a gentler, less natural, hiss. That would be the static, he thought grimly. And if that was static, then the other sound was real. And it did, in truth, sound like a huge sea approaching with a pretty stiff wind behind it. Suddenly her voice was back; the clear, crisp and decisive tone she reserved exclusively for the most dire of emergencies reduced to a whisper that echoed as though she was speaking from the bottom of a well somewhere on Mars. 'Get down,' Robin advised whoever she had been talking to. Captain Toro, perhaps, or this chap Manuel – whoever he was. 'Get down and lie flat. This is going to be a rollercoaster ride.' And after that, there was only the gathering roar which *Sulu Queen's* radio officer had mistaken for static, the terminal *click* that broke the contact – and silence.

Richard threw himself back in the chair. His eyes opened beneath frowning brows and gleamed blue in the dull afternoon light. His mind raced. He had no doubt that Robin – and, indeed, *Maxima* – was in trouble. His first instinct was to go back and help her, in spite of the fact that there had been no distress call. But he knew that would not be possible unless he made certain of several other factors. First, he had to establish where she was – and whether she was still going to be there when he arrived, which in turn would depend on how he travelled and when he left. And he needed to know, at the outset if possible, precisely what the trouble was. Though, of course, he could guess. Or he thought he could, but he still had no idea of the fates of *Katapult8* and *Maxima* in *Pilar's* rogue drift net. And he had no knowledge at all of *Pilar* herself. His main temptation was simply to pull his mooring lines back aboard, call for the engine to be powered up and go down there in *Sulu Queen* to help her out. But then, he would have to establish that she wanted help, and whether a bloody great container ship could offer the help she needed. And whether he could find her – wherever in the east Pacific she was likely to be in the forty-eight hours it would take him to get down there. Not to mention the fact that he would probably find the National Guard coming after him mob-handed, demanding their containers back.

But he knew how to take care of at least one problem: that of finding her. Especially as he would be trying to find Nic and Liberty into the bargain. He pulled out his cell phone and hit predial. As the signal went through he took off the headset and put the cool crystal surface to his ear.

'Greenbaum International, Glendale offices,' came the reply. 'My name is Martha. How may I help you this afternoon?'

'This is Richard Mariner. I need to talk to Biddy McKinney.'

'Just a moment, Captain Mariner. I'll put you straight through to her.'

When Richard finished speaking to Biddy, he hit Robin's number on the off-chance. 'Stranger things have happened at sea,' he said to himself. But the connection went straight to her messaging service. He dialled Nic. The same thing happened. He tried Liberty, thinking, *third time lucky*. But again with no result. So he put his phone away, put the headphones back on and started through the recording once again, eyes closed, concentration absolute.

He did not hear Major Guerrero come into the radio room. The major saw how fiercely he was concentrating and, uncharacteristically, hesitated to disturb him. Instead, the major leaned back against the doorjamb and rehearsed what he had come here to say, concerned that Richard – who had done nothing but try and help the National Guard so far – would be upset, perhaps angry, at the news he was bringing. After a while, Richard threw himself back in the chair, putting the whole structure at some risk of coming apart. His face dark with thought and worry, he pulled the headphones off his ears and threw them on to the table with enough force to send them skittering across the surface and into the radio with a considerable *bang*. 'Shit!' he said.

'Captain Mariner,' said Guerrero. 'Excuse me, but I have some news.'

'Oh. Sorry, Major. I didn't know you were there. What can I do for you?'

'I've just had new orders, sir, and as they affect you and *Sulu Queen* I thought I'd better alert you at once.'

'I see. Carry on.' What the major could see of Richard's expression looked almost dangerous. Since assuming command, thought the major fleetingly, Captain Mariner seemed to have become even more decisive and dynamic, growing into his concept of the role.

The major cleared his throat. 'As you probably know, sir, our President has promised *el Presidente* that we will offer all the help we can to Mexico – it looks as though the ARkStorm predicted for California will actually hit there instead. *Is* already hitting there, in fact.'

'Yes, I was aware of that. I flew through some of it coming back up here.'

'Of course. Well, my command and my supplies have been designated as a part of that help. We are geared up and ready to go.'

'Very good. What is supposed to happen next, then?'

'The current idea is that we unload the containers, put them on trucks and drive them down. A team has already been dispatched to Baja California *Norte* and another one is heading into Baja California *Sur*, though they're having bad trouble with the roads.'

'Bridges washing away all along highway one.' Richard nodded. 'I saw it.'

'Quite, sir. Well, the mainland behind the Baja hasn't been hit too hard as yet, but apparently USGS and NOAA predict that when the storm arrives south of the final section of the Baja at Cabo San Lucas and comes over the mainland there without the Baja to protect it – especially as it will go straight up against the Sierra Madre coastal mountains – the states of Sinola, Nayarit and Jalisco will be in trouble. The plan is to drive a convoy down through Mexicali, Hermosillo, down to the coast road through Los Mochis and Culiacan, then into Mazatlan, Tepic, Puerto Banderas and Guadalajara.'

'I see. You have enough trucks to do this?'

'Well . . .'

'When you didn't have enough to get the containers out of the docks?'

'I understand the regular army will be helping, sir.'

'I see. So, how are we going to get your containers off my ship and on to the army's trucks, if and when they appear?'

'Apparently I'm to request that you move to another berth – one with a functioning crane, as soon as one can be liberated. Though effecting repairs to this one has apparently been moved up the list of dockside priorities—'

'I have to observe, Major, that those two things were precisely what Captain Sin was trying to arrange when he had his stroke. Apparently brought on by the authorities' refusal to admit that either one was possible.'

'I know, sir. As with you and the bridges on the Baja, I was here myself and saw what happened.' The major's tone was frosty. He, too, was beginning to run out of patience.

'Let me shine a cold light of reason on to these proposals, Major,' said Richard, swinging the chair round fully to face the major squarely as he counted off the points on his fingers. 'First, it will take time to liberate a berth or repair the crane – Captain Sin proved that. Then it will still take a good while to unload your containers, especially as I can't see the army coming up with the better part of a hundred trucks with drivers anytime soon – even if they try to commandeer them from local freight haulage companies and deal with the lawsuits later. Then I think you will find that the rundown to Guadalajara will be a long, slow and dangerous process, unless you take a regiment of sappers with Bailey bridges to get you across all the arroyos where the original ones are history.'

'That's as may be, sir, but we can't just leave these people to whatever this ARkStorm is going to throw at them.'

'I agree, Major. And, therefore, I have a counter-proposal for you to put to your commanders. Bring as many more people aboard here as you think you will need. Leave your containers where they are and let me take *Sulu Queen* south to Puerto Banderas. I can guarantee to have you there in forty-eight to fifty-five hours from the moment of departure.'

'You'd be willing to do that?'

'Major, I'd be *keen* to do it. My wife and business partner are down there and they may be in serious trouble. When you arrived just now I was within a whisker of cutting my shorelines and heading south.'

The major paused, thinking rapidly. Richard watched him narrowly, trying to assess whether his words would be enough motivation to make the officer put a strong case to his superiors. Because, if push came to shove, Richard really had no intention of taking *Sulu Queen* from one dock to another in the hope that the army and the National Guard could get their act together. But he was wary of getting confrontational before there was any real need to do so. Besides, he had grown to like and respect the major. And, to be fair, he had put a good case to him – and had little doubt that he would pass it on up the chain of command pretty smartly. 'Well, I guess it would save a shedload of time, sir,' agreed Guerrero at last. 'As long as we can get the containers ashore when we get down there.' He straightened decisively. 'I'll put it to my superiors.'

'Put it to them quickly, Major, or you may find I've stolen a march on you.'

While the major went off to contact his superiors, Richard went first to Antoine Prudhomme. The pair of them talked through what Richard was planning to do – and its legal and financial consequences. 'You think I should draw up some kind of contract?' asked Antoine.

'With the army and the National Guard? I wouldn't have thought so. See what the legal eagles at head office think, then alert me and we'll take it from there. But the bottom line is that I'm taking *Sulu Queen* south as soon as I can. It's been too long since I've had direct contact with Robin or Nic. I feel in my bones – in my *water*, as the Irish say – that there's something wrong. I want to get down there as fast as I can. But I need to be sure that it's all legal and above board in terms of contract and insurance.'

'I see that, Richard. But I have to say I think you're looking on the dark side. Why make sure your insurance is OK if you think nothing will go wrong?'

'Sod's law, Antoine. The absolute certainty that if cover is *not* in place then something *will* go wrong . . .'

'OK. I take your point. I'll get straight on it.'

After his brief chat with Antoine, Richard went out on to the poop deck aft of the bridge house. The poop was level and fully decked – not open for container use like the foredeck. The metal decking was painted with green non-slip and marked with a white circle that had a huge capital 'H' at its centre. He had hardly had time to appreciate that the clouds were at last beginning to break up and there was the promise of a rose-red sunset in an hour or so when the Bell 429 dropped out of the last of the overcast and settled on to the 'H' close in front of him. He thrust his hands deep into his pockets and waited. A moment later, Biddy had climbed out of it and run across to his side.

'I'm all fuelled up and ready to do some searching if you need any – and if the weather permits. You heard from *Maxima* or *Katapult8*?'

Richard just shook his head.

'What about *Sulu Queen*? We good to go?' she asked.

'Yes, I think we are,' he answered. 'Maybe even before the end of the watch. The major's just dotting a few i's and crossing a few t's. And so is Antoine Prudhomme of Southey-Bell, my local shipping agents. Hopefully we're off with the tide at the end of the watch.'

'Great,' she said, with only a trace of disquiet in her voice.

'Yes.' He nodded, agreeing with her unspoken concern. 'It'll be worse than it was coming up along the Baja. Maybe a lot worse. But if it gets too rough then you'll be staying safely aboard. In the meantime, I think we'd better get the Bell lashed down tighter than she's ever been lashed before.'

THIRTY-ONE

R ichard's cynical thoughts about the ability of the army and the National Guard to get coordinated proved unfounded, though it was at the beginning of the last dog watch rather than at the end of the first that the trucks started pulling up beside *Sulu Queen*. And, in the pink light beneath a rose-red sunset, the trucks deposited squads of soldiers. Male and female. Regular and National Guard. They came at the double up the gangway, with their kitbags on their shoulders and the unfortunate Mr Cheng began trying to accommodate them all.

'Any more supplies to come with all the new personnel?' Richard asked Guerrero as they watched from the bridge.

'No. They carry what they need for themselves in the way of rations and so forth. They go into their target areas self-sufficient. There's no use going somewhere where the basics are in short supply and then start asking for food and water. What they need to help other people is all in my containers.'

'Still,' said Richard, 'we'll work out a rota for the showers, heads and dining areas – unless they're happy to eat their rations in their bunks.'

'They will be if they're ordered to,' said Guerrero.

'I suppose so. But there's no need if we can exercise a little forethought. Things will get pretty bad even before we get to Puerto Banderas if the forecasts are anything to go by. Let's let them at least start out in as comfortable a way as possible.'

'I'll get someone right on that.' Guerrero crossed to the back of the bridge, heading for the lift and the companionways back there.

'And I'll come round on inspection before the end of the watch,' Richard called after him, causing him to pause in the doorway, half-turned to listen. 'Just to see how they're settling in before we actually set sail.'

'Right. Captain's inspection at nineteen thirty. I'll warn them.'

After Guerrero vanished, Richard looked across at Biddy, who was the only other person on the bridge except for the second officer, who looked even younger than Cheng. 'Don't worry,' he said. 'I've put you in the owner's suite. I've moved into the captain's cabin, double-bunking with Antoine, who seems to be set on accompanying us. You have en-suite facilities all to yourself.'

'On the other hand,' she said, 'I guess I could make contact with some of the other girls and share my good fortune around a bit.' Then she too was gone.

Richard crossed to the bridge communications console and opened a channel to the engine control room. 'Time to start warming up the engines,' he ordered. 'I'll want to move out by the end of the watch. That will put us at the top of the tide and give us a good, fast start.' Then he walked through to the radio room and made contact with the harbourmaster to bring him up to date with *Sulu Queen*'s new schedule and to organize a pilot.

During the next hour, Richard checked the Bell was lashed down as tightly as possible. He had a quick chat with Antoine, who had put all the problems involved in Richard's proposed plan of action to the legal team at Southey-Bell and was in hourly expectation of enlightenment. 'Don't forget to remind them that I only want one set of answers from them and those are *Fine, Captain Mariner, full steam ahead,*' he observed, only half jokingly. He went round Guerrero's augmented command, which seemed to be equally split between engineers and medics, men and women. He approved Guerrero's competent arrangements for their comfort, smoothing over any friction he sensed between the soldiers and the crew, who were now more than a little overwhelmed. He visited the galley and put the cook's mind at rest about having to feed a complement that had mushroomed from less than forty to more than eighty. Then he used the cook's glow of relief to warn him that the deep-fat fryer would need to be cooled and stowed after tonight, and that the big wok would only be used for modest stir-frying and steaming from tomorrow, when they could expect to start catching up with the bad weather again. He did not use the opportunity to grab a bite to eat himself because he was too busy – something he mildly regretted later. However, his abstemiousness meant that he was able to check on the engine control room and on the engine room itself before he was called up to greet the pilot but not the group of officials from the port authority, customs and immigration, homeland security and so forth, who needed to check and stamp his paperwork. Far fewer going out, he thought with some relief, than there had been on the way in, according to poor old Captain Sin.

Sulu Queen pulled in her fore and aft moorings, broke the shorelines that supplied direct power and communications through the dock facilities and engaged her thrusters under a clear sky with rising moon at eight p.m. The dock was open and easy to exit, so she did not require much in the way of tugging, and Richard stood beside the pilot as he guided the ship out through the main channel, past the increasing bustle of pleasure and commerce reawakening after the fear of the ARkStorm. Richard then accompanied him to the head of the companionway and watched him walk down to the platform at water level where he stepped aboard the cutter, passing out of Richard's purview – and out of his mind. Then, even as the cutter pulled away towards the San Piedro pier, he was hurrying back to the bridge. Cheng was there, though technically it was the third officer's watch. 'You know the course, Mr Cheng,' said Richard. 'Compass heading one hundred and eighty degrees. Due south. And ask the engine room for full ahead.'

The voyage proper had no sooner started than Guerrero was on the bridge. 'Captain,' he said, 'my people are all fed, watered and quartered. Our next duty is to check the contents of the containers. I have a manifest, but it would be wise to double-check. It's twenty-one hundred hours now. If you could switch on your deck lights, we can at least get started before we bunk down.'

'Fine,' said Richard. 'I can supply light and the crewmen you'll need to get into the most accessible containers, but we'll have to take more time to get you into the ones that are harder to reach. It looks like the weather is going to be calm until mid-morning tomorrow, so if you start now with the easy ones you can finish going through the hard-to-reach ones after breakfast. And of course, you're right. If we're going to do any good down there, we need to be absolutely certain of what we're taking and what we can do most effectively with it.'

It was only when Guerrero bustled off and Richard had a moment to himself that he realized how hungry he was. He toyed with the idea of having something sent up, but decided that it would be better to let the watch officer take the responsibility, even though the third officer looked little more than a child. But the weather was calm. There was little traffic. The course was clear and unvarying. The only complication was that the deck lights were all on full while Guerrero and his command sorted through the contents of those containers that they could most easily access. He was all too well aware that he had been fussing around the bridge like an anxious parent, checking the course and heading, making sure no radio contacts had come in without his knowledge. He satisfied himself that the engine settings were running at the top of the green and *Sulu Queen* was heading south along the south-flowing California current at speeds well in excess of her optimum – the better part of twenty-five knots, in fact; and sod the expense. 'If you need me, I'll be on the foredeck with Major Guerrero, then down in the canteen,' he said.

The third officer nodded silently.

The foredeck consisted of the tops of the Chinese containers *Sulu Queen* had brought from Hong Kong. But it was possible to walk on it with care. And even to open and part empty the National Guard containers stacked around the outer edges – those that could be accessed easily, at any rate. Richard came down and joined the busy soldiers with a lively interest that quite overwhelmed his hunger pangs for the time being. The containers all seemed to be of the same basic design. They were specialized twenty-foot equivalent units with sides, tops and bottoms that had been corrugated for added strength. They could be opened from both ends, with pairs of doors that were twenty feet high and ten feet wide, meeting in the middle where they were locked and bolted. The stevedores working the huge cranes at Long Beach had stacked them end to end, two deep, round the outer edges of the foredeck in a kind of palisade. This arrangement reminded Richard of the battlements of a castle as he came into the middle and looked up. But it meant that only some of the lower ones could be accessed – where they hadn't been placed so close to one another that it was impossible to open the doors. The contents of these were laid out carefully on the makeshift deck, well clear of the narrow canyons that plunged down towards the keel between the Chinese containers' sides and ends.

As Richard walked among the soldiers, heartened and impressed by their focus and care, he began to make a mental list of his own. There were tents with inflatable skeletons, shelters of all kinds, large and small, judging from the descriptions on the packaging. Chemical latrines. Washing facilities lacking nothing but water. Containers of various sizes full of fresh water. Distillation kits to make fresh water from soiled or salty. Bundles of food in self-heating packages. Mealspec flameless food heater systems. Collapsible clinics, liberally

supplied by the looks of things. Generators. Solar panels. Lamp-
lights and torches. Wind-up radios. Everything that might be
required to offer help at a kind of paramedic or first-aid level
in a situation where the basic systems such as gas, electricity,
communications, road and rail had all broken down. But the
soldiers had opened less than a quarter of the containers, as
Guerrero pointed out, his voice tense, when Richard finally
caught up with him.

'I'll have a word with the lading officer and see what we can
do to help,' promised Richard. 'We'll leave it till morning and
hope the weather stays fair.'

'Lading officer?' snarled Guerrero. 'What good will he be? I
mean, have you seen the size of these things? Have you calculated
the weight? We don't have the muscle power to move even one
of them.'

'Oh, yes, we do,' said Richard gently. 'Look.' And he gestured
to the big square gantry sitting hard up against the front of the
bridge house. 'All we have to do is decide where we want them
and how we want them – especially as we'll have to secure them
as tightly as we secured the Bell on the poop deck – and that
gantry will place them absolutely precisely.'

Part of Guerrero's problem was that he, like Richard, had had
nothing to eat in a long while. As soon as Richard discovered
this, he persuaded the major to leave the foredeck under the
control of his new second in command, a regular army first
lieutenant called James Harding who seemed to be competence
personified. The pair of them walked back to the ladder leading
up to the level of the train-track runners that the gantry moved
along, then went side by side into the A-deck corridor and down
to the canteen. They were lucky. Cook was just getting ready to
clear away, but there was deep-fried Kung Po chicken, stir-fried
rice, spring rolls and wontons. And toffee bananas to follow. As
the two commanders ate, so their energy levels began rising.
After a while, Biddy joined them, and that geed them up even
more. 'I know what the immediate priorities are,' said Guerrero.
'But what's the long-term plan here?'

'To go south as fast as we can,' said Richard. 'With the current
behind us – and the wind – soon enough we'll be making more
than twenty-five knots or thirty miles an hour. That'll put us off

Cabo San Luca at the southern end of the Baja just after midnight tomorrow night and get us to Puerto Banderas by six or so the next morning. Unless we get sidetracked or held up at all.'

'Sidetracked,' said Guerrero. 'Held up. By what?'

'There are pretty bad conditions down there,' explained Richard. 'Not just on land but at sea as well. If we get a distress call we'll have to answer it.'

'You expecting any distress calls?' asked Guerrero, his eyes narrowing.

'Maybe one,' inserted Biddy as she arrived carrying a plate piled high with toffee bananas. 'That's what I'm here for. With the Bell. Search and rescue.'

'Search and rescue?' wondered Guerrera. 'What are you up to, Captain?'

'Call me Richard,' said Richard blandly. 'And your first name is?'

'Juan Jose,' answered the major, suddenly very much on his guard. 'But I must ask again: what are you up to, *Richard*?'

'You know there are several people and two vessels I care about somewhere down there,' answered Richard. 'I'm proposing to check on them as I run south. Shouldn't hold us up or slow down your mission, Juan Jose.'

'Especially as the plan is that I take the Bell out and scout around their last known location as *Sulu Queen* here steams on past it,' said Biddy, her mouth full of banana, toffee and sesame seeds. 'Weather permitting and all.'

'That's a big piece of ocean down there,' said the major.

Something in his tone made Richard ask, 'Do you know it, Juan Jose?'

'Born and raised in Puerto Banderas. Fished it till my teens when I came north with my mom,' he explained.

'Sill got family down there?' asked Biddy.

'Father and baby brother,' he answered shortly. 'Miguel-Angel. We haven't visited, Skyped or even called in years. I guess the break-up of the marriage was pretty acrimonious. I just know my father runs the ship chandlery on the Malecón down by the docks in Puerto Banderas and my little brother helps him, I guess. He must be about the age I was when Mom and I came north.'

'Well,' said Richard. 'Don't worry. We'll get there as quickly as possible.'

Juan Jose Guerrero was still nodding thoughtfully when the ship's tannoy broke the silence. 'Captain to the bridge, please. Captain to the bridge.'

'No rest for the wicked,' said Richard, rising. He hesitated for a second, then picked up his half-finished plate. On his way to the door he passed it in to the cook. 'Fill that up, please. Put it on a tray with some of that coffee from the filter there and send it up to the bridge.'

Richard stepped into the lift and pressed the button for bridge deck, but before the doors could close Guerrero pushed in. 'Mind if I come up?'

'So long as you keep your hands off my Kung Po chicken.'

'I give you my word. As an officer and a gentleman.'

This conversation was enough to take them up on to the bridge. The deck lights were off, Lieutenant Harding having closed everything down and sent the major's command to bed. The bridge lighting itself was on night setting, all reds and shadows, except for the banks of screens showing the course and disposition of the ship. Richard planned on assuming the watch. It was a good way for him to get to know the vessel he was commanding – even though he had already done a first inspection of the new guests and planned on a full Captain's Inspection before breakfast. Given the weather they were heading into, it was vital that he knew the ship and the crew as well as possible in the time he had available. When he took over on the bridge, he would check all of the screens and go out on to the bridge wing and use his human senses to augment the electrical information as he made up the logs. First, however, Richard walked to the third officer's side. 'Captain on the bridge,' he said quietly. 'And happy to take the rest of this watch. What did you want me for?'

'This, Captain.' The third officer crossed to the screen that showed the collision alarm radar settings. He punched a sequence of buttons and the range of the radar leaped out to its widest setting, where electronic information about what lay ahead was largely supplied by satellites rather than by the ship's own equipment. 'There,' said the third officer, quietly. 'You see it, Captain?'

'I see it,' said Richard. 'Even going all out, that'll take almost a day. I'll check with the coastguards nearer and see what other vessels are in the area.'

'I have done, Captain. There are none. None willing to go there, at any rate – they're all heading for safe haven.'

'I'm not surprised. So, set a course and we'll at least supply back-up.'

'What is it?' asked Guerrero. 'What does the machine show?'

'It's an emergency beacon,' said Richard. 'There's somebody in bad trouble in the middle of the ocean seven hundred miles dead ahead of us.'

THIRTY-TWO

Robin stood on the exposed aft end of *Maxima*'s middle deck. Above her was the bridge deck where Biddy's Bell 429 sat when she was aboard. Below her was the half-empty swimming pool and the lowered bathing section that was beginning to look as though it had seen better days, which was stuck until power was restored. Inboard of this, on either side of the heaving, slopping pool, harnessed to safety lines, stood groups of crewmen. Robin would have gone down to be with them but both Toro and Nic roundly refused to let her take such risks. So this was as close as she could get to the action. All around her was the vast storm of the late afternoon, which seemed set on destroying the battered but still beautiful vessel. Despite her almost limitless experience in nautical matters, Robin was only partially aware of the physical forces that held *Maxima* in their grip. Physical forces that reached far beyond the meteorological turmoil they were battling. The wind gusted again, making her stagger, even in the wind shadow of the bridge, and she mentally thanked heaven that she was secured to the lifeline and wearing a full safely harness. Except for the fact that she was wearing Aquascutum rainwear rather than neoprene wetsuit, she was as well secured as the divers whose work she was watching.

Two of the crew, Raoul and Emilio, had worked in the past as rescue swimmers. They had jumped from helicopters into the middle of tempestuous oceans to check the hulls of upturned vessels for signs of life. They had taken panicking men and women in hand, given them reassurance in the midst of great storms in huge seas and helped them put on the harnesses that allowed the winchmen above to lift them to safety. Swimming in near hurricane conditions had been their bread and butter. Even so, they had baulked at going in the water under these conditions. But the facts were simple: if they didn't get the screws fixed they were all dead anyway. And Nic, open-hearted and open-handed, had made them a financial incentive that they simply could not refuse. So they had agreed to do it one more time, to try to cut the nets free and, if possible, get the Spurs line-and-net-cutting equipment back online in preparation for the moment that the engineers got the Caterpillars running and the propellers turning. It was becoming increasingly vital that these things should happen soon, for *Maxima*, which had ridden over the first series of waves at the front of the storm through a combination of good luck and the fact that the water missing from the pool kept her stern buoyant enough to counter-balance the downward drag of the nets. But now, for reasons Robin could not fathom, *Maxima* was moving slowly south and beginning to turn beam-on to the big seas. Once she was positioned so that her side rather than her bow or stern met the great wave-sets, she would simply roll over and die. Hence the desperate lengths Toro was reduced to now.

The wind gusted once again, driving a combination of rain and spray into Robin's face like a handful of sharp gravel. There was an explosion of sound above her, and one of the communications golf balls sailed away down the wind, looking ridiculously like a big white balloon. It was well clear of *Maxima*'s stern before it hit the water, bouncing off into the driving spray and vanishing. With any luck, that was the one Manuel had been working on, she thought. And it seemed likely – she hadn't seen the electrician secure the cover when they'd come back inside. If it was the twin to the one Manuel had been working on, then its departure meant the end of all of their electrical navigation and communications equipment. She was thinking of staggering up to the bridge and asking what equipment had just gone west when *Maxima* swooped down the back of the next wave and buried her poop in green water. The men on the lower deck ran back, trying to keep their feet as the water boiled up past the base of the pool. *Maxima* heaved. Then she began to rise again. There was a sharp *crack* from below and astern, louder than the noise that had signalled the departure of the golf ball. When *Maxima* finally shrugged off the green water and began to sail steadily up the face of the oncoming wave, Robin saw that the lowered bathing section had been bodily torn away. The teams ran back to the stern and began to pull the divers aboard, clearly fearing that the missing section might have hurt them as it tore free. But no. Both men came back aboard unharmed. And Robin could have sworn that one of them gave a weary thumbs up.

As the teams on the lower deck were heading in, Robin decided she no longer had any business being out here. She turned and walked forward, following the hand rail to which her safety line was attached. In the shadow of the bridge house, she paused to unclip. As she did so, *Maxima* reached the crest of the wave that had torn her bathing section off her. She hesitated, see-sawing there. A flaw in the storm wind cleared away the rain for an instant, and there, surprisingly close, a couple of hundred metres to the south and on the crest of the third wave further on, Robin saw the unmistakable ruby gleam of an emergency beacon.

'I cannot help,' said Toro a couple of minutes later. 'Raoul has chopped away most of the net and Emilio believes he has fixed the Spurs cutters, but we are not yet entirely free. And I am reluctant to take the chance of starting the motors quite yet, although the engineer says he believes the repairs will hold. You know it would be foolish of us to try a rescue before we ourselves are safe. You know how many people drown each year during heroic attempts to save children and pets who survive anyway after their would-be rescuers are dead.'

'That's true. But you'll have to risk it soon, because for some reason I still don't quite understand, we're drifting round to beam-on to the wind and waves. The seas will kill us pretty quickly if we don't do something.'

But in fact, as they were talking, a chain of circumstance that neither was really aware of came to its culmination far below them. Ever since the waves pooped *Pilar*, she had been sinking deeper and deeper into the Pacific. As they talked, she was half a kilometre below them and still heading rapidly for the distant ocean floor. The nets were still attached to her winch, and the dead weight of the wreck was more than enough to overcome what little buoyancy was left in the floats on the float line. The pull of the sinking vessel on the nets still attached to *Maxima* was the force that was dragging her southwards and swinging her round, pulling her towards Miguel-Angel, who was bobbing in the water precisely above the point at which *Pilar* had sunk.

And as Robin and Captain Toro discussed what to do next, the simple physical laws that had governed the relationship between the two vessels came to their inevitable end. *Pilar*, precisely below *Maxima*, completed Raul's work for him. The tension she exerted on the nets peaked at the very moment the extra-lightened stern – with half of the pool water missing and the bathing platform gone – was thrust upwards by the face of the next wave. The strain between the sinking vessel and the floating one reached its peak. The last section of net between them, hooked round *Maxima*'s propeller, snapped. The whole tangle jerked free to plunge on downward with *Pilar*, taking the fish and the fishermen, all tangled in the billowing mesh, to their final resting place at the bottom of the ocean.

Everyone on board *Maxima* felt the jerk of freedom. Her stern jumped up by a metre and more, easily overcoming the downward pressure of the wave. 'That's it!' said Robin. 'We're free!'

Toro nodded and put his walkie-talkie to his mouth. 'OK, engine room,' he said. 'Let's try for slow ahead. And once the motors are running I'd like power and heating restored. But one thing at a time.'

'When we get power back we should get communications,' said Robin. 'Unless it was the communications gear that went west with the golf ball just now.'

'I don't know what it was,' said Toro.

'You want Manuel and me to go up and see?' asked Robin.

'Maybe later. Right now, I want you here. Your experience may prove useful.' *Maxima* used her new freedom to start a series of increasingly wild corkscrew movements that amply emphasised what Toro was saying.

'I'd have said *may prove vital*,' said Nic as he staggered through the door. 'What's going on? Even my intrepid yachtswomen are feeling seasick.'

'We are trying for steerage way,' said Toro. 'We should have full control in a few minutes. Then, I believe, Captain Mariner wants us to investigate an emergency beacon she believes she saw nearby.'

'That I do,' she said. 'In fact, I think, if you'll lend me the walkie-talkie there, I'll ask Raul and Emilio to stay in their wet suits for a little longer.' As Robin spoke, the heaving deck beneath her feet began to throb. Everyone fell silent, as though their group focus on the vibrations would help the engines start up successfully and keep running. And perhaps they did, for, little by little, the rhythm of the Caterpillars quickened like the beating of a wakening heart. The propellers span, beginning to bite into the water. The vessel's motion steadied and she began to move forward more purposefully. Robin and Toro both went to stand at the shoulders of the helmsman. Still three-quarters on to the sea, with the waves coming in on her port quarter, *Maxima* began to get properly underway, answering to the dictates of the helm as well as to those of the wind and the waves.

'We have a problem, Captain Mariner,' said Toro, the first to speak.

'I know,' Robin answered. 'Our best and safest course will take us away from the distress beacon.'

'As soon as we start running with the sea behind us,' Toro agreed. 'And I dare not try and turn around in this. If we get caught beam-on to these seas . . .'

'I know,' said Robin. 'But there must be a way . . .'

As she broke off, the power came back on. The lights blazed and the bridge equipment sprang to life. Robin was at the radar screen before it had even finished loading and updating. 'There!' she said as it cleared. 'The radar set has the beacon placed at one hundred and twenty metres off our starboard forequarter. I can give you a precise bearing in a minute. I think the sea will push us in that direction anyway, but the chances are we'll sail straight past . . . Look, Captain, I know we'd be foolish to risk so many lives trying to save one, but that beacon is so close. The Cats seem to be purring . . .'

'And pushing us well clear of him,' warned Toro.

'Yes, but . . . Wait! You have the top-of-the-range propulsion system down there. Variable pitch, the works.'

Yes, but . . .'

'It's a hundred metres, Captain. You could swing us into position, surely. Go to full power.'

Toro frowned as he assessed the implications of Robin's idea. 'Mr Greenbaum? It's your call in the final analysis.'

'Ask the engineer, Captain. If he says he can do it without any more damage to the motor, and if you're satisfied it won't add significantly to the hazards of an already dangerous situation, then I think we should go for it.'

'Swing? And at full power?' The engineer's answer came over Toro's walkie-talkie so loudly that they all heard it. 'We've only just got the motor going!'

'There could be someone in the water a hundred metres or so off our aft starboard quarter. Would it be possible to get back close enough to be certain without damaging the motor?'

'Someone in the water? In *this*? Hell, yes! I think we could give it a try. What are the sea conditions like? It feels like a fairground ride down here.'

'Hairy. But that's my call. You just get ready to start reversing on my command. And thanks for giving us power and light.'

'That's OK. We'll try for heat later. Out.'

'Right,' said Toro. 'We'll try. I need someone on the radar who can feed me precise headings and distances.'

'I can do that,' said Nic. 'I've spent enough time with Liberty—'

'Someone mention my name?' asked Liberty as she came on to the bridge. 'I've left the others below either asleep or crouched over sick bowls. This is sure as heck one rough ride! What's going on?'

Two minutes later she was at her father's side poring over the collision alarm radar, calling out headings and distances even more expertly than Nic could have done as Toro began to position *Maxima* for a run back to where the beacon was located.

'This is all very well,' said Robin, 'but you really need eyes out there too. I'll take the walkie-talkie and go aloft. I want to see which of the golf balls went west anyway.'

'OK,' said Toro. 'I'll send Manuel up after you in a minute.

I don't want anyone out on deck alone. Really and truly, I don't want anyone out on deck in the first place.'

'I'll hook on to the safety lines and take extra care,' promised Robin.

Robin was careful to do what she promised because the moment she stepped outside it became clear to her that the wind was picking up even further. *Maxima* was running south-eastwards and the wind was coming from behind her now. One glance at the sea told Robin that they were up to a steady nine or ten on the Beaufort scale, gusting to eleven, perhaps. It would only take one even stronger hurricane-strength gust to blow her away, but she was still able to stagger across to the starboard side of the top deck and clip on to the safety rail beneath the headless stub of the communications mast where Manuel had clearly failed to secure the golf ball covering after he had facilitated Robin's brief contact with *Sulu Queen*. One glance served to settle her mind about that. Then she was looking back over the starboard, hoping to catch another glimpse of that lone red light.

She saw it almost at once, closer now, but still three wave crests away, almost lost beneath the spume torn off the wave-tops and hurled towards the distant shore of Mexico. Somehow, amid all the howling, screaming, thundering batter of the storm, she felt the engines go into reverse. *Maxima* did not begin to climb the wave-fronts crowding in behind her easily or quickly, but she did begin to slide sideways, slipping along the troughs of the waves towards that intrepid little light which continued to flash, beating like a heart exposed to the elements. She estimated the distance with a practised eye, even as she strove to make out what the flashing light was attached to. 'Seventy-five metres,' she called. 'Has Liberty given you the heading, for all the use it is? I think I see a lifejacket and a head. Keep coming on that, keep coming on that . . .'

Something struck her on the back and she jumped. But it was only Manuel, trying to attract her attention. He gestured up to the headless communications mast and gave a pantomime shrug.

She shook her head and turned back. 'Fifty metres. That's good. Can you alert Raoul or Emilio, or do you want me to?'

The blow on her shoulder came again and she turned angrily. It was Manuel again, warning her by gesture that he was going to check on the other golf ball. 'For heaven's sake, be careful!'

she screamed and he nodded. She turned back – and gasped. The
brief distraction had been enough to bring the flashing light
almost within touching distance. And now she could see clearly
the inflated lifejacket, the dark head slumped on to the bright
orange cushion of the neckpiece. 'Raul!' she shouted into the
walkie-talkie. '*Go! Go! Go!*'

Maxima hesitated partway up the wave, then began to slide
down it again. The man in the water was also slipping down the
face of it. Suddenly he was no longer alone – Raul and Emilio,
adding exponentially to the fortune already promised by Nic
Greenbaum, were swimming rapidly towards him, their lifelines
dragging across the surface behind them. A moment later they had
him and the three of them were being pulled back towards the
side. Robin felt her heart swell with pride and relief. In the worst
of all possible conditions, *Maxima* had put aside her own danger
to come to the aid of someone who would otherwise have died.

Robin watched, entranced as the two swimmers and the man
they had rescued were pulled back to *Maxima*'s side. She strained
over the top of the safety rail, watching Raoul and Emilio handing
him up to the team waiting there, then begin to start scrambling
aboard themselves, a process complicated by the fact that the
bathing platform had gone. And that became briefly significant
because, as the rescued man was lifted aboard, something dropped
from him. Robin recognized it as the EPIRB beacon that had
guided them to him in the first place, and shouted 'Catch it!'
without thinking. It skittered into the scuppers and was swept
back overboard. Raoul tried to catch it but failed. It fell into the
gap left by one of the big hinges when the platform was torn
off. And there it stayed, wedged tight, well beyond anyone's
reach, flashing red, broadcasting its emergency signal. The swimmers came aboard. The rescued man was carried into the deck
house and the motors were switched from reverse to full ahead.
Maxima settled into a steadier motion. Robin knew that Toro's
best hope of keeping them all alive now was to try and match
the speed of the waves surrounding them, running in towards the
distant shore at a knot or two faster than the wave-sets. But it
would take a little time to get to that speed. In the meantime,
Maxima would see-saw sickeningly. But she would soon settle
down. They had saved a life and were running for shelter.

Robin swung round, unable to contain her elation any longer, needing to share her joy and relief with somebody. Anybody. But the only person nearby was Manuel at the top of the ladder leading up to the undamaged golf ball. As she turned, another gust of that near-hurricane wind arrived. The strongest gust yet. It brought with it a haze of spume as thick as an old-fashioned pea-soup fog. And, weirdly, it brought a sound Robin half recognized. A wailing sort of a song, as though there was some kind of musical instrument out there, playing a mad, stormy tune, as though a singing whale could fly. Frowning, Robin looked around. The ghostly music got relentlessly louder. Robin's mouth went dry. Her heart fluttered. She felt she should recognize the sound, but she simply couldn't put her finger on it. It frightened her. As she staggered over to the bottom of the undamaged ladder and began to climb up after Manuel, the only way of communicating her concern was by touch. She hammered on the back of his leg as though it was some kind of door. He looked down. She gestured wildly: *come down.* And he obeyed. In an instant they were standing side by side on the deck. He pushed his lips against her ear and shouted, 'What?'

And out of the heart of the murk, there came the answer. Something more solid and more lethal even than the storm wind. It smashed into the golf ball Manuel had been preparing to work on. The sound was deafening, overwhelming. But nothing compared to the sight of it. It beheaded the communications mast as efficiently as a guillotine and carried the top away in an instant, even as Robin, horrified, recognized what it was. It obliterated the golf ball that contained the last of their electronic equipment. Then it span, end over end, away down the wind, hurling the dead wreckage of the electrics away into the sea.

Katapult8's massive jet-wing sail.

THIRTY-THREE

'**I**s there a problem?' asked Guerrero the next morning, looking over Richard's shoulder at the radar display.

'Nothing for you to worry about. How's the container-sorting going? From the look of the weather forecasts you'll have to be quick.'

'It's going well, in spite of rapidly worsening conditions. With Lieutenant Harding and First Officer Cheng in charge, and that wizard who's driving the gantry, lifting and laying the containers at record speed, we should have done everything by the time we catch up with those nasty-looking clouds dead ahead. But why the worried face, Richard? Something disturbing ahead? Other than the weather?'

'No. It's just that the emergency beacon we're heading towards is now moving eastward at a steady ten knots. I logged it as being dead ahead when I went off watch last night. Now it's miles east of that position.'

'How's that possible? I mean, I guess whoever's got the thing can't be swimming at that speed. Unless it's Michael Phelps or Mark Spitz.'

Richard gave a grunt of laughter. 'Even those two would find it hard to keep that speed up! No, there's only one explanation I can think of – the beacon, and hopefully whoever's holding it, is on a vessel.'

'If he's on a boat, why hasn't someone switched it off?'

'Heaven only knows. But there's no other explanation I can think of.'

'OK. So the beacon's on a boat. And where's the boat headed?'

'Eastwards. Towards the coast. Towards Puerto Banderas, actually.'

'And the boats most likely to be out here are . . .'

'*Katapult8* and *Maxima* are the only ones we know about. And *Maxima*'s the most likely of those two. I can't see Liberty and *Katapult8*'s crew being able to pick anyone up, no matter how much they might want to.'

'So . . .'

'So, in the absence of any contact from either one of them, we have to assume that everything down there is now resolved, and we'll return to the original plan of meeting up in Puerto Banderas. Helm, alter your course to the south-east. Steer one hundred and thirty degrees, please.'

'That looks as though it will take us further into the rough weather even more quickly,' said Guerrero. 'I'd better go down and chivvy them along.' He vanished.

Richard noted the changes of the beacon's position and the ship's bearing in the log, then he walked to the starboard side of the bridge and stepped out on to the open bridge wing. He was at once overwhelmed by a range of sensations that the quiet of the bridge had kept at a distance. The smell of the ship itself, all oil and rust, was overlain by the odour of the ocean, the ozone; the salty tang that was half smell, half taste. The feel – almost the taste – of the new wind, partly originating in the fact that its direction had swung into a new quarter and partly because of *Sulu Queen*'s new heading. He could feel it gusting stormily at his back, like a drunk pushing past him to get to the bar. The fact that it was unexpectedly cool, even beyond the expectation of wind chill. The noise it made as it buffeted past his ears. A noise subsumed in the bustle ahead and below him. He put his hands on the white-painted metal safety rail, leaned forward and looked down.

The gantry was in operation, lowering the last of Guerrero's containers into its new position. When fully laden, *Sulu Queen* accommodated fourteen containers across her deck, twenty-foot equivalent units stacked lengthways. The stevedores and crane men at Long Beach had stacked the new ones lengthways, two containers high, in a kind of wall all around the edge of the deck. They were twice as long as they were wide, so Guerrero had asked the gantry operator to swing them round so the long sides were facing inwards. Now they sat snugly side by side, one level high, reaching in twenty feet from the ship's sides, with an open area between them made up of the tops of the original cargo. Richard had OK'd this arrangement because it was clearly much more stable than what the guys at Long Beach had done. Though to be fair, they hadn't envisaged taking the vessel into the conditions she was heading for now. While *Sulu Queen*'s crew bustled about making sure the new arrangement was secure, placing stacking cones, securing lashing rods, tightening twistlocks and turnbuckles, Guerrero's men were opening the doors on the inboard ends and pulling the contents out to check against their manifest. The foredeck was crowded and bustling. Richard looked up, sniffing the gale-force wind. The sky ahead was full of clouds and looked deeply threatening. It seemed to him that they would be in some very serious weather by the end of the watch. He hoped with all his heart that the signal from the emergency beacon heading east towards Puerto Banderas was safely aboard *Maxima*, and that the super yacht's continued silence – like that of the beautiful multihull – meant that all was well with them. Still, he thought, straightening and turning to step back into the clinical confines of the bridge, he would be in a position to check. And he had aboard everything he needed to find either or both of the vessels and to come to their aid if anything had actually gone seriously wrong.

THIRTY-FOUR

axima had been running east at ten knots since she had picked up Miguel-Angel Guerrero sixteen hours ago. And, by the end of that time, Robin for one was getting worried, even though she had not spent much time worrying in the interim. *Maxima* was riding more easily – especially after the downpour filled her pool to overflowing and rebalanced her hull. She seemed unlikely to succumb unless the force ten storm got a great deal worse. She was well out in a notoriously empty ocean, and now that the last of *Katapult8* was gone there wasn't much she was likely to collide with. They wouldn't be anywhere near the coast for the better part of twenty hours. And she found she had a lot to do.

She had led the shaken Manuel below after saving him from *Katapult8*'s rogue sail, and took him down to the sick bay. Here they found the lad Raoul and Emilio had just pulled out of the water, suffering from shock and mild hypothermia but bubbling with the excitement of having survived his adventure. Then, just as Liberty and her crew had preferred to be treated by a woman, she had left the two young men to the attentions of the male medic. With the power back on, it had been possible to prepare hot food and she had welcomed Liberty, Flo, Maya and Emma to the dining room, glad to see that even those who had suffered motion sickness were beginning to feel better. She had also welcomed the young survivor, who had told them his name and stretched his command of English to the limit as he recounted his horrific story while consuming a bowlful of chilli large enough for four hungry men. They all packed away more ladylike helpings, marvelling at the resilience of youth while subject to delayed shock, and beginning to look out for it in him. They went through the story of *Pilar*'s final moments several times, trying to assess whether anyone else could have made it out alive. Then they discussed their current position and where they were heading. How close, in fact, to Puerto Banderas they would be coming, hour after hour as time passed. Shock and food made them all sleepy, especially after the stress of their adventures so far, and even Robin finally bunked down, feeling vaguely guilty that she had not offered to relieve Captain Toro on the bridge.

She had sprung awake a little less than an hour ago – fully awake for once, with her heart racing. She'd come hurrying up to the bridge as fast as her rudimentary ablutions allowed, informed by her trusty wristwatch that the time had come to start worrying about what might be lying immediately ahead of them. Toro confirmed that they were still following the eastward set of the sea at ten knots, which was still the speed *Maxima* had to maintain to run just ahead of the big storm waves. And they had been running at that speed all night, she discovered in her conversation with a clearly exhausted Captain Toro, who had been on the bridge for two consecutive watches. *Maxima* was also running deaf, dumb and blind since the beheading of the second communications mast. Even considering keeping a human watch seemed to be a waste of time – nobody could stay outside for any lengthy duration. And there was nothing to see but wall after wall of rain and spray. But even had she been fully equipped and her state-of-the-art electronics all working, there would have been little chance of doing anything other than what she was doing now, Robin observed wryly.

'We could have called for help,' admitted Toro, his voice gravelly with fatigue. 'But we would still have to stay in front of the storm exactly in the way we have done until that help arrived. Of course, we could have done with radar and sonar to tell us what's ahead. But the chances of altering course are limited.

If we turn by more than five degrees – or do so too quickly – the sea is likely to overwhelm us.'

Deep in thought, Robin moved to the front of the bridge and tried to look through the windscreen, but the heavy downpour had returned fiercely enough to overwhelm the wipers and render the glass opaque. 'We were just over four hundred and fifty miles out when we recovered the boy,' she estimated. 'We must have come the better part of three hundred and twenty miles, therefore, which has brought us to the point at which our blindness is becoming something of a concern. The coast – and Puerto Banderas, with any luck – might be little more than one hundred and thirty miles ahead, but the islands named the Tres Marias are likely to be dead ahead. Maybe five miles, maybe ten. But that close. At this speed, maybe quarter of an hour away. Half hour tops. And even if we manage to miss them, there's Isla Santa Isabel with its outlying walls of dangerous reefs behind them. And Santa Isabel is less than thirty miles offshore. Even if we miss her, we hit Puerto Banderas or the coast pretty close to it before the end of this watch.'

'I know. I know this coast quite well,' said Toro.

'Our survivor probably knows it even better than you do,' said Robin. 'He's a local fisherman, after all, even if he is just a kid.'

'You think he's well enough to come up and see if he can help?'

'I can find out. If yesterday evening was anything to go by he'll be in the canteen if he's up and about. You want me to have anything sent up for you?'

'Bacon sandwich and coffee. *Tocino graso*. Big. Black. Four sugars.'

'It's on the way,' she said and walked briskly off the bridge. The way *Maxima* was riding – even though she was doing her best in the high seas – made Robin decide against the lift, and so she ran down the companionway to the canteen. And there, indeed, was Miguel-Angel, looking lost in clothes borrowed from the crew that were far too big for him, just finishing a massive plate of *chilaquiles*. The look and smell of the tortilla casserole tempted Robin, especially as it had obviously been topped with fried eggs and grated cheese. But she was vividly aware that if she sat down to eat a serving, *Maxima* could well be aground on one of the Tres

Marias before she finished. 'The captain wants a bacon sandwich
and coffee,' she told the chef. 'Both big. *Tocino graso . . .*'

'I know how he likes them,' the chef answered. 'I keep some
fatty bacon especially for him. It'll be up on the bridge in five.'

'Thanks. Miguel-Angel – up to the bridge. The captain wants
a talk.'

'I think he wants me to work my passage home, no?'

'Not in the way you think,' said Robin. 'We'd better stop off
on the way up and get wet weather gear and safety harnesses for
the pair of us.'

'*Si*,' said Miguel-Angel five minutes later as he stood on the
bridge after Toro had explained their problem. 'I can guide
you past the Tres Marias. They sing to me and I know their
voices.'

Ah, the confidence of youth, thought Robin, who was still
finding it hard not to laugh at the sight of him in a gigantic
yellow jacket that was only held on his slight frame by a safety
harness tightly fastened over it. 'They sing to you even in conditions like these?' she asked, meeting Toro's sceptical gaze.

'*Es verdad*,' insisted Miguel-Angel. 'The fiercer the storm the
louder their songs. I also know the voice of Isla Santa Isabel.
Capitan Carlos taught me. I can guide you into Puerto Banderas,
even if I cannot see Dahlia Blanca.'

'Who's talking about Dahlia Blanca?' asked Nic as he and
Liberty came on to the bridge.

'It is I,' admitted Miguel-Angel. 'Dahlia Blanca makes a fine
beacon to guide us into the harbour at Los Muertos, day or night.
You know this house?'

'I built it,' said Nic. 'It's mine.'

'*Es verdad?*' asked Miguel-Angel. 'Is a fine house. *Capitan*
Carlos, his daughter and son-in-law, they work there.'

'Right,' said Robin, before the discussion got sidetracked into
gossip. 'If we want to be sure of seeing it again – as a beacon
or as home – we'd better get out and listen for your singing
islands, Miguel-Angel.' She led him down to the main deck level,
and they went out side by side into the wind shadow of the bridge
house. She stood still while Miguel-Angel strained forward into
the blast, listening with all his might. Robin pushed her walkie-
talkie to her lips. 'Can you hear me, Captain?'

'I can hear you.'

'Well, it all depends on what the boy hears now . . .'

No sooner had she finished speaking than Miguel-Angel was gesturing to her.

'Listen!' he shouted. 'You hear her?'

Robin closed her eyes, concentrating as fiercely as she could, sifting through the overlapping waves of sound. The buffeting bellow of the wind – big, deep blasts from behind exploding over the deep ocean; piercing, keening whistles from above as it howled through the ruins of the equipment masts. The throbbing of the racing motors that fought to keep the boat alive in the mountainous seas. But then, to her right, she suddenly heard another sound altogether. A deep, percussive booming that echoed almost to silence before it was repeated. 'You hear!' shouted Miguel-Angel, mightily pleased. 'This is Maria Madre. She has the deepest voice of all. She is away to starboard, perhaps a kilometre south of us. We will run safely past her on this heading and through the Isla San Juanito Passage. But I would tell your *capitan* that he needs to ease us five degrees northward to port as soon as he comes into her wind shadow, which will happen within half an hour. That way, he will run north of the reef at Isla Santa Isabel, which he will reach in two more hours or so. Only then can he turn ten degrees southward to starboard and take us south into the harbour at Los Muertos an hour after that.'

Charily at first and then with growing confidence, Captain Toro followed Miguel-Angel's instructions and took *Maxima* through seas that behaved precisely as he predicted. Robin offered to relieve the exhausted captain on bridge watch between the islands and he snatched a couple of hours' sleep as *Maxima* ran on, her heading north, from Isla Maria Madre to Isla Santa Isabel, even though the fat bacon sandwich and creosote-dark coffee had invigorated him. Robin was so impressed with both the boy and the butty that when Toro came back on to the bridge after the better part of three hours' sleep, he found a tray awaiting him with an even bigger bacon sandwich and another cup of coffee. And a walkie-talkie, through which Robin informed him that she and Miguel-Angel were on the deck in the wind shadow of the bridge house again, listening to Isla Santa Isabel singing.

No sooner had they rejoined him on the bridge than he used

the quieter water in the lee of the reefs to order the helm ten degrees south to starboard. But the stormy waters soon reasserted themselves, and so *Maxima* ran on down towards Puerto Banderas at a good ten knots once more. 'If we cannot see Dahlia Blanca,' Captain Toro asked Miguel-Angel an hour later, 'how will we know how to approach the harbour? Is there another landmark that might help or guide us?'

Miguel-Angel nodded. 'There is the Faro on the big breakwater. But on this heading, *Capitan* Carlos was always able to guide *Pilar* into the dock at Los Muertos. The harbour is wide because of the Rio Cortez, which flows down from the Cordillera.'

'Can we slow down?' asked Robin. 'At this speed we'll be in serious trouble if we hit anything.'

'Yes,' said Captain Toro. 'We will need to risk slowing in any case, because as we come closer to the coast we will get caught up in the surf if we're not careful. But from what Miguel-Angel says, it seems likely we'll be able to get into the shelter of the harbour without getting involved in the surf line.'

'Would you like us to go out to the foredeck again?' asked Robin.

'That would be helpful,' answered Toro. 'As we close with Puerto Banderas we will need to be clear about where we are and where we need to head next.'

Robin and Miguel-Angel returned to the sheltered section of the foredeck. This time, however, they were not listening out for the songs of the islands they were passing. Instead, they were looking out for anything that would lead *Maxima* into her safe haven in the harbour past Los Muertos. Lookouts such as they were should have been up at the point of the forecastle, but had they ventured there they would have been blown bodily into the ocean. They had a clearer view here, however, than Toro through the spray-smeared bridge windows, so they were relying on their eyes rather than their ears. It was ironic, therefore, that it was a sound that alerted them to what was going on. Toro had throttled back and was allowing the storm waves to run under the keel a good deal faster than *Maxima* was moving. This made things even more uncomfortable for anyone aboard not yet used to the pitching and tossing which the big waves generated, and meant that the foredeck moved up and down a great deal more wildly than it had done even while going past Isla Maria Madre. And the result of that was that *Maxima*'s forefoot suddenly smashed down on to something so forcefully that both Robin and Miguel-Angel thought they must be holed. But no. *Maxima* had simply smashed down on to an upturned rowboat, which sank so fast after the collision that the two watch-keepers only just saw what had been hit as it blundered along the boat's sleek side. The next few minutes brought more debris that *Maxima* smashed her way through increasingly noisily.

'What's going on?' asked Miguel-Angel, awed.

'I'm not sure,' answered Robin soberly. 'But it looks as though a good deal of debris from Puerto Banderas is being washed out to sea. From what my husband Richard said about what he saw on his way up the Baja, there may have been serious flooding, especially down your Rio Cortez.'

And even as she said this, *Maxima*'s cutwater bashed up against a more substantial piece of flotsam. As it washed past the two lookouts they saw that it was – a wooden section more than two metres high and a metre and a half wide. A construction of teak planks and crosspieces, clearly the main gate to a considerable *inmueble* estate, with the ruined remnants of black metal hinges torn bodily off a gatepost down one side. And, on the front of it, in letters formed of black-painted wrought iron, were the words: *Dahlia Blanca.*

THIRTY-FIVE

Sulu Queen fell off the top of a big sea like a base jumper diving off a cliff. She corkscrewed, seeming to go through all of the six degrees of freedom as she pitched, rolled, yawed, plunged, heaved, swayed and surged. She smashed head-first into the trough and huge fans of white spray exploded on either side of her bow, just visible beyond the torrential downpour until the wind whipped the spray back and smeared it over the clear view like ice. There was a distant crash and some swearing scarcely audible beneath the bellow of the storm. The mugs on the bridge coffee table all slid forward and crashed silently into each other. Richard staggered slightly. 'Come round to ninety degrees,' he ordered.

'Ninety degrees, due east,' said the helmsman.

'She'll settle now,' Richard informed Guerrera and Antoine, who were both fighting to stay erect. 'Half a cargo still stuck aboard makes good ballast at least, and she'll steady with the sea running up behind her.'

'As long as we go north of the Tres Marias,' said Guerrera.

'That was the objective behind that uncomfortable readjustment of the heading,' said Richard. 'The Tres Marias are just to the south of us. We're just entering the San Juanito passage, following the same course as *Maxima* – or the beacon, at any rate. I'll adjust our heading again in the calmer water in the lee of Maria Madre then swing round Santa Isabel and into Puerto Banderas before the end of the watch.'

'*Maxima* might not be there,' warned Guerrero. 'The course we're following is the one the local fishermen use. I don't remember a vessel of this size ever coming in this way. They don't like the reefs and shallows off Santa Isabel. It's a ships' graveyard. From what I remember the big vessels either come north or south parallel to the coast, and only those steaming up from Acapulco and Vallarta actually come into port at Puerto Banderas. Or, if they're coming eastwards in from the ocean they tend to run south of Maria Cleofas, the southernmost of the Tres Marias, and then swing north into the harbour past Los Muertos beach and dock against the breakwater.'

'We'll keep a sharp eye out,' said Richard. 'We have collision alarm radar and forward-facing sonar. All mod cons. And radio, of course. If we could actually *raise* anyone south of the border, down Mexico way. Well, anyone we want to speak to, at any rate.' In fact, *Sulu Queen* had registered her presence with a number of Mexican authorities. Authorities who had not been able to advise them as to the current state of things in their destination. And they still had not managed to make contact with the men and women they needed to speak to in Puerto Banderas itself – or aboard whichever vessel was sitting in harbour there with the tell-tale emergency beacon aboard.

'We'll be going in relatively blind,' warned Cheng, who seemed to have grown into his post as Richard's first officer. He looked older, sounded more competent and decisive. And he was no longer shy about offering his opinions. 'That lack of contact with anyone in Puerto Banderas is worrying. Not the coastguard or the harbourmaster. All the local radio stations are off-air. Even the local news channels FOROtv and Azteca13 have stopped broadcasting from there. It's as though the whole place has shut down.'

'Or been drowned out,' added Antoine. 'Washed away, maybe . . .'

'Point well made,' said Richard. 'We'll slow down and take care as we pass Santa Isabel, then we'll positively tiptoe into the harbour on slow ahead, or as close to slow ahead as we dare go in these seas. It'd be a pity to come all this way and then go down with all hands as we approach our final destination. Which reminds me, now that *Sulu Queen* has settled somewhat, you and I need to go over the chart of Puerto Banderas harbour and its approaches – because, under the circumstances, I'm not expecting a pilot to come out and guide us in. Juan Jose, you know this place best – would you give us the benefit of your experience?'

The major followed Richard and Cheng across to the electronic chart and waited while Richard found the details of Puerto Banderas harbour. 'OK,' said Richard as the schematic filled the screen. 'As you can see, it's a sizeable, combined harbour. The outer area is the commercial dock and the inner is the marina. They are separated by this bridge here which takes a six-lane highway out to the breakwater here. The whole thing has been extended from the mouth of the Rio Cortez. The breakwater's been built out in an L-shape on the Pacific side, turning the westerly flow of the river to a southerly one. The breakwater runs parallel to the Malecón as far as the Playa Los Muertos beach on the mainland. The actual harbour mouth is a five-hundred-metre-wide channel between the breakwater and the Malecón, dredged to a considerable depth, especially against the inner side of the breakwater, which is long, high and very robust, ending in the Faro, or lighthouse, here. The breakwater is substantial enough not only to have ship-handling facilities but also

warehousing on the inner side, and even two or three hotels on
the outer side looking out over the Town Beach to the Pacific
on one aspect and over the marina up into the Rio Cortez and
the Sierra Madre behind it on the other. All served by the six-
lane highway coming over the bridge. The commercial section,
the Malecón, is on the inland side here, and it stretches right
from the left bank of the river mouth all the way along to Los
Muertos beach. Is this all as you remember it, Juan Jose?'

'Yes. But the chart gives little idea of the scale. The Rio Cortez
is quite a big river. It drains straight down from the watershed
among the peaks of the Sierra Madre in a series of waterfalls
and lakes.'

'That's right,' said Richard. 'It's by the lowest of those lakes
that Nic Greenbaum built Dahlia Blanca, right up there in the
jungle, reaching out to the edge of the cliff. Apparently you
can see it from the harbour. The locals use it as a landmark,
according to Biddy McKinney. I'm looking forward to seeing
it. I've only seen pictures so far. But you were saying. About
the river itself . . .'

'So, it comes down from the mountains quite powerfully. And
it keeps everything pretty well dredged by the strength of its
current, especially along the outer edge of the main channel,
which is the inner edge of the breakwater where the commercial
docks are. The breakwater is the better part of a kilometre long
and half a kilometre wide; a little narrower than the harbour
mouth. It's manmade but very substantial. It would be possible
for several vessels of this size to berth along the inner side of
the breakwater. As I said, I remember seeing big cruise ships
docking there in my younger days. And these little squares that
represent the hotels you were just mentioning – they are the
likes of the Westin, the Marriot and the Hilton. Some of them
are twenty stories high. And they have substantial grounds.
Swimming pools. Decorative gardens. All on the widest section
of the breakwater.'

'OK,' said Richard. 'So access should be easy enough, though
you see the recommended routes on the chart all come up from the
south, as you were saying, Juan Jose. They come straight in past
the lighthouse and harbourmaster's offices at the point of the breakwater on one side and the port authority building part way down

the Malecón on the other. If we go in on that heading we should end up here, where the loading and unloading facilities are located. But, of course, we don't know what state the facilities are in, though if no one there is answering our radio calls then I guess they'll be deserted. I hope *Maxima* was careful going in.'

'If that is actually *her* sitting in the outer area where the beacon's signal is coming from,' added Antoine as he joined them. 'I'd have thought a yacht like *Maxima* would have gone under the road bridge and into the inner marina. Always assuming she doesn't have a private, secure dock.'

'Which I know she does. But let's just assume it's her for the time being,' suggested Richard. 'We'll find out the truth one way or another pretty soon. And she must have been careful, because I doubt the emergency signal would still be broadcasting so clearly if anything too terminal had happened to her. Now, Mr Cheng, let's get some good old-fashioned ship-handling planned. After we get past Isla Santa Isabel we'll use the quieter water in the lee of the island to swing south, track south-east across the harbour itself – still well out – swing round and head back in from the south along the recommended route on the chart here, keeping an eye out for the Faro lighthouse on our port beam and the port authority building to starboard. Slowly and carefully. Hoping that the dock we need is clear. And that *Katapult8* and *Maxima* are waiting.'

Once the immediate plans were made, Richard used the slightly less stressful period between their passage past the Tres Marias and towards the reefs at Isla Santa Isabel to try and work out something more long term. He had experienced a wider range of weather conditions than most, but he had never had to face an ARkStorm before. He really had very little idea of what to expect beyond the threat of a truly biblical downpour lasting in the region of forty days and forty nights, as it did for Noah in Genesis. But he knew a woman who did. And Dr Jones was happy to take his contact, for she was prioritizing the National Guard and those like Richard, who were trying to help them, consumed with unreasoning guilt that she had warned California of the imminent disaster but not warned Mexico, where the real damage was being done.

'I believe you have already experienced the primary storm front,' she said quietly, her face on his Skype contact frowning with concern. 'It was you, was it not, who reported the precise height and nature of the storm surge and the effect of its first impact on Baja California *Norte*?'

'I flew over it in a helicopter,' he admitted. 'I'm on shipboard now, and much further south. I'm at one hundred and six degrees west, twenty-one fifty-five north, coming up to the reefs at Isla Santa Isabel. We still have high seas, though the storm surge has passed. The general conditions are severe storm, but everything except the rain seems to be easing. What I need to know is: what do I have to expect? Medium term and long term, if possible?'

'The primary storm front is the one with the hurricane winds and the worst seas, and the storm surge. We estimate that once this is past you'll be looking at moderating conditions. Moderating through severe storm to storm. Winds coming down from gusts of over one hundred miles an hour to between forty and fifty. From twelve down to nine or maybe eight on the Beaufort scale, moderating further in time. With increasing periods of calm, perhaps the occasional dead calm, especially at ground level, though there will be strong winds higher up. But even if the wind moderates and the seas begin to settle, the rain won't stop. What you have above you is what I described at the Chamber of Commerce. A river of warm, saturated air stretching from where you are right the way back beyond China, and it's going to come across the ocean non-stop and precipitate everything its carrying as it hits the Sierra Madre.'

'Yes. I've seen it.'

'No. That's my point. With respect, Captain Mariner, I don't think you have seen it. So far, bad as things may have been for you, you haven't been at the leading edge when it hits land. That's where the real downpours are occurring. And that's where the big winds are too, though up high for the most part. We're looking at precipitation rates of one, perhaps two inches an hour. Have you any notion of the damage potential of precipitation of that intensity? How long has this incident been going on so far? Three days? Seventy-two hours. One hundred and forty-four inches of rain. That's *twelve feet* of rain.'

'No wonder it flooded California in 1862. But, Doctor Jones . . .'

'Yes, Captain?'

'On the west coast of Mexico there's no big central valley like the one stretching down from Sacramento to Bakersfield. The mountains in Mexico come right down to the beaches. I'm not sure whether that's a good thing or not.'

'We're hearing here that the Mexican authorities have advised anyone who can get away to run south or east over the Sierras to Guadalajara. They're setting up temporary evacuation centres south of the main storm front from Vallarta on down to Acapulco. But there's been nothing from Puerto Banderas.'

'There's only one way to be certain. And I'd like to be more certain than I am now – before I take *Sulu Queen* into Puerto Banderas harbour.'

'Good luck, Captain Mariner, whatever you're planning. Stay in touch.'

'I will, don't worry. All relevant details will be exhaustively logged and passed straight along to you and your colleagues at USGS and NOAA.'

Richard broke contact and sat back for a moment, looking at the blank screen of his laptop. Then he pulled himself upright and strolled through on to the bridge with studied nonchalance. 'Mr Cheng,' he said. 'We have agreed the course we want *Sulu Queen* to follow during the next couple of hours?'

'Yes, Captain,' answered Cheng. 'Why do we need to agree this?'

'Because, Mr Cheng, you have the con. I'm stepping out for a while.'

'Stepping *out*?'

'Precisely. Major Guerrero, would you like to accompany me?' He walked forward to the communications console and pressed the All Hail. 'This is your captain speaking. Would Biddy McKinney report to the bridge, please? I repeat, Biddy McKinney to the bridge . . .'

THIRTY-SIX

The Bell 429 skipped low over the round lake in the dead volcanic crater of Isla Santa Isabel and settled towards sea level beside the sheer, rocky islets of Las Monas. 'You were right, Richard,' called Biddy through the earphones. 'The air is quieter just above the waves – as long as I keep clear of the spray and foam. Do you think the rain is beginning to ease a little too?'

'Looks like it,' answered Richard. A flaw in the wind combined with the easing of the downpour giving him a glimpse of the high white surf-line stretching away northwards, where the reefs reached out from the little island. Even in these conditions, the air above the boiling water was dark with flocks of boobies and frigate birds hunting the breakers. He turned his attention to Juan Jose Guerrero, who still looked more than a little shaken from the scarily stormy lift-off. 'This take you back to your youth, Major?'

'A bit. Though I have to admit I was never out here in a chopper. And, given half a chance, I won't ever be again. Getting the Bell ready for take-off and then lifting off in this weather has aged me by decades. Not years. Decades. Anyhow, it all looks different from a fishing boat. Bigger. And, of course, I've never been out in conditions like these.' The cabin tilted slightly as Biddy put the Bell's nose down and pushed her airspeed up. The grey corrugations of foam-webbed wave-sets sped past at hypnotic speed. The bellow of the wind quietened and the rainfall seemed to ease a little more. But Richard could see the major's point. Nobody in their right mind would bring a boat out in this. He was even beginning to have second thoughts about his own massive ship. But he was committed now; he had given his word. And there was the matter of finding Robin . . .

Biddy was taking the Bell on the route by which Richard was proposing to bring *Sulu Queen* into the harbour at Puerto Banderas. Conditions in the air were not quite as bad as those they had experienced over Baja California *Norte*, Richard thought. But they were still a way out from the land. And if what Dr Jones said was accurate, it was where the aerial river of the ARkStorm met the ten thousand foot wall of the Sierra Madre Occidental that he would find the heaviest downpours. He tried to imagine what twelve feet of water poured on to the west-facing slopes of those massive mountains would unleash. Only to give up. Speculation was a waste of time. He would see the reality of it soon enough.

See it at once. 'What's that?' demanded Guerrero. 'A whale?'

Richard strained to see what he was pointing at. A long black shape was tossing in the grip of the waves. 'No,' he answered. 'It's the keel of a boat.'

The upturned wreck was only the beginning. As the Bell sped shorewards the rain began to intensify again. But it was still possible to see everything in the water beneath them. The waves steepened. The colour of the water changed – from grey-green to grey-brown. And the pieces of flotsam became more numerous. More varied. 'What's going on here?' asked Biddy.

'It's the outwash,' said Richard grimly. 'The eastward set of the ocean is being met by the westward flow of floodwater washing out from the land, bringing with it anything that will float.'

'Anything that's been washed off the hillsides – whether it's from the jungle or the town.' Guerrero nodded.

'With, first of all, anything that's been washed out of the harbour by the floods coming out of the river or down off the land. Hence the boats. There's another. At least it's the right way up. Looks abandoned, though.'

There was almost a surf-line where the waters of the ocean and of the flood fought for supremacy. A solid-looking band of rubbish heaved and rolled, defining the line where the waters met. 'You'll have to take *Sulu Queen* through that pretty carefully,' said Guerrera.

'I was thinking the same thing. And from the look of some of the ropework, tackle and netting down there I was thinking, thank heavens for the Spurs cutters on my propellers.'

'I don't know about your propellers,' Biddy added, 'but it looks as though an ice-strengthened bow would be useful. Is that a *car*?'

'Looks like a Volkswagen,' said Richard, as precise as ever. 'Heaven knows how it's floated out this far.'

'This is like pictures of the sea beside Japan after the tsunami in 2011,' said Guerrero. 'Could the flooding be that powerful? Like a tsunami?'

'Looks like it,' answered Richard shortly.

'God help them.'

'That's what we're here to do,' said Richard. 'Give the Almighty a hand.'

'But what can we do?' demanded Guerrero, suddenly over-- whelmed by the enormity of what they appeared to be facing.

'Make a start,' said Richard. 'Make a difference, no matter how slight. No matter what, it's better that we're here to help than the alternative, which looks like *nobody* here to help. For the moment, at least.'

'I guess,' said Guerrero, but he didn't sound convinced.

And Richard could see his point. The rubbish on the water beneath them grew thicker. Prompted by Guerrero's thoughts, Richard suddenly remembered a story Liberty Greenbaum had told him about something she had seen when sailing the North Pacific. She had come up against what appeared to be an uncharted island in the middle of the ocean, only to discover that it was several acres of floating rubbish from the Japanese tsunami on its way across to North America. Thinking of Liberty made him wonder about *Katapult8* and how she could have made her way through this – if, indeed she had done so. And thinking of *Katapult8* made him think of *Maxima*. And of Robin. Suddenly he found he was short of breath, with an actual ache in his chest.

'You OK?' asked Guerrera, seeing the change in his expression.

'Yes. I was just wondering about *Maxima*.'

'She'll be in the harbour. That's where the beacon is.'

Yes, thought Richard. But what if the beacon's not on *Maxima* at all? What if we've been on a wild goose chase all along and she's still out there in the deep ocean – on the top or at the bottom?

He gave voice to none of his fears. It was not in his nature to do so. Once a decision was made he stood by it. It was not his style of leadership to be constantly second-guessing himself and agonizing over *what if?* or *what might have been*. But he had never been this worried about Robin before; never felt that she was at so much risk. So, instead of continuing his conversation, he leaned over and pushed his face close to its pallid reflection in the glass, staring through his ghostly profile down at the debris and the almost pitch-black water on which it heaved sluggishly, as though its buoyancy was being overcome by the weight of the lashing rain.

'There,' shouted Guerrero, who had been looking shorewards rather than downwards. As he spoke, Biddy called, 'Land-ho!'

Through the driving downpour, the coast looked at first like another low thunderhead sitting just above the sea, its normally vivid green seemingly washed out by the grey rain. The drab spectacle swung round as Biddy adjusted her course to run northwards towards Puerto Banderas itself. As she did, the Bell came over the main coastal highway and Richard was given a brief but vivid view of the tail-end of a slow-moving traffic jam being pounded by the downpour and blasted by the wind. 'Looks like some people have managed to get out of town,' he said. 'Where does that road lead to?'

'San Blas,' answered the major. 'Then Tepic and Guadalajara if they can get over the mountains; Vallarta and Acapulco if they can't.'

'If they can get ahead of the weather somehow, as long as the road holds out. I'd say there was a considerable outwash flooding down off the coastal mountains. The same here as there was on the Baja California.'

The Bell swung out over the water then, and Richard put the caravan of refugees out of his mind, returning to the matter in hand. The flotsam began to take on a pattern, spewing out in a widening fan from the still-distant mouth of the harbour. Its outer edge, to the left, formed that strange surf-line where it met the incoming rollers. Shorewards, on their right, it washed towards the long, grey-gold beaches. But they were themselves awash with run-off that spewed at first from the jungle and then – as they flew further northwards – from the tarmac and concrete acreages of the town's roadways, yards, flat roofs and over-brimming swimming pools, pouring down with sufficient force to keep the beaches awash but clear of rubbish. At first glance, Richard felt heartened. The town looked to be in better condition than the junk in the ocean had led him to expect. 'Biddy, can you take us closer in?' he asked. She complied. The two men strained to see though the rain and to stay focused as the buffeting wind returned.

'Where is everybody?' asked Guerrero.

'Indoors if they've got any sense. Or on their way to the government evacuation centres. Just look at that!' A wide boulevard led straight downhill towards the beach and a line of tall hotels and apartments. A river of runoff was cascading down it, making rapids where anything stood in its way or where the sewers overflowed like geysers, throwing yellow foam high into the air.

'That's Avenue Sixteenth September,' said Guerrero, awed. 'It's always packed with cars. It leads past the *mercado* market to the beach at Playa Camerones.'

'Is that the market?' asked Richard, pointing to a great square black lake which appeared to be still – until the chopper passed above a line of corrugated-iron roofs over which the water boiled like the reefs by Santa Isabel as it poured away downhill. 'And there are your cars,' Richard added as they skimmed just above the hotels standing behind Los Muertos beach and saw piles of vehicles forming dams and barriers across the bottom of the avenue and all the roadways running down parallel to it. It seemed incredible that there should be so many still left when they had just seen so many more heading south.

Biddy took matters into her own hands then, taking the Bell to the right, rising up the hillside until they were over the jungle immediately above and behind the town. Then, in spite of the buffeting of the gusty wind and the renewed intensity of the precipitation, she raced them over to the Rio Cortez. What had been a sedate stream falling in picturesque waterfalls and sluices from one pretty lake to another was now a non-stop torrent. The lakes had all spread along the hillside steps, as though even the speed at which the river was roaring down was not enough to keep them contained within their natural shorelines. 'Mother of mercy!' she whispered as she came over the last of the lakes, familiar from the film she had shot for Nic. Except that Dahlia Blanca was no longer there. The lake that had lapped so sedately near the beautiful building now filled its grounds, brimming over the tall wall that had edged the cliff at the end of the massive estate. And the house, like the market, was little more than a reef over which the water boiled in a cataract that would have been at home on the Nile or the Colorado as it rushed through the Grand Canyon. 'Mr Greenbaum is going to be *pissed* when he sees this!' said Biddy.

'Right,' said Richard, unable to bear the suspense of not knowing *Maxima*'s fate any longer. 'Let's go down and tell him. He's in the outer harbour.'

They followed the rampaging river on down to the ocean, keeping low, especially when the buildings began to break up the brute force of the wind. But they paid for the protection by coming face-to-face with yet more destruction. Long before it reached the harbour – before it had reached the outskirts of the town proper – the river burst its banks once more. Riverside houses, hotels and condominiums became reefs, wrecks or islands in the foaming stream. Items of furniture joined the vehicles swirling in the flood. Chairs, sofas, tables, televisions, stereos, beds. But so far no bodies, living or dead.

It was hard to see where the inner harbour began, for the water level was high above the marina's jetties and only the occasional boat on a long, strong mooring gave the position of the facility away. The roofs of the marina's restaurants and shops gave some sort of definition to the shoreline, apparently floating like terra-cotta rafts on the swift current. But that was all. The only real definition of the end of one and the beginning of the other was the tall arch of the single-span road bridge that leaped upward out of a welter of foam at the foot of a six-lane highway running parallel to the Avenue Sixteenth September. 'That's the Boulevard Centrale,' said Juan Jose. 'It was built to link the breakwater hotels with the centre of town.'

'The bridge seems to be holding up well, though,' said Richard.

'That's because of the high curve on it. They built it like that so even quite large vessels could get into the inner harbour. They wanted Puerto Banderas to be the next billionaires' playground on the Pacific coast.'

The outer harbour beyond the high arch of the wide bridge was much broader, and had fared better in consequence. The L-shape of the breakwater was above even the swollen water level, and the Malecón opposite was built on top of a high embankment. Even so, runoff gushed off the Boulevard Centrale and between the buildings, pouring out into the dock as though the entire Malecón was the side of a ship frantically pumping out its bilges.

But Richard had no eyes for any of this. He was instead focused on the inner wall of the breakwater. His plans dictated that he should be searching for the great dockside cranes like the one he had left in Long Beach, big enough and strong enough to lift the National Guard containers off his deck. But no. He was focused entirely on his increasingly desperate search for a multihull with a tall black solid sail and a sleek white billionaire's plaything. And, sure enough, there were some vessels tethered to the outer dock. But all of them looked deserted and none of them looked like *Katapult8* or *Maxima*. His heart sank painfully again as Biddy skimmed as low as she dared over the filthy, battered derelicts. But then: 'Oh! Sweet suffering Christ!' she said. And the Bell whirled, nose down, settling towards one of the worst-looking wrecks. Richard stared at it, wide-eyed with shock, wondering what Biddy was up to. The state of it! he thought numbly. Its communications gear was gone. Two stumpy masts ended in tangles of twisted wire-work. The stern section, from midships back, had clearly seen better days. There had apparently been an on-board pool but it was a total wreck now. There had been an aft section that folded down to water level; it had clearly been torn away. The hull looked rust-streaked, salt-grimed. Little better than a hulk on its way to the breaker's yard.

It was not until the Bell settled on the third deck up like a homing pigeon returning to its roost that Richard realized. Heart suddenly lifting, he unstrapped his belt, tore off his headphones and opened the side. Oblivious to the deluge, he jumped down and ran forward. The familiar glass doors slid open and Robin was standing there. He stopped. Stepped forward, feeling that his chest was going to explode. 'Christ,' he said. 'I've been so worried about you!'

'Me too,' she said with a pale grin. 'I've been really worried about us. And with good reason. You don't know the half of it!'

He really felt as though a weight had been lifted from his shoulders. She was safe. She was here. There was nothing they couldn't tackle now. Nothing they couldn't overcome. 'Tell me all about it later,' he said, taking the last step forward so he could slide his arms round her and hug her with all his strength, looking over her shoulder at Nic and Liberty as they stood smiling on the battered bridge. 'We've got quite a job to do. A ship full of relief supplies and soldiers to bring in. A great deal of reconstruction work too, by the look of things. And a whole town of people to find and to help – those that aren't on their way to Guardalajara or Vallarta. Let's get this show on the road!'

THIRTY-SEVEN

Biddy flew Richard, Robin and Guerrero back to *Sulu Queen* almost immediately. But there was more than one couple reunited before the Bell lifted off. For no sooner had Richard and Robin greeted each other than Miguel-Angel appeared, summoned by the sound of the helicopter and brimming with questions, none of which he ever asked. Because if Juan Jose hardly recognized his little brother, Miguel-Angel knew his elder sibling at once. One glance at the tall, dark officer and the boy burst into tears. Between sobs, he tried to explain in a mixture of broken English and guttural Spanish that the sight of his brother made him realize how terribly he was going to miss his *capitan*. Juan Jose swept his little brother into his arms as though the tall youth was still a child. 'And Father?' demanded the major. 'How is Father?'

Miguel-Angel shrugged. '*Where* is Father? The shop is locked and empty. *Señor* Greenbaum sailed close by the Malecón on the way in and I ran ashore and knocked. But there was no reply. He must have gone. So I came back on board.'

'We saw a convoy of refugees on the flight in.' Juan Jose nodded. 'The local authorities are beginning to get organized, I think. But it is impossible that everyone will have gone. There are always people who will not or cannot leave. These are the ones we are here to try to help, for things will get worse.'

At the major's request, therefore, Biddy did not simply reverse her incoming flight path. Instead of following the river and going over the jungle, she took the Bell as low as she dared over the apparently deserted town. 'I calculate,' Guerrero explained, 'that anyone still here is likely to try to communicate with us if they hear the chopper passing.' And so it proved. Especially as he and Miguel-Angel, now inseparable, dictated the course using their superior knowledge of the town. 'Follow Los Poetas,' called Miguel-Angel. 'It runs parallel to Boulevard Centrale. It is where the main hospital is. There will be people there who cannot easily be moved.' The Bell skipped low over the tall, square building and paused, hovering so that they could look in through the windows – and, sure enough, there were people waving. Miguel-Angel waved back.

'Where next?' asked Biddy. 'If I go straight up I just get back to Dahlia Blanca, which I still have not dared tell Mr Greenbaum about. Any volunteers?'

'The Malecón? Los Muertos?' suggested Juan Jose.

'No. There are three CMQ hospitals in the centre of town,' said Miguel-Angel. 'And there are the Buena Vista health clinics which are high up near the beginning of the jungle. If the rain continues, they would be at risk first, no?'

'Yes,' answered Juan Jose. 'But they will also be the hardest for us to reach.' His observation was borne out as Biddy took them up to Buena Vista at the jungle's edge. 'What we need is some kind of transport that can get up and down these hills, even when they are flooded. Something amphibious, maybe.'

'The Mexican Navy has amphibious vehicles,' Biddy said knowledgeably. 'They have BTR-70 eight-wheelers and some Gama Goats still in commission.'

'Their main Pacific base is in Manzanillo, just south of Vallarta,' said Juan Jose. 'Though they also have bases at Ensenada, Puerto Cortez and Vallarta.'

'Good,' said Richard. 'But what we could really do with is more choppers.'

'I tell you what you need,' said Robin. 'You need that airship we saw.'

'Dragon Dream? It would be perfect if it can handle the conditions.'

'I could ask,' called Biddy. 'I mean, there will be guys up in LA who'll know the contact. Like I said when we saw her, Dragon Dream has fans there.'

'Worth a try,' said Richard. 'She was heading for Mexico City. She could conceivably be quite close by if she can get over the Sierra Madre.'

'I remember a briefing,' added Juan Jose, 'that suggested one of the best uses for dirigibles like that is in emergencies. They don't need any major ground support and yet they can move things the size of containers.'

'So we have some priorities,' said Richard. 'Check the last hospitals. Get back to *Sulu Queen*. Contact the navy at Manzanillo. Contact Dragon Dream.'

'Aeroscraft are the guys who built her,' Biddy added. 'I knew it would come to me. They're out in Montobello. I can get through to them.'

'Right. But, unless you're confident about multitasking, I suggest we leave the radio contacts till we get back aboard, except for alerting Cheng that we're on our way. Then we can start to call our priority list as we bring her in.'

By the time Richard eased *Sulu Queen* past the Faro lighthouse at the end of the breakwater and into the flotsam-thick relative calm of the outer harbour a couple of hours later, Juan Jose Guerrero had contacted Manzanillo, explained who he was, where he was and what he was doing. Already on high alert, under direct orders from the president to cooperate as fully as possible, the admiral he finally talked to warned that the commands on the Baja were already fully committed and Vallarta was filling up with refugees so swiftly that the naval contingent down there was going to be needed onsite. But he agreed to load one of his venerable Papaloapan-class tank landing ships with as many BTR-70 amphibious vehicles and Gama Goats as he could spare. And with drivers and support teams. Already well versed in such work and holder of a Humanitarian Service Medal, the vessel had an emergency routine practised after Hurricane Katrina and again after the Haiti earthquake. She could be with them in twelve hours, depending on sea conditions.

Biddy's contact with Aeroscraft seemed equally positive. Dragon Dream was indeed on her way to Mexico City. 'She's currently at Durango International Airport,' Biddy explained just after she broke contact. 'That's just the other side of the mountains, about two hundred and fifty kliks north-east of here. Of course, they're keen to help in any way they can. Dragon Dream is a scaled-down version of the craft already in production, but she can still help. They're trying to find a way over the Sierra. As soon as they do, they'll be here. Dragon Dream can fly at more than one hundred and fifty kliks per hour. And she can carry up to sixty tons payload – that's three fully laden TEUs – or a hundred or so passengers. Sounds like the answer to your prayers, Richard. If she can get here.'

As the helmsman eased *Sulu Queen* into the empty dock in front of *Maxima* at Richard's command a couple of hours later, however, the next set of problems became obvious. The amount of rainwater draining between the containers and collecting in the bilge beneath the ship's hold meant that the pumps were on full. At sea this was not a problem, but as the big freighter came close to the dockside, the bilge water flooded the facility even further, adding to the deluge and washing away towards the warehouses. Furthermore, although there was a crane large enough to lift Guerrero's containers ashore, there was no one to man it and nothing to transport them – always assuming the roads were passable. 'As I said,' observed Robin as her husband stood thinking the problems through, 'we either need some big choppers or Dragon Dream.'

'But in the meantime,' frowned Guerrero, 'what can we do? We have focused so much on getting here. And now that we are here, we cannot get our help to the people who need it most!'

'Not for eight to ten hours, maybe,' added Miguel-Angel, looking on the bright side as ever. 'Then the navy will be here.'

'But the National Guard is here already,' snapped Juan Jose.

'Tell you what,' said Richard. 'How about this? The way we have your containers secured means that the only thing stopping us opening them up again and really starting to get things moving is the rain. How about if we moved them into the dry? Then your people could get out some of the supplies – tents, say, heating units, medicines, so forth. And then we could see about bringing people to us, aboard here, if we can't get the containers to them.'

'Like a real *arco de Noa*!' said Miguel-Angel.

'But where is this dry place?' demanded the major.

'Under the road bridge,' answered Richard. They all turned round to look at it. The arch of the single span was dead ahead. The outwash from the town joined with the current of the river to make the landside rough and dangerous-looking. But where the span swooped down to settle on the breakwater, things looked much calmer. And on that side, too, the dock had been built out under the span into a broad walkway with a series of bollards. It was clear that, with care, Richard could get a good deal of his ship in there and use the bollards to moor her securely in place. 'I can't get *Sulu Queen* right under because her bridge house is too high,' he was saying. 'Even with all our thrusters and the manoeuvrability of the engine it will be really tough. But I reckon we could put all of her foredeck under. Use it as a roof, effectively. Tie up so that my bridge house here is as close to the road-bridge wall as possible and keep a close eye on the way the flood and the tide make the water level rise and fall. Biddy can still come and go off the after deck, taking your experts out and bringing emergencies aboard, and in the mean-time we can try and get the foredeck bright, as warm as possible and dry. Come to that,' he continued, following his train of thought further, 'once you've started emptying your containers of their emergency supplies you could even use some of them as individual refuges. People all over the world are using containers as houses, schoolrooms, hospitals. Why not stock each one as you empty it with a chemical toilet, a heater, some bedding and put people in them until the authorities get on top of the situation?'

'Jesus,' said Juan Jose. 'When you start thinking, Richard, you think *big*.'

'It's something that's been at the back of my mind for a while. As I said to Nic Greenbaum when Robin and I were still staying aboard *Queen Mary*, we were the only people in Long Beach who didn't need to fear a flood, because we were in the only local hotel that was actually designed to *float*.'

'Right,' said the major. 'If you think you can pull it off then go ahead. In the meantime, my next move is to get some teams looking through those warehouses for anything we can use – including more shelter. I've always wanted to get into the hotel business, and if the Westin, the Hilton or the Marriott are empty then now's the time. They'll make great evacuation centres, independently of the fact that they make great wind-breaks to give us some shelter here. Also, I need to take some of my medics in the Bell up to the hospital where we saw those folks waving.' He saw the look on Miguel-Angel's. 'OK, kid, you can come.'

'I'm trained up to accident and emergency level,' added Robin. 'And I can fly choppers. I'll sit in the co-pilot's seat and see where I can be most help.'

'Take a walkie-talkie,' said Richard. 'Stay in touch.'

'I've got fuel in the tank,' added Biddy. 'I can take you three and four others then hop back for seven more as many times as you like. Just get it organized. Or get that super-efficient Lieutenant Harding to do it for you.'

'That's settled, then,' said Richard. 'Let's get to work.'

THIRTY-EIGHT

Upslope of the hospital building in Puerto Banderas was a car park that was both in the wind shadow and the rain shadow of the building. It was relatively dry. Biddy landed there while Robin, the Guerrero brothers and the first four American medics got out and ran for shelter. Then she lifted off and hopped back towards the harbour and *Sulu Queen*. Robin ran up the eight steps that took her from ground level to the ground floor of the building and paused in the covered outer entrance as she watched the helicopter lift away. Her gaze swept up the slope to the edge of the jungle and the long white wall at the end of Nic's Dahlia Blanca estate. It had almost become the lip of a waterfall now. Runoff overflowed in a steady stream and swept on down the hill. She wondered briefly about the state of the beautiful house she had admired in Biddy's video. Then she turned and ran in through the automatic glass doors.

Robin arrived partway through a conversation between a tall, fine-boned woman in a white coat who looked like an Aztec princess and the major, who looked more like a Spanish conquistador. '. . . When the power went out we switched over to our backup generators on the roof,' she was saying. 'But they're not working properly so they only give us emergency power. And we started moving all the patients we could downstairs to wait for transport out. But then the cellar flooded and that's where the main generator is. We've been without heat, light or power since. Luckily there was no one in the lift when the generator went down but we still have patients trapped on the upper floors. And, needless to say, you and your men are the first people we've seen.' She looked closely at his ID badge and glanced across to Miguel-Angel, who had wandered away and was looking around. 'One of our patients may be a relation. *Señor* Guerrero who runs the ship chandlery down on the Malecón. He broke his leg trying to help a friend whose boat was being carried away by the flood. He is on level three.'

'Miguel-Angel, our father is in one of the beds upstairs. See if you can find him. Tell him we've come to rescue him,' said the major. 'Don't worry,' he continued, turning back to the woman and pulling one of the ship's walkie-talkies from his belt, 'we'll get a generator up here and restore power. Then we'll see about moving your staff and patients out.' He turned away and spoke into the walkie-talkie. 'Richard? When Biddy gets back, tell her the next load has to include the biggest generator Lieutenant Harding can find – that Biddy can lift in the Bell – and people to run it.'

'But where will we go?' asked the woman in the white coat. 'There is nowhere nearer than Vallarta!'

Her words were more a spoken thought than a question directed to anyone, but Robin answered. 'To my husband's ship. It's a bit like Noah's ark from the Bible . . .' Then she started to explain about *Sulu Queen* and Richard's plans for her.

Some of the hospital's maintenance staff had stayed along with some of the medical staff and, by the time Biddy returned, they had shown two of Guerrero's engineers the best place to patch in a generator – at the major's insistence up on the second floor *just in case*. 'Then I'll get men up on the roof to see what we can do with your back-up generators up there,' said Guerrero. 'But if we target at least one lift shaft with this one then we can get you moving. And maybe we can get light and heat running with the ones on the roof.'

The engineers promised that the generators would be working

in a very short time and with luck would have the lifts serviceable within the hour. Robin watched work on the first begin at a fuse box on the second floor then went down and found the striking-looking white-coated administrator. She explained her qualifications and offered her help. As she did so, she finally got a look at the woman's ID badge, which identified her as Dr Citali Potosi. Ten minutes later she was three storeys up, looking for Miguel-Angel with orders to check on his father's leg. The moment she saw the boy she knew his father must have been badly hurt. She had expected to find Guerrero senior on crutches or in a wheelchair. But no. Miguel-Angel, framed against a window at the end of the ward that overlooked the jungle slopes and the low grey sky, was sitting beside a bed whose covers had been tented from halfway down. As she walked swiftly up the ward, Robin glanced at the other three occupants. They were all bed-ridden for one reason or another. Two were asleep. One, like the boy's father, was sitting up. *Señor* Guerrero was propped on a pile of pillows, grey-faced with discomfort, his pallor emphasised by the darkness of his thick hair, heavy eyebrows and deep chocolate eyes. He was the major in twenty years' time. Miguel-Angel clearly favoured a finer-featured mother resembling Dr Potosi. 'How are you feeling, *señor*?' she asked solicitously. 'May I take a look at your leg?'

Miguel-Angel excitedly introduced her and explained how they had met as she folded the blanket back to reveal a leg that had been secure by old-fashioned splints. It was a good job but it was not really good enough. His foot was black with bruising and – more worryingly – his hip looked out of shape. She began to wonder at once whether there might be damage to the pelvis and hip joint as well as to the leg, but without removing the man's hospital gown it would be impossible to be certain. And, thinking of recent examinations she had done – and not done – for reasons of gender, she realized all too clearly that she was not the person to remove *Señor* Guerrero's gown. 'Miguel-Angel,' she said. 'Would you run and find a doctor, please. A male doctor.'

'*Si*,' said the boy and ran off, clearly pleased to get away.

'*Señor* Guerrero,' said Robin, 'can you tell me exactly what happened?' As the ships' chandler began to explain, Robin pulled up the chair the boy had been sitting in. She half turned it so she could see the rest of the ward. But she had only just sat down to listen to his story when a strange flicker in the light from the window behind her made her turn. She caught her breath with a mixture of surprise and wonder. She stood, leaving her patient stammering into silence, and went to the window. And there, seemingly immediately outside, apparently just above the hospital's flat roof another ten stories up, the three hundred foot body of the Aeroscraft dirigible Dragon Dream was sailing steadily and silently down towards the docks, looking like a space ship made of mercury, the rain exploding off its skin, giving it a kind of silver halo.

Looking straight ahead out of the bridge windows, Richard could see nothing but the concrete wall of the bridge's side, even though he was more than sixty feet above the dockside. He could see little more from the port-bridge wing which overhung the concrete sixty feet below and was hard up against the concrete of the road bridge, which was close enough to touch. The starboard wing, however, gave a view beneath the rising span, and from here it was possible to see the bustle of the foredeck as, under the ship's deck lights, men and women from Guerrero's command were working on the relief containers. They were sheltered from the rain by a combination of the bridge's broad span and *Sulu Queen*'s tall bridge house. In spite of the fact that the underside of the span rose over one hundred feet above the deck at its highest point, only the most occasional gust came anywhere near pushing the precipitation past the six-deck-high white wall of *Sulu Queen*'s accommodation and command areas or in from the far side of the road bridge, in spite of the fact that the span was high above – especially near the centre of the arch. But in fact, things beneath the span of the bridge were relatively calm as well as being warm and dry. The wind was coming out of the west, in from the ocean. And between *Sulu Queen* and the main force of the storm stood wall after wall. Tall, strong-sided warehouses standing along the western dockside. Wide, solid, skyscraper hotels beyond them that lined the land-side of the beach. Richard was just stepping back in from this vantage point, thoroughly satisfied with the way things were progressing, when the radio operator called to him. 'I have someone on the radio who wants to speak to you.' And that was how he learned that Dragon Dream had arrived.

Ten minutes later, Richard was running along the gangplank on to the wide, sheltered walkway between two of the bollards to which *Sulu Queen* was secured. He ran back along the great ship's length and out into the stormy afternoon, slowing beneath the shelter of the port-bridge wing to watch as the dirigible's pilot brought the massive silver craft to rest on the top of the dockside. Guerrero's team exploring the warehouses crowded the door, looking on. Massive though she was, Dragon Dream sat sedately outside the hangar-sized warehouses, sheltered from the worst of the wind if not the rain. With hardly a pause, Richard was running forward again through the downpour and across the dock towards the beautiful craft. Stooping beneath its overhanging side, he carried on in until he reached the low-hanging cabin which housed the two pilots. Richard opened the door in the side of the cabin and stepped into the future. The cabin was small but roomy enough for the three people occupying it. There were windows all round it, giving a clear view of the four big motors – two in front and two behind – that gave Dragon Dream her vertical take-off capacity. Above the forward-facing windows a bank of instruments led round to a big screen in the centre of the pilot's view. Below the windows there were square touch screens for both pilot and co-pilot, who occupied two big seats that could have come from a jet fighter. Between them there were more instruments and controls convenient to the pilot's right hand.

The pilot stood up and turned towards him, a tall, slim, dynamic-looking man with short, greying hair and rimless glasses. 'Hi,' he said. 'You must be Captain Mariner. I'm the guy you just talked to – Erwin Creech. This is Gene Rogers. How can we help?' he asked as the co-pilot also stood.

They shook hands. 'I'll know more about that when I've had a quick look over your dirigible,' answered Richard.

'We can do that from here,' said Creech. 'All the main areas aboard have cameras fitted.' He crossed to the big screen. 'Video feeds show up here. You'll be most interested in the cargo bays, I guess. The plan is to put passenger facilities in

some of the bigger craft that are in production now. But we
just have the basics.' As he spoke he tapped the screen, which
was showing a video of large, empty spaces that looked like
the insides of Boeing C17 transport aircraft. 'Of course, people
can go in there in emergencies,' Creech continued. 'It just
won't be so comfortable. But I guess you could easily get a
hundred people in there.'

Richard opened his mouth to answer but he was interrupted
by the walkie-talkie. 'Excuse me a second,' he said and put it to
his lips. 'Mariner?'

'This is Biddy. As you have your heavy lifter in place now,
Nic wants me to hop him and Liberty up to Dahlia Blanca for
a quick look-see. Won't be long.'

'OK,' said Richard. 'Take care. And get ready to see a grown
man cry.'

Richard, Gene Rogers and Erwin Creech were still discussing
how Dragon Dream could be of best use when the Bell lifted
off the helipad behind *Sulu Queen*'s bridge and powered away
through the storm. 'I can place her with absolute precision and
hold her absolutely still,' Creech explained. 'That's part of how
we got here. The weathermen at Durango warned us the really
big winds were up at the tops of the sierras, so we followed the
river valleys up one side then down the other. Stayed a couple
of metres above the flow. We had lots of protection from the
valley sides – interlocking spurs and what have you. Even this
side, where the bad floods are. You'd be surprised.'

'The only bad moments we had were up at the watershed,'
added Gene Rogers. 'But once we managed to squeeze over we
just sat on top of the Rio Cortez and down we came.'

'She's what, fifty feet high? Maybe sixty counting the
turbofans?'

'Fifty's nearer the mark,' said Creech. 'What have you in
mind?'

'Still follow the river. She could fit beneath the bridge. Maybe
even hover over *Sulu Queen*'s foredeck and load or unload directly
from there.'

'We could certainly try,' nodded Creech. 'She'd fit under the
centre of the arch above the water easily. It must be more than
a hundred feet high. It's certainly more than ninety-five feet

wide – and Dragon Dream's ninety-three, including the propellers. We've – what – five hundred metres to play with? It'd be easy as long as there's no very gusty winds under there.'

And that was as far as discussions had reached before Biddy was back on the walkie-talkie. 'Richard, we're at Dahlia Blanca and you got bad, *bad* trouble.'

THIRTY-NINE

Miguel-Angel arrived with a harassed-looking young doctor just as the Bell clattered overhead. The medic pulled *Señor* Guerrero's bedding back impatiently and reached for the hem of his gown. Robin turned away and went to the window, watching the helicopter soaring up the drenched hillside. She could think of only one reason for the flight: Nic was going to look at his beautiful estate. She shook her head, empathizing with the shock and sadness he would feel. To have lost *Katapult8*, to have all but destroyed *Maxima*, and now this. Talk about a bad day, she thought. On the other hand, he still had a daughter snatched from the jaws of death – almost literally. So there was a silver lining even to these black clouds. Idly, she watched the chopper as it slowed, hovering above the long white wall that was currently acting as a kind of dam at the edge of the flooded garden.

As she watched with growing horror and incredulity, the overstressed structure finally yielded to the relentless pressures of holding back all that water. As though Biddy and the Bell were somehow members of Guy Gibson's Dambuster squadron, the wall immediately beneath them abruptly sagged forward, hundreds of gallons of water spilling over its lip. Robin watched, frozen; scarcely able to believe what she was seeing. In an instant, the whole wall was gone and the hundreds of gallons were thousands. Hundreds of thousands. And the hospital was standing directly in their path.

Robin pulled out the walkie-talkie and pressed *transmit*. But she couldn't connect to Richard. Someone else was talking to him, she realized. With any luck it would be Biddy. Her mind raced. There were streets and houses – hopefully empty – upslope from the hospital. Then the car park that Biddy used as a landing field. Would all this be enough to turn the tide? Probably not, she thought. And now that the wall was gone and what looked like an entire lake was on its way down, she reckoned that there would soon be more than water. Mudslides. That was what they had been worried about in those suburbs of Los Angeles, she remembered numbly. Glendora, Azusa. Oso in Washington state, where between forty and ninety people had died. And the one in Collbran, Colorado. How many had that killed back in May 2014?

Suddenly the line to Richard was open. 'Richard—' she said.

'I know,' he interrupted. 'You'll be hit by water. Then probably mud. Are the lifts working?'

'Just about—'

'Get everyone you can up on the roof.'

'Is that the best plan? Most are on the ground floor already. There's a car park. Biddy can land there. She's used it already.'

'The water will be moving at more than fifty miles an hour. Mud the same. The car park will be underwater in a couple of minutes and buried soon after. Get them up on the roof and pray the mudslide's not strong enough to make the place collapse. It's their only chance. And for God's sake, get up there yourself.'

Robin turned. *Señor* Guerrero was exposed from the waist down, his hip swollen and dark. But she didn't even notice. She was running for the door at the far end of the ward, switching the walkie-talkie to the major's channel and sorting out priorities in her mind as she went.

'Guerrero.' The major answered Robin's call immediately.

'Major, there's a flood and a mudslide heading towards us. The lower floors, at least, are at imminent risk. Can you ask Doctor Potosi to get everyone there to move up as fast as possible? And move the generator too if you can, so we can keep the lifts running for as long as possible.'

The major wasted no time on pointless questions. 'Move up how far?'

'Richard says to the roof, but I guess to the top floor and stay in the dry until we know precisely what he's planning. Are the generators on the roof working yet?'

'Barely. Doctor Potosi is here. How long have we got?'

'Before the flood, no time at all. Before the mudslide, who knows?'

She reached the door, only to be stopped by Miguel-Angel's cry. '*Señora!* There is a wall of water . . . It is coming over the car park . . . *Madre de Dios!*'

The whole building shook as the water hit. The sound of breaking glass echoed up the stairwell. My God, thought Robin as she span through the door and went racing down the stairs. If that's how it reacts to a flood, what's it going to do when a mudslide hits? But when she reached the ground floor, things were not quite as bad as she had feared. The steps up from the car park had saved them from complete inundation for the time being, but a glance through the shattered doors showed only a sea of brown water that seemed hardly less threatening than the huge waves which had nearly destroyed *Maxima*. Then, as she looked through the wreckage and up the hill, she realized that one of the houses a couple of streets up, in the forefront of the flood, was beginning to collapse. The mudslide was on its way, she reckoned. And the only thing stopping it moving as fast as the water was the resistance being put up by the buildings upslope of the hospital. But behind the tinkling of the glass still falling out of the doorframe, the rumble of the flood and the hissing of the downpour she heard the welcome wheeze of the lift coming into operation. And, nearer, the chime that announced that the lift car had arrived. She followed the sound and found Dr Potosi in charge of several hospital staff who were wheeling beds into a sizeable lift car as fast as they were able to. There was a crowd of walking wounded behind them, waiting to squeeze in round the beds. Robin opened her mouth but her words were cut short by another chime as the car in the second shaft arrived. The fact that it was working made Robin think Guerrero's men on the roof were getting the generators back online. The walking wounded crowded into this. 'Top floor,' called Robin, and Dr Potosi translated, '*Al ultimo piso,*' then stepped back to join Robin as both sets of doors hissed shut.

'My husband says we may have to go out on the roof soon,' said Robin.

'That is *al azotea* in Spanish. Have you any idea why he wants us there?'

'No. But it'd be good to get away from this.' Robin looked down. The muddy water was already around her ankles. There was a roaring sound as it went pouring down the lift shaft. 'It is fortunate,' observed Dr Potosi, 'that the lift motors are in water-tight housings with the back-up generators on the roof.'

'Yes,' said Robin. 'Are there many more people on this level?'

'We need only worry about the bedridden, I think. Those on crutches and frames are willing enough to attempt the stairs. I have sent everyone I can spare down here to bring the beds to this place. We should get them all in two lifts. Could you start organizing the same thing on the next level up?'

'Yes. And don't forget the third level. That's where the major's father and brother are. How many levels are there above that?'

'Seven. But they are all empty.'

As Dr Potosi spoke, the first of the lifts returned. The doors opened. The water, which was now well over the women's ankles, washed over the lift car's floor, forming little whirlpools and rapids as it continued to cascade into the shaft. 'I am glad this is the last set of patients from this floor,' said Dr Potosi. 'This water is becoming unnerving.'

'And there's worse on the way,' warned Robin. 'I'll go upstairs and see how things are proceeding.'

'And check with Major Guerrero as to how long we are likely to be able to run the lifts,' advised the doctor as Robin turned to dash up stairs. But as she passed the rear of the reception area on her way to the staircase, she couldn't resist another look outside. The water was deep enough to be forming waves now, and they were washing in through the shattered door. It was also deep enough to begin to carry rubbish and worse down the hill. As Robin paused, she saw the first tree trunk coming across the drowned car park. And, beside it, what looked like an entire A-frame roof – terracotta tiles and all. She looked up. The furthest line of houses had vanished now. Only one flimsy street stood between the hospital and the mudslide. She turned, slopped across to the staircase and ran on upwards, thanking heaven for her all but indestructible footwear. At the same moment as the tree trunk hit the front of the hospital like a medieval battering ram, the walkie-talkie sounded. She jammed it to her mouth as she dashed out on to the next floor. 'Yes?'

'It's Richard. How are things going?' The question was almost lost beneath the pandemonium of the A-frame roof tearing itself apart against the front wall of the hospital.

'Bad to worse. We're moving everyone up like you asked. I'm just about to find out how much longer we can keep the lifts running. Even if they can handle the flood, it's a hundred to one that the mudslide will screw them.'

'Biddy's on her way back down. Anyone she can pick up? The boy?'

'His father's here. Badly broken leg. The boy's waiting with him.'

'Can she take both, maybe? Or if not, is there anyone else?'

'No. She won't be able to land anyway. I'll get back in contact when we have people on the roof. She might be able to take some from there. Two of Nic's men are ex-storm swimmers. They might be able to help or advise.'

'I'll check. Good luck in the meantime. And for God's sake, take care.'

She broke contact. 'Chance would be a fine thing,' she said to herself.

She found Guerrero and the hospital's electricians at the junction box nearest to the lifts. 'How long can we keep these running? Doctor Potosi needs to know.'

'For a while. We gave lifts priority both here and on the roof as we fixed the generators up there. She should be using both shafts to get as many people up as possible.'

'That's what she's doing. They'll clear this floor next then the one above. Everyone's going up to the tenth level, then out on the roof when Richard says. He's talking about getting Biddy McKinney there with the chopper.'

'Fine. I estimate that we can keep things moving from here for a while, then. I don't think the flood water will reach this high. The hospital's on too much of a slope. It'll flood the lower floor and run on down the hill.'

'True. But we're just about to be hit by a million tons of mud. And that, more than likely, will take the hospital and all of us within it straight down the hill as well. It will probably smash up the lifts one way or another.'

'Then we need to get everyone upstairs as quickly as possible!'

The major had no sooner said this than Dr Potosi arrived with her helpers and the next set of wheeled beds from the wards on level two. The familiar chimes announced the arrival of the lifts and Robin left them to it. She ran on upstairs. Richard's suggestion put Miguel-Angel and his father at the forefront of her mind and of her conscience, as she had refused the help he had offered them. She ran into the ward and found little had changed. The young doctor was gone and *Señor* Guerrero's leg was covered. The other three occupants were sitting and lying exactly as they had been when she left. Miguel-Angel was by the window, staring down at the water with horrified fascination. 'How is your leg feeling, *Señor* Guerrero?' she asked as she came up to his bed.

'A little easier. The doctor gave me an injection. He has gone now.'

'Good. We'll be moving you soon. You may have to climb some stairs from the top floor on to the roof. Could you do this if you had support?'

'I could try . . .'

'Excellent.' No sooner had Robin finished speaking than the major arrived with several of his men. 'You take those three,' he ordered. 'My brother and I will see to my father. Be quick. Time may be short. Don't wait for us.'

Dutifully the others took the three beds and wheeled them out in the direction of the lifts as fast as they could. 'Miguel-Angel,' ordered the major, 'come along. It is time to take *Papa* to the roof.' He clicked the brakes off the bed's wheels with the toe of his army boot and eased the bed gently away from the wall. Miguel-Angel came at once, and Robin turned to follow him out of the ward. As they entered the passage she saw the other three beds being pushed into a lift at the far end. 'Send the lift back for us, please,' called the major, and one of the men raised a hand to show he had heard. It was precisely at this point that Robin realized she could hear a distant rumbling, as though a massive freight train was approaching or a jumbo jet was revving up for take-off. Her mouth went dry and her heart fluttered. 'Here it comes,' she called. 'We'll need to get a move on or we'll be too late – if we're not too late already.'

FORTY

The major broke into a run. Miguel-Angel followed him and Robin brought up the rear. But it was suddenly quite difficult to keep on her feet because the floor was shaking as though they were experiencing a minor earthquake. 'Too late,' she called, but realized that the major was unlikely to have heard her above the gathering roar. '*Major!*' she bellowed. He came to a stand outside the lift. The light was on. The arrow pointing down promised that the lift car was on its way from level ten. They hesitated, all of them watching the stately progress to level nine, then eight, seven . . . six . . . five. Level four . . .

The mudslide hit the front of the hospital. It was travelling at fifty miles an hour. It might not have weighed precisely the million tons Robin had described, but it was carrying within its first tall wave all of the timber and much of the concrete and brickwork from the two streets of houses it had destroyed on its way here. The steps in front of the hospital vanished in an instant. The windows of the lower storage areas exploded inwards and three underground levels filled almost instantaneously. The broken doors were swept aside with no hesitation. The foyer filled in a heartbeat. Semi-solid slurry burst into the flooded rooms and hallways. It smashed open the ground-floor lift doors and poured like molten magma into the shafts as it burst upwards out of the cellar. The whole building reeled like a boxer given a knock-out blow. The light on the lift went out. A massive roar came up the shaft as the air trapped within it became the plaything of the racing mudslide. The floor tilted so that the shuddering lift doors were at the bottom of a slight but decidedly downhill slope. The bed rolled out of the major's shock-slackened grasp and its foot slammed into the bulging metal.

The noise was enough to shake all of them out of their stasis. 'You two start helping your father up stairs,' said Robin. 'I'll try to find a stretcher. If I can't I'll follow you up.' She turned and ran along the corridor back to the ward, racking her brain trying to remember if she had seen anything that resembled a stretcher, or anything that could be used as one. She burst into the long, vacant room and started looking around. A tall cupboard by the window looked promising and she ran to that, thinking that even if there was no stretcher inside, the door itself would do if she could get it loose. She tore it open to reveal a pile of bedding. And as she did so she registered that what had appeared to be one six-foot door was two three-foot ones. 'Useless!' she shouted, turning. And as she did so, the building shook again. She glanced out of the window and gasped. The mud was piling up and up. The first wave of it had clearly been stopped by the lower floors, but more waves of increasingly massive earth were piling on top of the first one, forming an apparently solid brown storm surge armed with trees and house sections. She froze for a moment, realizing that the mud was going to burst in through the window any minute now. That the hospital was never going to stand against such a massive onslaught. But then she saw something that gave her hope after all. She saw Richard's plan. For there in the lower sky, close enough for her to see a tall, familiar figure standing behind the two pilots in the nacelle, Dragon Dream was sailing sedately into the maelstrom.

Forgetting all about stretchers, she turned and ran back to the stairwell. The whole building shuddered again. There was a huge crash as the window came in. The stairs in front of her leaned backwards at an even crazier angle. She threw herself up them at a flat run, keeping her right hand sliding up the banister in case the odd angle made her trip and fall. Six levels up she caught up with the Guerreros, who were making ruthlessly good progress with the major in charge. *Señor* Guerrero was in the middle with his sons under each arm, half carrying him. An innate sense of decency kept Robin a few steps back because there had been no chance to wrap the patient in a sheet and his back-fastening hospital gown was not designed to protect his modesty. 'Couldn't find a stretcher,' she called.

'Never mind,' puffed the major. 'Only level ten to go, then the roof. But we're slowing you down. You want to squeeze past?'

'No. I'll stay here. That way, if anything goes wrong at least your father will have a soft landing.' Both of his sons laughed breathlessly. The father groaned. The hospital reeled and started screaming. There were two massive rushes of reverberation as the big lift cars broke loose, plunging down to smash into the surface of the mud on level three. The physics of their destruction forced air through the rubber seals on the doors that were still closed. The howling shrieks were unnerving as well as deafening. The stairs reeled, groaning, and the three Guerreros fell backwards.

Robin just had time to grab on to the hand rail as tightly as she could before the bodies crashed into her. She was hit first by the slight Miguel-Angel, the back of whose skull clubbed her forehead with stunning force. Then the father crashed into the pair of them. Robin felt a sharp pain in her left knee. No sooner had it registered than it was made a great deal worse by the major's arrival. A scream rang out and, for a disorientated moment, Robin thought it must have been her. But no. It was *Señor* Guerrero, who took the full weight of his solid elder son on his damaged hip. But Robin's determined stance saved them. The banister groaned. So did Robin, feeling the full weight of them crushing her. The stairwell lurched again, throwing their combined weight forward. The three men somehow linked up once more and stumbled onwards on to level ten. Robin swung upright and stepped up in their wake. This time she did scream. Her knee gave out and she tumbled on to her face, compounding Miguel-Angel's Glasgow Kiss headbutt with the edge of a tread. But in among the cacophony all around, her cry of agony was lost. The Guerreros vanished round the corner on to the top level. She reached for her walkie-talkie but it was gone – probably while the Guerreros were piled on top of her, she thought.

Robin took a deep breath, shook her reeling head, crawled sideways and pulled herself up on the far-side banister. Using it as a crutch to support her damaged leg, she staggered on upwards once again. She was surrounded by the increasingly overpowering sounds of timbers groaning and shattering, light fittings dropping and smashing, concrete beginning to fracture, marble and tile to shatter. Rain beat against those few windows which had not broken. Water cascaded everywhere. And in the background, reverberating in a bass note so deep it could be felt as well as heard, the relentless mudslide sought to tear the building apart and bury it.

Robin reached level ten and looked around, still dazed. At the far end of a corridor, the major was just pushing his father up into a staircase that was clearly so narrow they needed to take it one at a time. 'Major!' Robin bellowed. But as she spoke, the whole level slammed down by more than a metre, as though the top half of level nine had just vanished. The major disappeared. Robin fell forward and just had the presence of mind to land with all of her weight on her undamaged knee. She looked around for something to support her. And there, just within reach, was a portable commode consisting of a chamber pot on a metal frame that made a rudimentary chair. It was about the same height as a Zimmer frame. She grabbed it, pulled herself stiffly and unsteadily on to her feet, put as much of her weight on it as she could and began to shuffle forward. 'You're a robin,' she said bitterly to herself. 'Pity you can't bloody fly.' Suddenly the mudslide which had been trying to kill her decided to help her. The corridor leaned sideways so that she and her makeshift walker were abruptly proceeding downhill. It was a big help, and she arrived at the door through which the major had vanished just in time to see him step out of a doorway at the top of a narrow flight of steps that clearly led to the roof.

Robin let go of the lifesaving commode and pushed herself into the narrow stairwell. Because of the angle of the building, she was able to put most of her weight on her right shoulder and pull herself upwards without having to rely on her damaged knee. But the increasing angle of the stairwell, though it was helping her, also made it brutally obvious that the hospital was falling over increasingly rapidly. Richard's madcap scheme to get people off the roof was likely to be history now. The hospital's top, like the stairwell leading up to it, would be falling sideways increasingly rapidly. Robin simply could not believe that the beautiful dirigible would still be close enough to help the last survivors with the hospital beginning to come apart beneath her.

And yet Robin refused to give up hope; simply would not stop. '"The impossible we perform at once,"' she quoted from Gilbert and Sullivan's *The Sorcerer*, saying the words aloud, unable to hear them among the sounds of the dying hospital.

"'Miracles take a little longer . . .'" Icy water dashed into her face, shocking her into full wakefulness. The doorway stood in front of her like a still from a German Expressionist film where everything was shot at odd angles. She pushed herself up through the last few steps and fell out of the doorway on to the roof. The rain that had woken her now tried to knock her senseless again, pounding down on her as forcefully as the back of Miguel-Angel's skull. She began to pull herself up but her knee gave out. 'Where's your commode when you really need it?' she asked herself dreamily, looking around. The whole rooftop was sloping down-hill at an increasing angle. Halfway down the slope, the nose of the massive dirigible Dragon Dream miraculously still nestled against the asphalt roofing. There was even a ramp leading up into an open hold and, as Robin watched, the Guerreros staggered up it into the dry security of the huge airship's interior. Helping them to safety were the familiar figures of Richard and Dr Potosi.

Robin pulled herself up once more and stood, like Long John Silver, one-legged but lacking a crutch. The fictional pirate – a childhood hero of hers – had been able to move quite easily on one leg, and it occurred to her that she might simply hop to safety. But the slope of the roof fooled her once more and she fell forward on the first attempt, skinning her hands on the rough roofing. Increasingly wildly, she rolled over and sat up, trying to work out whether she could skid down the slope like a child on a playground slide. But the roughness of the asphalt made any hope of it impossible. The roof lurched again. Dragon Dream moved several metres closer, keeping in contact with the increasing incline. 'Help!' she screamed at last. 'Richard! Help!' But Richard was in close conference with Major Guerrero, not that he could have heard her over the sounds of the rain, the flood, the mudslide and the destruction of the building. It was at this point that she began to understand the bitter truth: she was going to die with the hospital. But still she would not give up. With her bad leg sticking straight out behind her, she began to crawl forward on all threes. But this too was spoiled by the slope. She had moved perhaps two metres before she crashed forward, skinning her already battered forehead. She rolled over and sat up, her mind racing, feeling the roof beginning to tilt more rapidly, like a sinking ship going into its final death-dive.

Then she looked up and saw Richard running across the slope towards her. For an instant, she thought Dragon Dream was at last lifting off behind him. But then she realized that the airship was not lifting. The pilot was holding it hovering exactly in place. The hospital was finally falling. 'Go back!' she yelled. 'It's too late! Richard, go back!' But still he pounded towards her, sure-footed in spite of the increasing unsteadiness of the toppling roof. She closed her eyes, feeling hot tears burning on her cheeks amid the numbing chill of the downpour. But what about the twins? She thought numbly. Desperately. What will the twins do if we both die here?

'Here we go, old girl,' came Richard's voice, deep and calm, as always. She opened her eyes and he was standing immediately in front of her, his blue eyes dazzling in the dullness of the stormy afternoon. He must have jumped out of Dragon Dream and dashed across the roof to be with her in extremis, she thought. He stooped and caught her under the arms, pulling her erect and holding her in the tightest bear hug she had ever experienced, and which she returned with interest, for it was the last embrace they would ever share, she realized. He was too late. The roof gave way and they were both falling as the hospital was swept under the countless tons of mud that had once been Nic Greenbaum's lovely Dahlia Blanca estate. Robin had a moment of dream-like weightlessness, during which she thought that, after all they had been through, it was strangely appropriate that they should die in each other's arms. She opened her eyes and looked over his shoulder at the huge forepeak of Dragon Dream hanging in the sky seemingly just above them. So close, she thought, and yet so far.

Then their wild tumble was brought up short with a jerk that nearly tore her arms out of their sockets, and she realized that Richard was joined to the massive dirigible by a long line clipped to a safety harness. Wrapped around each other in an unbreakable embrace, they swung safely above the rearing waves of the mudslide as it rolled over the ruin of the hospital and on down the hill. 'A trick I learned from a bloke named Raoul,' said Richard. 'He used to jump out of choppers into stormy seas for a living.'

'You sod,' she said tremulously. 'I thought you were willing to die for me!'

'And so I am, darling,' he said sincerely. Then he grinned and added, 'Just not today! One way or another, we still have far too much to do.'

'Right!' she answered. 'Then let's get me back into the warm and dry aboard your bloody ark, then do the same for everyone else we can find in this godforsaken place, shall we?'